# Dreams Of Tamar

# Dreams Of Tamar

## A TALE OF REJECTION, REDEMPTION, RESTORATION, AND FAITH

## Darlene Pryor

Join the characters in this compelling and inspirational story of love, hope and deliverance.

Palm Arbor Press
Lancaster, California

©2016 by Darlene Pryor
Design and layout for cover; Naveed786 & Rightly Designed
Editor: Monique Nixon
Publisher; Palm Arbor Press

Printed in the United States of America
Palm Arbor Press
Lancaster, Ca.
ISBN: 0997930403
ISBN 13: 9780997930405
Library of Congress Control Number: 2016913031
Palm Arbor Press, Lancaster, CA
Visit us online at www.palmarborpress.com or call us at 661-237-3423

# Dedication

*This book is dedicated to my family. We are entrepreneurs, artists, writers, and most importantly, dreamers. To my mother and father, Lillie Watson-Pryor-Buchanan and Wilbert Pryor, who raised me to believe in my dreams, and continue to this day, to remind me that my circumstances never limit my potential.*

*To Gloria Pryor, you have become an integral part of our family and I am glad to have you as a step-mother.*

*To my five sons, Aaron, Timothy, Daniel, Benjamin, and Brian. Aaron, who never gives up: Don't stop pushing. Your greater is coming. Tim, the levelheaded one: the possibilities for you are endless. Daniel, you are more like me than you even realize: Dare to step out of your comfort zone and watch the world open up for you. Benjamin, the old soul: God's got big plans for you. And Brian, the practical dreamer: believe that you are destined for greatness. You guys are my inspiration and I pray that you never stop dreaming.*

*To my sister Linda, you have always been a trail blazer. My brother, Will, you have encouraged and supported me along this journey. My brother John, from the moment you read my first poem, you believed in me. My brother Tony, you have always been the voice of reason. And to my sister Deshaunda, you have listened to me gossip about my characters for years, as if they were old friends.*

*I am fortunate to have you all in my life, and each one of you has served as inspiration and/or encouragers at different junctures along the way. I thank God for blessing me with such a wonderful family to share this journey with.*

# Author's Note

WHEN I STARTED MY FIRST novel, it was initially a secular novel. A quarter into the story I got stuck. I had an idea where my characters were going, but I didn't know how they would get there.

Then I stumbled across two articles by TD Jakes pertaining to Tamar, David's daughter. I received so much revelation and insight from those two articles, I knew I would change the focus of my story. I prayed about it and I said Lord I know you have a story for me to tell. I will wait for you to give it to me and then I will finish. That was in 2004.

One evening in December of 2014 I was sitting alone in my empty house. My children had all moved out. AJ was working at an automotive plant in Tuscaloosa and Tim was in Texas working for a professional sports organization. Daniel, Benjamin and Brian had all moved into an apartment together near the local university where Benjamin was enrolled. And there I was, alone with my dog Jack, waiting for my divorce to finalize in January of 2015.

As I reflected over the state of my life I was reminded of the characters in my still unfinished book, Dreams. I prayed to God and asked "Is it time?" I believed that it was. I dug my manuscript from the bottom of a plastic tote in my living room closet and started reading through it. As I read the story, the characters who had lay dormant for 12 years, began to breathe again. As their story unfolded onto the pages before me I became more certain that *Dreams Of Tamar* was a story God intended to use to uplift and encourage others.

I picked up on the last page and as their story poured onto the screen, I knew this is what I was called to do.

Darlene Pryor

# Acknowledgements

I GIVE ALL THANKS TO God for entrusting me with the gift of expression. I thank God for giving me the rest of the story.

Denise Shelvin, Vanessa Wiggins, Monique Nixon, and the Antelope Valley Writers Association; editors, proof readers, and writers group. Thank you for embracing my vision and helping to fashion my dream into a reality.

Thanks to T D Jakes for the inspiration to turn my secular novel into an Inspirational fiction that will not only entertain, but will uplift and encourage readers, as well.

Thank you to all who invested the time to share in the story of *Dreams Of Tamar*. I pray that your soul was touched as we traveled this journey.

If you loved this book and believe that it will bless others, please feel free to leave a short review on my author's page at Amazonbooks.com and/or at goodreads.com. Your help in spreading the word is greatly appreciated. Reviews from readers like you make a huge difference in helping new readers find stories like *Dreams Of Tamar*.

Thank you,

Darlene Pryor

http://palmarborpress.com/authors/

https://www.facebook.com/tamarsdream/

https://www.instagram.com/darlenepryorauthor/

Darlene Pryor

# Prologue

### The 80's

"WHAT DO YOU WANT?" DIEDRA asked in a hoarse whisper, her voice barely audible. She was about to repeat herself when she heard the now familiar voice of Desmond.

"Yo, is me," he said in a voice that chilled Diedra to the core. His heavy Jamaican accent was cool and easy, and didn't offer a hint of the wickedness he obviously had in mind. He spoke as if it was the most natural thing in the world for him to lurk in the basement waiting for her, and then grab her in the dark and pin her up against the wall. "Me told you me soon come back for you," he whispered softly into her ear, as he rubbed his body against hers. Desmond held her wrists over her head with one hand and roamed his free hand across her body. A bell rang out in the background.

Diedra struggled as hard as she could to get away from him, but she couldn't move. Her body was frozen in place as she stared at Desmond's gold tooth twinkling in the dark. She opened her mouth and screamed, but her voice was drowned out by the ringing bell. *Where is Mike? He's supposed to be here! Lord help me please! Where is that ringing coming from?* The ringing became louder and louder until Diedra shuddered awake. She leaned over the side of the bed and saw the familiar number flashing across the caller ID. She quickly picked up the receiver. "Hello Mom!"

Two weeks later, Diedra and her twin sons, Adrian and Austin, piled into the back of her father's Ford Bronco Centurion and headed home to Alabama. She had sold her broken down Honda for parts. She gave her living room furniture to her Landlord, Chino and donated the rest of their household items to the church down the street. She also donated most of their snow gear but she decided to keep the sled because in Alabama, you just never know. Her best friend, Brea, had promised to send whatever wouldn't fit in the vehicle along with her own things, which she would ship shortly.

Her friend, Mike, had designated himself as her personal guardian. He had been sleeping on the couch in her living room every night for two weeks straight, after that awful incident with Desmond. During the day his friends on the police force would make extra passes in front of her apartment building in their patrol cars to insure that Desmond didn't attempt to return. Mike was a deputy sheriff who looked as if he'd fit more comfortably in a defensive lineman's uniform than his sheriff's department uniform. Although she felt safe with his massive frame on her couch, she knew this arrangement could not last forever. Besides, even Mike couldn't prevent Desmond from entering her dreams. Each night, in her dreams, Diedra would relive the terror of the day of Desmond's attack.

Mr. Davis pulled away from the curve and drove the Bronco up South Whitney Street toward Farmington Avenue. Diedra, Adrian, and Austin turned and looked out the rear window of the vehicle as their apartment on Warrenton Avenue faded away into their past. Finally, she was leaving Hartford, Ct. bad dreams, and memories, once and for all. Finally, she was leaving this place, bad dreams and memories, once and for all.

# CHAPTER 1

## New Year's Day

AT 7:15 FRIDAY MORNING THE sun peaked through Diedra's bedroom window, tickling her eyes open with its soft rays. As she slowly awakened from a restless sleep, she reached an arm high above her head, stretching and yawning, as she turned...over...in...her...bed.

*What's he doing here? Don't tell me he overslept again! That excuse about not knowing how to set the alarm is getting really tired. It's just one more attempt to make me responsible for his actions.*

*You'd think it being a new year... That's right! It is a new year. It's New Year's Day and neither of us has to work today. It's also our anniversary. I cannot believe I have been married to James for five years! Look at him lying there. Lord of all he surveys. Even in his sleep he seems to say, 'I'm the man! I work eight hours a day, I expect to have lunch brought to my job or at least a sandwich waiting for me when I get home. Dinner is to be served by six o'clock every evening regardless of anyone else's plans. I expect to know where my wife is at all times but I'm a man and I come and go as I please. I should not be expected to lift a finger around the house because I work an eight hour day and besides, that's what I have a wife for.'*

*He'd better get real. He wants a geisha girl not a wife. I work a twelve hour shift four nights a week, sometimes five. I am not about to spend my days chasing behind a grown man who is supposed to be an equal partner in this marriage and bending over backwards to make him feel more equal. Oh my head hurts! I'm going back to sleep.* Diedra's thoughts were so intense, she could feel her face tightening into a frown.

James awakened to greet the first face he saw every morning; that of the alarm clock on his side of the bed. *Its seven twenty-five already! No need to look, I know Diedra is still in bed sleep. That woman sleeps more than anyone I have ever seen before in my life. I guess it would be too much like right for her to get up and serve me breakfast in bed. I can't even get a sandwich when I come in from work.*

*The word says a wife should submit to her own husband. I don't think I ask for too much, just the wifely things any man would expect, but today of all days! It's our anniversary and so far it's proceeding true to form. I didn't get any loving last night and don't expect any this morning. She said, 'I do' just like I did, so why do I always have to be the initiator? Occasionally, I would like to feel like my wife has a physical desire for me and is not just going through the motions. No need to get worked up over that one bro. It's just not going to happen.*

James turned to Diedra and tapped her on the shoulder. "Babe, wake up."

"What's wrong?"

"We need some breakfast."

"Well get some." Diedra buried her head deeper into the down-filled pillow and James just sat and stared across the bed at his wife shaking his head from side to side. Suddenly he swung his legs over the side of the bed, snatched his pants off the footboard, pulled them on, and stormed out of the bedroom and into the hallway.

"Trevor, Travis, Tremaine!" James called to his four year old triplets. "Time to get up!" The boys, who had been awake for an hour already, toppled out of their room and into the hallway. The love in James' heart shown through his eyes as it always did whenever he looked at either of his sons. He felt a connection to these three little guys stronger than anything he had ever experienced except the bond that he once felt between him and his wife Diedra.

As he walked toward the kitchen his thoughts wandered back to his wife of five years and he asked himself a question he seemed to be asking more lately. *What's happened to my marriage and where do we go from here? Lately Diedra and I seem so far apart and the gap between us just seems to keep growing. We don't really talk anymore and when we try, simple conversations tend to explode into shouting matches or worse, dwindle into silence like this morning. I don't know how to reach her. I have tried to give her everything she's wanted. We have come a long way in the past five years. We've...*

"Are you going to give me my breathing treat Daddy?" James' thoughts were interrupted by the question asked by Trevor as he bound into the kitchen after his father, smiling that adorable single dimpled smile that was identical to his father's.

So deep in thought, James had not realized that he'd entered into their spacious kitchen. With all its modern amenities, it was Diedra's favorite room in the house. She had insisted on having it remodeled as soon as they were able. He had to admit it was a labor of love. He enjoyed working with his hands and besides, he liked the kitchen as well. There was a lot more shared in this room than meals and chores. The kitchen was the family meeting room as well as his special projects center. There had been many precious moments spent in this room.

James returned Trevor's smile and said cheerfully, (all thoughts of his troubles wiped away for the moment), "Yes little man, I'm going to give you your breathing treat!" James tickled Trevor playfully as he swooped the giggling boys up onto one of the kitchen chairs.

James announced in his commander voice, "Power Rangers check in!"

"Red Ranger here!" replied Trevor very seriously.

"How can I be sure you're not the Orange Ranger?" asked James.

"Because there is no Orange Ranger Dad-uh, Sir."

"Hmm, well how do I know if you are really the Red Ranger? Do you know the secret Red Ranger password?"

"Yes."

"What is it then?"

"Jelly Biscuits" replied Trevor with a twinkle in his eyes.

"Jelly Biscuit?!" exclaimed James in mock surprise. "Did someone change the password without telling me?" he asked.

"Yes," replied a beaming Trevor.

"Who could have done such a thing?" asked James.

"I did!" shouted Trevor.

"No?!"

"Yes I did!"

"Well just so I can be absolutely, positively, sure that you are the real Red Ranger, can you tell me the password?"

Trevor sat erectly and held his right hand straight up toward the ceiling and shouted out, "Power sword Whoaa!"

"Alright! Now we can get down to business," said James. "Red Ranger, are you ready for your life saving mission?"

"Yes sir!" With that, James proceeded to assemble the parts to Trevor's nebulizer machine and fill it with the prescribed 3 cc's of albuterol and saline mixture. Then he placed the mask over Trevor's face and turned the machine on. "Remember, Red Ranger, you must be very still and breathe slowly into the alien monitor"

The treatment took approximately five minutes. Funny how both Trevor and Tremaine turned out to have asthma, but as of yet, Travis had displayed no symptoms. Dr. Howard, the family physician, had told James and Diedra that since the triplets were identical, in all likelihood, Travis would eventually develop symptoms as well.

"Finished!" said Trevor.

"Fantastic!" said James. "Red Ranger, remove your mask and check your gauges." James said as he looked to see that all of the medicine was gone.

"All clear!" said Trevor.

"Congratulations Red Ranger, you have successfully completed another lifesaving mission. Report again in four hours."

"Right" said Trevor with a salute. "Daddy", he said,

"Yes?"

"When is four hours?" James smiled and said, "I'll let you know. Where is Tremaine?"

"In Mommy's room with Travis."

"In Mommy's room? You boys know you are not to disturb your mother when she's sleeping.'

"I didn't, Daddy."

"Well, let's go get them."

Diedra was kneeling on the ground in the middle of a grassy field, underneath a palm tree, of all things, holding her head between her hands and rocking back and forth, moaning softly, "Ooooh it hurts so badly! Why won't it stop?" Suddenly she heard voices.

"She seems to be in great distress old friend," said a soft masculine voice.

"Yes she does." Replied an equally gentle voice

"What? Who's there?" asked Diedra as she looked around her, confused, because she knew neither whom the voices belonged to, nor where they came from.

"It's going to be alright Dee. Don't you fret anymore." Then she saw them; two men walking toward her. The man on the left wore faded grey slacks with gray suspenders and a white shirt. A light grey fedora tilted slightly to the left on his head, and his sockless feet were cradled in a pair of brown leather house shoes.

"Big Daddy, is that you?" Diedra recognized her father's father who looked exactly as she remembered from her youth; a gentle faced, fair skinned man of medium height and slender stature.

"So you do remember me," said Big Daddy.

"Of course I remember you."

"Do you remember me?" asked the man on the right. His khaki pants and shirt coordinated with the safari hat perched above his bespectacled face. He was even fairer than the first man, about the same height, but of a sturdier build.

Diedra stared at the man curiously, "I'm sorry but I don't believe I do," she said. Then she turned to Big Daddy and asked "Who is that with you, Big Daddy?"

"Are you sure you don't recognize him, Dee?" Big Daddy prodded gently.

"I'm sorry..." Just then, Diedra was overcome by the intensity of the pain in her head. It seemed sharper, more intense, like heat! She felt as if a fire was about to explode behind her eyes. She dropped her head down to her knees and closed her eyes saying, "This is more than a headache."

The man in the khaki outfit looked at Diedra tenderly, and softly told her "Don't you worry Baby Girl. It's going to be alright."

Diedra looked up at him, "Baby Girl? They used to call my mother that when she was a girl. Even though she was the second of four girls, everyone called her Baby Girl."

"That's because she always looked so innocent. Strangers often mistook her for the youngest of her siblings. You look just like LB all grown up."

There was something vaguely familiar about this man. Something about the way he looked at her. Diedra gazed into his eyes and then she saw them, her mother's eyes. "So do you," she said.

He chuckled and said, "Well I wouldn't say I look just like her. Your mother's a might prettier than I am." Diedra blushed.

"Are you her…"

"Yes child, I'm your granddaddy Lawrence."

"I'm sorry I didn't recognize you."

"No need to apologize Baby Girl. You don't mind if I call you Baby Girl do you?"

"Not at all"

"You were such a little thing when I went away. I can understand how you might not remember me."

"I remember you, Granddaddy." At that point Big Daddy interjected.

"Well, now that we're all reacquainted, why don't you come along with us. Dee?"

The next thing Diedra knew, she was riding in a car between Big Daddy and Granddaddy. She didn't happen to notice whom, if anyone was driving. But she did notice that the road was lined with palm trees. Then they traveled through a vast field, a faint scent of citrus leading the along.

"Where are we going Big Daddy?" Diedra asked, just as she realized the car was being propelled by foot power like a Flintstones car. Diedra heard Big Daddy answer her, but she didn't understand him. She turned to Granddaddy and asked "What did he say?"

At that point, Granddaddy, who was on the front of a motorcycle with Diedra in the middle and Big Daddy in the back, said "Take care child." They continued along the winding highway; gliding over a steep hill that dipped down into a green valley, through forests and open air.

As they traveled, their mode of transportation continued to regress. They were all on bicycles, then running, and finally, they walked into a shopping mall. Big Daddy said "Come swing with me awhile Dee." He sat on a white porch swing that seemed to fit his proportions perfectly, but was so big to Diedra that Granddaddy had to help her climb up before he sat down on the other side of Diedra. There she sat on this big white swing between her two grandfathers, both of whom had died years before, her feet swinging high above the ground while theirs rested comfortably on the floor, as they gently rocked the swing back and forth. They continued for a while until Big Daddy turned to Diedra and said, "Dee, your Granddaddy Lawrence and I want to tell you something."

"What is it?" asked Diedra.

"Child, we want you to remember that tomorrow isn't promised. You have to go for your dreams now, but you also have to take time for the really important things in life, like your family. You have to remember that you are just as important to them as they are to you.

"Yes!" added Granddaddy. "And we also want you to remember to open the door.

"Do you know what opportunities are in store for me Granddaddy?" Diedra was almost begging him for answers.

"Of course we do."

Diedra looked at both her grandfathers and said, "Seriously, that one question has been the source of so many headaches. If you could please tell me what my purpose in life is, maybe I would be relieved of some of the stress I've been under."

At the mention of headaches the two men exchanged a concerned glance and Big Daddy turned to Diedra and answered her question. Then Granddaddy said "Mama, when life knocks" Tap! Tap! Tap! Diedra heard a light knocking from out of nowhere. "You gotta answer the door."

"Mama? Why did you call me Mama?" Diedra asked.

"When opportunity knocks, Mama"

Tap! Tap! Tap! There was that knocking again. "You've gotta open the door. Open the door Mama, open the door." His voice rang deep, resonating in her ears.

"Wha-!" Diedra awakened with a start. Tap! Tap! Tap! "Mama, open the door!" Diedra looked around her bedroom and slowly raised herself up in her bed. She sat there for a moment, dazed.

"Who is it?" she asked as she realized someone was knocking on her bed-room door.

"Me," said a child's voice.

"And me too" piped another small voice.

Diedra shook her head and asked, "Who is me and me too?"

"Travis!"

"And Tremaine too!"

Diedra laughed aloud, reached up and gingerly massaged her throbbing temples and said, "Come in Travis and Tremaine too." The boys opened the door to their parent's bedroom, rushed across the room, and leapt simultane-ously onto the bed. "Whoa!" Take it easy! This bed's not pulling out anytime soon." Diedra gave each boy a hug and a kiss.

"Pulling out?" the boys chimed in unison.

"I mean it's not going anywhere and neither am I." she said.

"Are you going to stay in bed all day?" asked Travis, as he and Tremaine snuggled up beside their mother.

"No, I'm not going to stay in bed all day," replied Diedra.

"Where's Austin?" asked Tremaine.

"With his dad," replied Diedra.

"Where's Adrian?" asked Travis.

With Austin and their dad," she answered.

"I want to go with my dad too," said Tremaine.

Diedra said, "Go with him, he's right down the hall."

Tremaine said "No that's Daddy."

"And Adrian and Austin's dad is their daddy," she answered.

"Daddy is their daddy," argued Travis.

Diedra looked at her boys and thought for a moment. She didn't know if they could understand. "You know, Adrian and Austin have two daddies. They have your daddy, James, and Derek. Since Derek doesn't live with us, he likes to come and take them to his house sometimes, so they can get to know him as well as they know us. I know you probably think it would be fun to pack a suitcase and go away with your daddy. In fact, I'm sure your daddy would love to take you on a trip sometime. Just you boys."

"He said he was going to take us to the circus!" said Travis.

"There you go!" exclaimed Diedra. Tremaine looked thoughtful and asked, "Can you come too Mommy?"

"I wouldn't miss it for the world," she replied, and gave both boys another kiss on the cheek.

James tapped lightly on the door as he stuck his head in the room. "There you are." He said to Travis and Tremaine. And to Diedra he said, "Mind if we join you?"

James was taken aback by how tired and worn his wife appeared, but he chose not to say anything in front of the boys. He just looked at her sitting in the center of their king-sized bed with the rose patterned linen with ruffles. He would have thought it too frilly for himself, but Diedra loved the way it looked and he loved the way she looked in it, soft and delicate. But now she looked fragile and vulnerable. Terms not usually associated with his wife, despite her petite frame. He and Trevor walked across the room to the bed. James leaned over and kissed Diedra lightly on the forehead. Trevor climbed up on the bed and did likewise. Diedra gave Trevor a squeeze and looked lovingly at her husband. "I'm sorry I fell asleep last night."

"Why didn't you tell me you were having headaches again?"

Startled by the question, Diedra was silent for a moment, and then "How did you know?" The question was barely audible. James' gaze displayed that crooked grin that Diedra used to swoon over.

"Woman I'm your husband. I'm supposed to pay attention. Sometimes I may be a little slow, but I usually catch on to what's happening with you." He reached over, gently massaged the back of her neck, and asked her if she had taken anything for her headache. As expected, she had not.

"I really don't understand why you would suffer needlessly, refusing to even take pain relievers. If the pain is so severe that over-the-counter medications can't help, then you definitely need to see a doctor."

Diedra could see that James was concerned. "I hear what you're saying. It's just that these headaches are so irregular that I would feel foolish going to a doctor and trying to explain them. Uh, I sometimes get these headaches. No, I don't have one now. As a matter of fact, I haven't had one in a few days, maybe weeks. But when I do get them, they're really bad."

"Don't you think a physician could help you pinpoint the source of these headaches?"

"Possibly, but you think you already know the source don't you James?"

"Well yes, since you ask. I think you try to do too much. Between your job, the track team, and your business, you barely have anything left for your family. Babe, you have to remember to take time out for the really important things like your family and yourself."

Diedra massaged her temples with a slow, meticulous, motion as she stated her position for what seemed like the thousandth time. "My job takes up more time than energy and it provides me with an opportunity to work on my book. The track team only takes a few hours a week and it helps me to stay in shape as well as presenting an opportunity to spend time with all five of our sons. My business is little more than a hobby and takes no more time or energy than I choose to give it. As far as the family goes, if you weren't so rigid you would see that our family is my top priority and even though I may not always conduct myself in the manner you have determined to be ideal; everything I do is with thoughts of you and our boys. And James, I really resent you implying otherwise."

Through the entire speech she kept her eyes on the boys, not wanting to meet eyes with James for fear he might notice that his statement unnerved her. Why would he say that now, this morning? Those were Granddaddy's words practically verbatim. Was there some connection between the events that occurred in her dream and this morning's conversation with James? She didn't feel she was neglecting her family. She wasn't neglecting herself either. True enough, she did have quite a few things going on but she felt she had to pursue all avenues in search of that ever elusive niche. She had always felt she was destined to make a difference in the world, but she never had a clue as to what that might be. In her dream Big Daddy told her what her destiny was, but she was unable to remember what it was he said.

"Babe, did you hear me?" James looked searchingly at his wife. She hadn't heard a word in the last few moments. Trevor, still on her lap, smiled. Travis covered his mouth as he giggled, and Tremaine laughed out loud.

"James shook his head and said, "We'll talk later. Let's get some breakfast. I'm starved." Diedra agreed and the five of them went to the kitchen where Diedra prepared the meal with a little help from Travis and Trevor while James gave Tremaine his breathing treatment. Shortly, they sat down to a tasty breakfast of French toast, bacon, milk and sliced oranges.

"Finished," said Travis.

"Finished" said Trevor.

"What? Are you two racing again? How many times do your father and I have to tell you to take your time and eat?"

"Finished" said James with a sheepish grin.

Diedra smirked and turned to Tremaine. "I guess we'll still be sitting here by the time they get the dishwasher loaded," she said with a wink. Tremaine beamed as he continued to eat his breakfast. By the time Diedra and Tremaine finished eating and scraped the scraps off their plate into the garbage disposal, James and the other two had practically finished cleaning the kitchen. Diedra rinsed the last of the dishes and put them in the dishwasher while Tremaine wiped the table.

Diedra sent Tremaine to the den to watch television with the others before she gave the kitchen a final once over. She thought of how blessed she was to have such a wonderful family. It wasn't by chance though. It had started with Adrian and Austin. As a single parent of twins, she learned rather early to encourage independence at every opportunity. That is not to say that she didn't start out overindulgent.

In the delivery room with the twins Diedra was so exhausted after the ordeal of giving birth to two full-sized babies, (Adrian was five pounds, Austin was six) that she did not have the strength to do anything more than take a quick look at each baby before he was whisked off for bathing. The next thing she remembered was waking up in her maternity room to see Derek sitting in a chair next to her bed, talking on the telephone. When he realized she was awake he ended his call and congratulated her on a job well done. He called the nurse and told her "My fiancée and I would like to see our babies now."

Diedra glared at him coldly, and said, "Your fiancée? Our babies? You might want her to wheel you on down to the emergency room because obviously you have fallen and hit your head… hard!"

"Dee you know I'm going to marry you someday. And you didn't make those babies by yourself," he admonished.

"Oh, I can't tell!" she replied as she counted off on her fingers. "I carried them by myself. I went to each and every one of my prenatal appointments, by myself. I went to birthing classes, by myself. And you can bet I'll be raising my sons the same way…By myself! And by the way Derek, in case you hadn't heard, bigamy is illegal!" Diedra angrily retorted.

"I see you're still talking crazy. If you don't chill out I might end up taking those babies and raising them myself."

"Ha, ha, ha, ha…" Diedra laughed in spite of her aching body. She slowly eased herself up straighter as she raised the top half of her hospital bed. She looked at Derek, shook her head from side to side and laughed again. "Derek, by the time you grow up and become responsible enough to raise anybody's children, yours will be grown men themselves. Hopefully trying to teach their own sons not to be like you. But today, you can get the he…"

"Here they are!" the nurse said as she wheeled the babies into the room. Diedra and Derek both fell silent as the nurse wheeled the twin boys across the room toward them. She picked the larger of the two infants up and placed him in Diedra's arms. Diedra kissed him on the forehead and said "Hello Austin." Ignoring the surprise that registered across Derek's face she turned to the nurse who reached into the other bassinet to pick up the second baby boy.

"And how about one for Daddy?" she asked Derek.

"Let me please?" Diedra asked, reaching out for her other son with her free hand.

"Are you sure? You don't want to overdo it so soon after delivery." replied the nurse.

"Yeah, and that's a lot of baby for someone as small as you Dee," said Derek.

"I carried them both into the delivery room. I don't think they've gained very much weight in the hours since."

Derek laughed and said "You done good Dee. Give the boy to her, would you nurse?" Diedra positioned Austin in one arm and the nurse gently placed his brother in her other arm.

She kissed this baby and said, "Hello Adrian." She sighed, looked at her twin baby boys, and shed soft tears of joy.

Derek was startled to hear Diedra use the names they had come up with as teenagers. He leaned over and hugged her. "Yeah, you done real good," he said through tears of his own. They sat there for a moment until the nurse reminded them that the babies needed to be fed. Diedra gave Austin another kiss before Derek took the baby into his own arms and sat down to feed him. With a little assistance from the nurse, the two young parents fed their babies.

After they fed and burped the babies, Diedra and Derek held them and compared family traits. Derek insisted that both boys looked just like him, but Diedra said that was impossible since they didn't even resemble each other very closely. They agreed they had two beautiful baby boys.

When the babies fell asleep Derek moved to return Austin to his bassinet but Diedra insisted that he place him back in her arms.

"Dee, I thought you were so mad at me that you would come up with totally different names." He was silent a moment, then "I'm sorry I wasn't with you throughout your pregnancy. Girl, I've been in love with you since I was fifteen years old. You just don't know how happy I was when you told me you were pregnant with my child. You know we talked about one day getting married and having kids. So even though this pregnancy wasn't planned at this time, it wasn't unwanted."

"Then why did you leave me, Derek?" she blurted.

"I'm trying to explain!" He took a deep breath. "I was ready for one baby but when you told me you were carrying twins I panicked. Dee, I didn't know what I was going to do with two children. Man, I'm only twenty-one years old. I'm just graduating from college this year. I just didn't think I was ready for this responsibility."

"Derek, I'm nineteen. I had to drop out of college. If you didn't think you could handle two babies along with me, what did you think I was going to do by myself?"

"I don't know Dee. I guess I was only thinking of myself. I'm sorry, but I'm here now."

"Yes you are, but for how long?"

"I'm here for the duration. I want us to get married and raise our sons together."

"I don't think your wife would appreciate that very much, Derek. Do you?"

"I told you I was running scared. Alicia offered me a refuge from reality but I didn't marry her. You are the only woman I want to marry."

"Yeah, I could just feel the love the entire time I was pregnant"

"I said I'm sorry. What more can I do? I can't take back the past"

"No you can't. But what you can do is get out of my life now, before you break my sons' hearts the way you broke mine." Derek winced as if she'd struck him. He stroked Adrian's head. "Dee, I know I hurt you, and I can understand your anger. Maybe you don't want me back in your life but you can't keep me from being a father to my sons."

"Okay Derek, what is it you propose to do with this new found sense of responsibility to your sons?"

Derek looked at Diedra's petite frame sitting in the bed with his two sons in her arms. It was true. He had loved her since he was fifteen years old. He still loved her. He loved their sons too. But he was so scared. He sighed softly and said. "I want us to be a family Dee. I want to take care of you, Austin, and Adrian. I want you to know that no matter what, I will always take care of you."

Diedra looked at Derek for a long moment before she replied "I wish I could believe you Derek but I just spent the last eight months alone and pregnant. Nightly, I have prayed for you to come and take care of my babies and me. Even when I realized you weren't going to be the man I always thought you would be, deep down I continued to hope. But you never came through Derek. You never came through." She sighed, heaving her shoulders before she continued. "Now, here you are promising everything I ever asked for. I'm sorry, but I just can't…"

Diedra shook her head and gave the kitchen counter one last wipe. *There's no point in dwelling on that day. It was one of the happiest and saddest days of my life. My babies were healthy and beautiful, but it was no surprise Derek couldn't live up to his promises. I knew the moment he walked out of the room that he wouldn't be back. To this day I don't understand why I was so devastated when he didn't return. But I was, and I got over it. More importantly, I got through it. Here it is fifteen years later. Adrian and Austin have grown into fine young men. They are the best big brothers the triplets could ask for. They have a great relationship with James and…*

"Oh James!" Diedra folded the towel and placed it over the rack. She turned toward the den where she heard James and the boys laughing. She smiled as she hurried into the room. She walked across the room to James who was sitting on the sofa with the boys, watching television. Diedra grabbed his hand and led him out into the hallway.

James asked, "What's going on babe?"

"Shhh," Diedra replied, as she reached her arms around his neck and proceeded to give her husband a long, slow, kiss.

# CHAPTER 2

"Let's see, all the sockets have safety plugs, the cabinets are locked and all my crystal is safely put away." Lee-Beverly Daniels was teeming with nervous energy as she bustled around her home, checking to insure that each room was child-proofed. "Robert did you lock up your liquor cabinet? Don't forget to check the back gate. I wouldn't want my babies to wander off. And Robert, please don't leave the Ex-lax on the kitchen counter. I'd hate for one of my babies to come across it and think he's lucked up on some chocolate."

Robert Daniels sat at the kitchen table reading his newspaper. He didn't even look up as he spoke. "Lee, would you calm down? Every time our grandsons come over you act as if they're still two years old; fussing over them like a mother hen. You won't let them do a thing for themselves. The boys are four years old. I would think they'd know the routine by now. They're not going to come in here and wreak havoc all over the house. Just this once, would you please relax and enjoy their visit."

Robert smiled at his wife of forty years. He knew he was wasting his breath. Although Lee was a levelheaded and composed lady, who was hard to unravel; when it came to their grandchildren she was a bundle of raw nerves. He knew she didn't doubt her daughter's ability to take care of her children; but she felt that as their grandmother, it was her responsibility to protect all of her grandchildren from any and every unforeseen mishap. Lee-Beverly was only slightly ruffled by his comments.

"I can't help myself. I want the boys to enjoy themselves but if anything happened to one of them I'd never forgive myself."

"I don't understand it. We raised Reggie, Diedra and Beverly, and they turned out fine. Nothing has happened to Adrian or Austin as of yet, and they are fifteen now. So how is it that you have come to be so apprehensive about the little ones?"

"I honestly don't know, except for the fact that I feel somewhat responsible for Diedra having to spend all those years alone raising the twins. I'm her mother. I should have been there."

"Well she's not alone now and the twins are fine."

"Yes, well that is what you keep telling me, but we can't exactly depend on Diedra to let us know when there's a problem. Why, the twins were practically a year old before we ever became aware of their existence. I just don't understand that daughter of ours sometimes. We could have helped her through what had to be a traumatic period in her life. But not only did she shut us out, but she walked away from a very good man as well."

"Diedra is a grown woman. We raised her to be independent and self-sufficient, just like her mother. As for Derek, we don't know what her reasons were for leaving him but we do know that whatever happened, she felt it was best to leave that relationship alone. Lee, there comes a point in time when we have to rest in the knowledge that we did our best to raise our children and realize that our job is done. From that point forward we have to have faith in God to watch over them and trust in them to put all of our life lessons to use. One of those lessons being to think for themselves."

"I understand what you're saying but sometimes it is hard to sit back and watch my child make mistakes."

"Lee, life is about making mistakes. We can't always expect people to learn from the mistakes of others. I think the important thing is that we all learn from our own mistakes."

"Okay Robert, you're right as usual. And how did you become so calm and practical regarding our children?"

Robert smiled at his wife as he folded up his paper and said, "Well don't you know Lee? I know you'll do enough worrying for both of us."

"Oh Robert!"

# CHAPTER 3

JAMES LOOKED QUIZZICALLY AT DIEDRA. His wife, she never ceased to amaze him. There were times when he felt as if she really didn't want to be married to him; as though she just put up with him because he was there. But then there were times, like right now, when he felt as if nothing else existed beyond what the two of them shared. He felt like she was an extension of himself; as if each breath she took carried life through his lungs. It felt as if his heart pumped blood through her veins. He loved Diedra with all his heart. He had never felt so strongly for another woman before and didn't believe he ever would or could again. The power of the emotions that erupted inside him when she held him like this was mind-boggling.

"What's that look all about?" Diedra asked softly. "You looked as if you were light years away. I thought I'd lost you for a moment there."

"Not hardly! Dee, you could never lose me. You are me, and I am you." Then he kissed her again holding her so closely that he didn't know where he ended and she began. They stood there in the hallway embracing one another until James felt something tugging at his pants leg.

"Daddy, Mommy! Granny's here!" It was Travis. "Can you let her in? She's at the door."

"Just a minute," James said to Travis as he shot a questioning look at Diedra over his head. Diedra smiled, shrugged her shoulders and addressed Travis, "Go into the living room and tell your grandmother we're on our way."

As soon as Travis rounded the corner out of the hallway James started toward his and Diedra's bedroom rattling on, "Dee you really need to talk to your mother now. I thought we made it clear that we wanted this day to ourselves." James was whispering to ensure that his sons didn't hear him. He reached into a drawer and snatched a shirt out. "How's she going to just show up on our doorstep unannounced? Just once I'd like to see her respect our wishes. Now that would be cause for a holiday all its own," he pulled his shirt on, punching his arms through the sleeves.

"James, I know my mother can be a little overbearing at times but what makes you so sure that's her at the door? She's not the only granny they have you know." Diedra reminded him in a weak attempt to calm him down.

"Oh, I know it's her. I specifically told my family I wanted to spend my anniversary alone with my wife. Besides, my mom and dad are on that cruise, remember?"

"Oh yeah," replied Diedra. "Well maybe something's wrong. I also told my parents we wanted to celebrate our anniversary alone. I don't think my mom would blatantly disregard our wishes. Now come on so we can let her in before she starts thinking something is wrong with us." Diedra said as she pulled James back into the hallway.

James fumbled with the buttons on his shirt as Diedra led him down the hallway. "Something is wrong with us," he grumbled. "We just can't seem to get a moment to ourselves. You would think that people would realize that five children do not leave us with a great deal of personal time."

James opened the door to greet his mother-in-law. The triplets jumped up and down cheering "Granny, Granny!" All three boys pounced on their grandmother as she walked in the door.

"Hello Lee-Beverly." James said coolly as he let her in the house, giving her a slight peck on the cheek. "What brings you by today?"

Diedra gave James a little nudge as she greeted her mother. "Happy New Year, Mom! Have you gotten the new year off to a good start?"

"Yes dear, your father and I enjoyed a wonderful service at church last night. We brought the New Year in splendidly. You should have been there," she said pointedly. "But that's not why I'm here. I know you said you wanted to spend your anniversary alone without any interruptions."

"Yes, I do believe I told you that," replied Diedra as she led her mother to a seat on the couch.

"Tell me, how can you do that with these little ones underfoot?" Lee-Beverly asked.

Diedra grinned over at James as she responded to her mother. "What do you mean?"

"Your father and I thought a nice anniversary gift to you and James would be to give you the rest of the weekend alone. We'd like to keep them at our house until Monday, if that's alright with you."

"Alright?" James asked. "That would be fantastic! I'm sure they would love to spend the weekend with you. I can't tell you how much I appreciate your thinking of us like this. But what about daycare? How are they supposed to get there Monday morning?"

"We could keep them Monday. It would be no problem. Or, if you prefer, Robert can drop them off at the Center that morning."

James smiled broadly at his mother-in-law and said, "This is really generous of you. I have to say you really surprised me this time, Lee-Beverly."

Lee-Beverly said, "James, you didn't have to be surprised. You could have asked us to keep the boys. We are always willing to spend time with our grandchildren. Frankly, we don't get to spend enough time with them."

James said, "We realize you're here for us Mom, but with the hectic schedules that Diedra and I have we hardly get to spend any quality time as a family."

"But James and I are extremely grateful to you for giving us this weekend to ourselves," interjected Diedra. She stood up and walked across the room. "I'll just go and gather some things for the boys." Diedra went into the triplet's bedroom, opened the closet, and found a blue duffel bag sitting on a shelf. She opened it, only to find that it was already full. Upon further inspection, she found the bag contained three days' worth of clothing and supplies for each of the three boys. There was also a note from Austin folded around a recent picture of him, Diedra, and Adrian, standing on Ladiga Trail. Austin, who boasted a height of 6'1 in his socks, was a head taller than Adrian who stood 5'7" in his Nike Air running shoes. They both towered over Diedra as they draped an arm on either of her shoulders. The note read:

Mom and James,

We don't often get an opportunity to let you know how much we appreciate the sacrifices that you make on our behalf. Together the two of you have worked above and beyond the call of duty to see that the five of us are provided with not only the basic necessities to grow and thrive, but you always seem to put our wants at the top of your list of priorities as well.

We hope that this weekend you will concentrate on each other.

HAPPY ANNIVERSARY!

Austin D.


Diedra sat down on Trevor's bed and read the note a second time. "My child," she whispered softly to herself. She was always overwhelmed by Austin's maturity. "How did someone so young get to be so wise? He is so sensitive and sincere." From the time he and Adrian were toddlers he always seemed to be attuned to Adrian's emotions, but it went beyond that twin connection. That boy had an uncanny insight into the feelings and needs of others. In fact, it could be quite unnerving at times. Diedra heard the telephone ringing in the hallway. She smiled to herself as she went to take her son's call.

Adrian and Austin were calling to wish Diedra and James a Happy New Year and a happy anniversary. Before they left to go visit their father. The twins had called their grandparents to suggest that they get the triplets for the weekend. When Lee-Beverly said she thought James and Diedra would think her pushy, Austin had insisted it would be the perfect anniversary gift. He was right on the mark as usual.

James, Diedra and Lee-Beverly all expressed their appreciation to the boys for their suggestion. Adrian congratulated Diedra on her ability to let go of her babies for three whole days. And, Trevor, Travis, and Tremaine, all wanted to know when Adrian and Austin were coming home. They informed them that they were having the time of their lives in California and were in no hurry to return to the routine of school and its related activities.

Derek, who had done quite well for himself as a sports agent, was pulling out all the stops for his sons' visit. Professional basketball games, plays, comedy shows, movie premiers, and whatever entertainment he could squeeze into their three week visit. If it was going on, they were there. He took them to UCLA and USC to tour the campuses. He took them to a record company and finagled introductions to a hot new girl group. Needless to say what the highlight of their visit had been thus far. They also spent plenty of time with their Uncle Reggie, Diedra's brother, and his family. They even saw Aunt Shar, one of Diedra's oldest friends, out there. James and Diedra told them they were glad they were enjoying their vacation. They exchanged their goodbyes and ended the call. Once again Diedra and James thanked Lee-Beverly for taking the little ones. The boys literally dragged their grandmother out to her car as they waved goodbye to their parents.

Diedra and James walked out behind them and helped get the boys settled into the car. When they were off and away they walked back into the house to enjoy a quiet weekend alone.

The couple stood in the middle of the living room floor grinning at each other for several minutes. "What do we do now?" asked Diedra.

James looked at her with a mischievous grin and said, "I can think of a few things"

Diedra smiled back at him, took one step toward him and said,

"Hmm, do pray tell."

James grabbed Diedra's hands and led her over to the couch. He sat down and looked intently into her eyes with that look. That look that made Diedra feel as if she were sixteen years old all over again. The one that always seemed to sear straight through to her soul. He would cock his head slightly to one side and let that wicked smile play around one corner of his lips. The side with the little dimple that Diedra thought was so sexy. And his eyes, those gorgeous eyes would never leave hers.

Diedra and James spent the rest of their anniversary weekend rediscovering why they were married. They reminisced about their first meeting, their first date, their first kiss, and all the other firsts that were important in their relationship. They shared their hopes and dreams for themselves and their children as well as their fears. They spent time loving and teasing each other. They laughed together and they cried together. They both realized that this time alone was something that would be vital to their very survival as husband and wife.

By Monday morning they had taken their relationship to an entirely different level. The two of them realized that the connection they shared was something more powerful than they had ever realized previously. They shared a bond that went beyond words and promises. It was about something deep within their souls. For the first time in five years, they truly believed that this marriage was something that God had put together and they were bound and determined to make it work.

# CHAPTER 4

THE BELL ON THE ALARM clock rang at 5:30 Monday morning. James reached over and turned it off. He turned over to face Diedra, who was still fast asleep and kissed her on the cheek before he hopped up and bound into the bathroom. James, who was usually a morning person anyway, was extraordinarily chipper this morning. He was actually singing. His smooth, strong, voice resonated through the room with the words to Larry Graham's, 'One In A Million'. He sang in the shower and he sang as he came back to the bed to wake Diedra. When he saw her face he stopped singing.

Her face was set in a tight grimace. She looked as if her jaws were closed tight enough to break a tooth. James knew she was going to wake up with another headache this morning. He wandered how often she was having them. He had a feeling it was a lot more often than she let on. He looked at his wife and he ached for her. He thought about calling her job and telling them she wouldn't be in that morning, but he knew her well enough to know that wouldn't be appreciated. So instead, he began to gently massage her temples and her neck which was tense as well.

Diedra awakened, smiling weakly, and asked what he was doing. "Just trying to wake you up," he said. "Babe, I know you have to be in pain this morning."

"Why do you say that?" she asked.

"Because I could see it all over your face. While you were sleeping you looked as if someone had your head in a vice or something. I'm serious now. I want you to call Dr. Howard today, and make an appointment for a complete physical."

Diedra actually was in a great deal of pain; so much pain that she didn't have the strength to argue with James. "Okay" she responded.

"As a matter of fact, I think you should stay home today,"

"Okay,"

James was really worried now. *That was just too easy*, he thought to himself. To her he said, "I'm going to call in as well. I want to stay here and take care of y..."

"Don't push it James," Diedra interrupted. "I will stay home today, and I'll call Dr. Howard for an appointment. Who knows, maybe he'll be able to fit me in. Whatever the case, you can go to work. Although I appreciate your concern, I don't need you fussing over me." Diedra attempted to smile at James, but she was just too tired. She hoped he was reassured by the fact that she was taking his 'advice' this morning.

He wasn't. "I don't think I should leave you alone like this. Besides, knowing you, you'll probably go back to sleep as soon as I leave and end up spending the rest of the day in bed suffering. And tomorrow you'll go back to work, still unaware of the source of these headaches." They both knew he was right.

"James, you know you need to be in the office today. This is the first day after the holiday and it's going to be crazy down there. Look! Would it make you feel any better if I had Brea come over?"

Breanna Thomas wasn't one of James' favorite people but she was better than nothing. Diedra called her a free spirit. He just thought she was wild. Diedra said that was just her way of covering all the pain she carried from growing up without a father and losing her mother while she was still in college. She had no family of her own and all the money in the world could not dull that pain.

"Actually, I would feel better if you had Cassandra come over." He felt she was the more stable influence. "But if she just can't, then Brea will have to do."

"I would have them both come over but Cassie has her children at home. So it's going to be 'three of a kind minus one' today," she said, referring to James' nickname for Diedra and her two best friends. "But I promise you I will call Brea as soon as you leave." James looked at Diedra skeptically as he leaned over to kiss her good-bye.

"I'll call and check on you," he told her.

"I know you will," she sighed, as she watched her husband walk out of the room.

Cassandra Smith and Diedra had been friends since they were the triplets' age. Now they were both mothers. Diedra had her five sons and Cassandra had two daughters, Nicholette, 14, and Jasmine, 4. It would have been nice to spend the day with both friends, but it wasn't going to happen. Not this day.

Diedra thought she would go ahead and call Brea but then her head began throbbing and she was overcome by a wave of nausea that practically sent her reeling. She lay back across the bed and closed her eyes, waiting for either the pain or the nausea to subside. Soon she was fast asleep. She must have slept for a good half hour before she was startled awake by the ringing of a bell. She rolled off the bed and hurried to the front door to answer it. There was no one there. She walked back into the hallway and picked up the telephone. "Hello," she said as she tried to get her bearings.

"Hello?" Babe, are you all right? Why didn't you answer the phone? It must have rung at least 20 times." It was James. Diedra sat down in the chair next to the phone stand and tried to clear her head. She was really out of it. "Hello? Diedra what's going on? John Michaels called me wanting to know why you didn't make it to your meeting this morning. He said he'd called the house but got no answer. I explained to him that you weren't well this morning and you must have fallen back to sleep as soon as I left. I also told him you wouldn't be in for your regular shift tonight. I thought you were going to have Brea come over. I'll tell you what; I'm coming home."

Anxiety rang palpably through his voice.

"James, you don't have to do that. I just fell asleep. I told you I would call Brea but don't you think it's a little early to be calling someone?"

"Diedra it's 9:30."

"What! I couldn't have slept that long!" Diedra was shocked to learn that she had slept for over three hours. "James thank you for calling me but you don't have to leave work. I'll call Brea right now. As a matter of fact, let me go so I can get myself together."

"Okay Diedra, and Babe…"

"Yes?"

"I love you."

"James, I love you too. I'll see you this evening." She returned the receiver to the cradle and then picked it back up. "I can't believe I slept that long. Brea must be going mad. She hates waiting even more than I do." Diedra dialed Brea's number and just as it started ringing, her doorbell rang. She put the receiver down again and went to answer the front door. She looked through the beveled glass and saw Brea standing out on the front porch. Diedra opened the door and greeted her friend. "Hey lady! I was just trying to call you."

Brea stood on the porch looking like a fashion model. She had a way of looking glamorous without even trying. She could make a jogging suit look dressy. The thing about it was that with Brea, it really was effortless. Diedra knew for a fact that Brea did not put half the effort into her appearance as most women. If anything, she put more effort into trying to downplay her looks. But it never seemed to work. She even made her Police uniform look sexy. This morning she was wearing a denim mini-skirt with a purple, oversized cowl-neck, sweater, and even though the sweater was too large, it still managed to hit all the right curves. Her olive complexion was flawless and a pair of Ray-Bans perched on the tip of her nose. As usual not a hair of her short hairstyle was out of place. She stood there with her hands on her hips frowning at Diedra.

"What are you doing in there? I have been out here for twenty minutes at least. I rang the doorbell and knocked, and after you didn't answer I walked around back. By the time I got around the house I thought I heard the door open. Then I came back around here and you still weren't here!"

Diedra smiled sheepishly and shrugged, "I'm sorry. After James left this morning I kind of dozed off. Evidently, you showed up at the same time he called to check on me. I was running from the door to the phone. I didn't know what was going on." she said, as she led her friend back into the living room. "I have had the worst time pulling myself together this morning. When I woke up I felt as if my head was going to explode. I was exhausted and I guess James could tell something wasn't right. I had the hardest time convincing him to go to work this morning. When I told him you were coming over he reluctantly agreed to leave me."

"Well that was close," said Brea. "But if you had told your husband what was going on like I told you to, he could have been a source of comfort to you this morning, rather than anxiety. I'm sure the stress of keeping secrets is not help-ing you at all." Brea walked past Diedra and headed to the kitchen. "Cause, I'm telling you girl, it's not even my secret but it's stressing me out to no end. I've been eating like a horse. What do you have in here anyway? I'm so hungry," Brea said as she jerked open the refrigerator.

Diedra smiled at her friend as she watched her stick her head in the refriger-ator. "In your case I don't think that would be indicative of stress. You're always hungry. I'll never understand how an individual can eat as much as you do and never gain a pound to show for it. You probably still wear the same size you did in high school." Brea pulled out a pack of ham cold cuts, a pack of cheese, the mayonnaise, the mustard, and bread, and took it all over to the table.

"Look who's talking," she said as she retrieved a knife and plate from Diedra's cabinets. "I know for a fact that you can actually wear some of the same jeans you wore in high school.

"Yeah, but I can't wear them like I wore them in high school," quipped Diedra. "Anyway, I sure am glad you're here this morning. I am so nervous. Do you know James wanted me to call Dr. Howard for an appointment today?"

"What? How did you respond to that?"

"I told him I'd try to get in to see him. And what's even worse, I forgot to tell John Michaels I wouldn't make that meeting this morning. I guess after he wasn't able to reach me, he called James, who told him I wouldn't be in for my shift tonight either. Thankfully he didn't tell James that I was already off tonight."

"Dee, you need to be straight with your man. I don't know why you couldn't have told him about your doctor's appointment today. What's the big deal anyway?"

Diedra looked at her friend, shrugged her shoulders and said, "The big deal is that I don't even know what's going on with me. But I assure you that what-ever it is, I will tell James as soon as I know and we will deal with it together. I just need a little buffer between the time I find out and the time he finds out."

"You talk as if you've already been given a terminal diagnosis. You're prob-ably just anemic or something. Ha! I wouldn't be surprised if you were pregnant again," Brea laughed.

"Hush your mouth Brea. I think I would know if I were pregnant. I don't know what it is, but something is just not right. I'm going to go get ready for my appointment and in the meantime, try not to eat me out of house and home, okay." With that, Diedra went out of the kitchen and headed for her bedroom. Brea had not changed a bit since they were kids. She was always bold and straightforward. Although some found her to be a little brash, Diedra felt that this forthright quality was one of the reasons their friendship had lasted so long

Brea sat down at the table and began to prepare a ham and cheese sandwich for herself and one for Diedra. After she'd made two double-stacker sandwiches she looked at them appreciatively and said, "That'll do just fine." She poured herself a large glass of milk and sat down to her meal. She devoured her sandwich and started on Diedra's without a thought. By the time Brea was halfway through the second sandwich Diedra walked back in to the kitchen dressed and ready to go. She wore a simple yellow sweater dress with yellow pumps and some yellow hoop earrings. Her brown shoulder length hair was swept back into a neat ponytail with bangs. Brea smiled at her friend and said, "You look like a little girl. No one would believe that you were a mother of five, with teenagers, at that."

"Well thanks a lot. You know my goal every time I coordinate an outfit is to walk out of the house looking like an adolescent." Diedra walked to the refrigerator and poured herself a glass of milk. She grabbed a napkin and sat down at the table. The two women sat in silence.

Brea continued to devour her sandwich while Diedra drank her milk, one small sip at a time. "How much time do we have until your appointment?" Brea asked through a mouthful of food. Diedra took a dainty sip of her milk and wiped her mouth primly with the corner of her napkin.

Brea eyed her friend with an amused glint in her eyes while she waited for her reply. Diedra looked at her watch and said "Well, it's 10:20 now and my appointment is at 11. I'd say we should be leaving as soon as you tell me why you are looking at me as if I'm the funniest thing since "In Living Color." Then she finished off her milk and began to gather up the mayonnaise and other items Brea had sitting on the table. Brea swallowed the last bite of her sandwich and laughed out loud. As she helped Diedra clear the table she explained.

"I was just thinking. For as long as I've known you, you have had one particular trait that always amuses me. Whenever you are nervous your actions become very prim and proper, prudish even. It's really cute."

Diedra shook her head and said, "I don't know what you're talking about." Brea laughed and said "I'm talking about the way you daintily drank your glass of milk just now. Any other time, you would have thrown that glass back and swallowed that milk down with gusto"

Even though they had been friends for most of their lives, Diedra was still surprised by Brea's acute since of perception. She had always been one to notice the slightest details in even the most obscure circumstances. Perhaps that's why it didn't pay to lie to her which was part of the reason she'd turned out to be a far better cop than anyone had expected. Diedra stammered, "I...I..." She dropped her head and shrugged her shoulders, smiled sheepishly and said, "I'm really not very hungry or thirsty this morning but I knew I should put something on my stomach." She hated to admit to any weakness at all, and that was why Brea always made a point to call her out.

Brea liked to remind Diedra that even she had to lean on others sometimes, and that she had people ready to support her whenever she needed. Brea placed a reassuring hand on her shoulder saying. "Everything is going to be alright. I know it. I already prayed about it. Now who's driving, me or you?" Brea flashed a radiant smile at Diedra.

The two women agreed that Brea should drive. They finished putting the things away, Diedra grabbed a coat and out the door they went. Even though the drive to Dr. Howard's office was only twenty minutes, it seemed to last a lifetime. Brea tried to keep the mood light, but it was hard to do since she was worried about her friend. She knew that Diedra had been in a great deal of pain for a while now. She was glad they would finally get some answers but she was apprehensive.

Deidra was her best friend in the world and she didn't know what she'd do if anything happened to her. Since her mother had died, Diedra, Cassandra and Shar had been the closest thing to family she had.

Brea tried to keep the conversation going all the way into town but was unable to get more than an occasional chuckle or monosyllabic responses out of

Diedra. When they arrived at Dr. Howard's office the two of them were both surprised and relieved to see Cassandra waiting in front of the building.

It was the first week in January and the weather was typical for a winter day in Alabama, but Cassandra looked as if she was suffering through one of those German winters they'd all experienced rather than the cool winds of the south. She was bundled in a heavy wool coat with a hood and a wool scarf. She had on gloves and boots as well. Despite all the bundling, she still seemed cold. Brea let Diedra out and went to park the car. Diedra greeted Cassandra with a quick hug. "I'm glad you're here, but how did you manage?" she asked.

Cassandra smiled warmly at her friend and responded, "I realized I had to be here for you. Girl, I've been up since five a.m. this morning going stir crazy. In between pacing and talking to myself, I've been cleaning, reorganiz-ing, and driving everyone else in the house insane as well. Nicholette begged me to leave. She promised she would take good care of Jasmine today and I could make it up to her by taking the girls out to dinner and a movie tonight. So I told her it was a deal, and I got myself together and got out of there. I think I was a little hasty though." She clapped her gloved hands together and blew onto her fingers. "I could have stood to put on a few more layers of clothes. It's freezing out here."

"More clothes? You already look like an abominable snowman!" cracked Brea as she walked up to them. "I swear, I barely recognized you underneath all that swaddling. You are worse than Diedra. How the two of you ever survived one winter in Germany is beyond me.

Brea stood there in her mini-skirt and sweater next to Diedra and Cassandra, bundled up in their coats. It was obvious that though her two friends were miserable, the weather did not bother her at all. She had always seemed to have more tolerance for extreme temperatures. When their families were in Nurnberg, Germany, Diedra and Cassandra would barely tolerate the winter activities while Brea thoroughly enjoyed them. Each winter they would usually get an extra week or so of winter vacation due to 'snow days'. The girls would get together with their friends and build snowmen, have snowball fights, go sledding or skiing, or indulge in some other winter sport. But Cassandra and Diedra would usually have so many layers of clothes on that movement was constricted and mobility was limited. They could hardly do more than huddle up on the sidelines. Alabama winters left Cassandra in the same predicament.

Cassandra shivered and pulled her scarf tighter, as she adjusted her earmuffs underneath her hood. "Brea, I realize that your reptilian blood keeps you comfortable in even the dankest weather, but you cannot expect me to believe that you are comfortable out here dressed as you are."

Brea winked at Cassandra and said, "Although I dressed quite comfortably this morning, it was not with the intention of lounging around outside half the day." She linked an arm inside one of Diedra's arms and said, "Come on ladies! Let's go on inside and see if Dr. Howard is about ready."

Cassandra laughed and linked on to Diedra's other arm saying "Not without a thirty minute wait."

"At least!" Diedra added. Then she laughed.

Upon entering Dr. Howard's waiting room they saw that it was not quite as full as usual. The tastefully decorated office had only a few patients scattered throughout the waiting room. Two small children played quietly in the play area in the far corner of the room, their mothers watching them from nearby seats. A young man and his very pregnant wife sat in front of the receptionist's window. An older gentleman with a walker sat in an armchair behind the young couple.

Dr. Rodney Howard was one of only a few African American doctors in Calhoun County. Contrary to what one might expect, his patient list was more diverse than the doctor's listing for this area. Dr. Howard was a widely respected physician. His practice so successful and his care so sought after, that generally the only new patients he could accept were the newborns of his current patients. Many of his current patients, such as Diedra and Cassandra, had been under his care since they were small children. Like their parents, Dr. Howard was a retired armed service member. When they returned from Germany they picked right back up with his care.

The old fashioned parlor-like décor in Dr. Howard's waiting room belied the sleek modern architecture of the building and the high tech equipment in the treatment area. This room had a quiet, comfortable atmosphere that made his patients feel as if they were visiting an old friend, rather than waiting for some clinical procedure. The comfortable armchairs were arranged in conversation groups around coffee tables centered with assorted hypoallergenic floral arrangements. The three women walked over to the coat rack and Diedra and Cassandra started removing their outer layers of clothing. "Hmm, maybe you'll get in to see the good doctor without such a long wait today Dee," whispered Cassandra.

"No, I think there's something in the Hippocratic Oath stating that all patients will wait a minimum of thirty minutes per visit. Regardless of the purpose of said visit," said Brea softly. Cassandra and Diedra laughed at that. "I'm serious! Have you ever come in here for any reason and got out in under thirty minutes?"

"Sure I have," said Cassandra as she tucked her gloves in her pockets and began to unwrap her scarf.

"No you haven't, and neither have I, nor has anyone else for that matter," said Brea.

"Hush your mouth!" said Diedra as she tried to contain her own laughter. "I for one am glad to know that my doctor is taking the time to thoroughly assess and evaluate my situation each and every time I visit his office." Then she hung her coat up on the rack.

Cassandra finished unwrapping her scarf, folded it, and stuck it in her pocket along with her gloves and pulled back her hood and removed her earmuffs.

"That's all well and good," replied Brea "but the majority of your time at the office, in most cases, is usually spent waiting, not being assessed or evaluated!' She nodded toward Cassandra and said, "Now if you wait for the mummy over here to finish unwrapping, you'll be a good thirty minutes late signing in for your appointment." Cassandra just stuck her tongue out at Brea as she continued to remove her wraps. Diedra laughed at her friends and headed over to the receptionist's window.

As she drew closer to the window, her feet felt like cement blocks. Diedra's steps became more hesitant as she approached the receptionist. *I don't know what I'm so nervous about. It seems like I've been to this office a thousand times.* First one step... *Between the triplets with their asthma, and the twins and James with all his minor mishaps, I probably have been here a thousand times.* Then another step... *Now is the time for me to take care of me.* And another step... *Once I know what I'm facing, I can deal with it!* Then she arrived at the window... *"So sign in already!* She addressed the receptionist, "Hello Candy, I uh, I'm..."

"Hello, Mrs. Davis," the receptionist greeted her cheerfully. "You are right on time, as usual. I know you have a long afternoon ahead of you so we'll try to get to you as soon as possible. Just have a seat and I'll let them know in back that you are here so you can get started immediately." Diedra walked back over to Brea and Cassandra who had just hung up her coat. Cassandra straightened her glasses and adjusted the arms. She smoothed her curly, sandy colored hair down away from her face. Her hair had never been cut and the easiest thing for her to do was to pull it back into a ponytail that hung down her back. This was usually her style of choice.

"Maybe it won't be too long a wait today after all," Diedra said as she approached Brea and Cassandra. "Candy says they are ready for me and I will be going back to an examining room shortly." The three of them headed toward a group of chairs.

"And...?" asked Brea. "That means what? Baby girl, you're still going to have to wait; whether it's out here or in one of the examining rooms, stripped down to your birthday suit!"

Diedra blushed, "That's not Dr. Howard's wa..."

"That's all doctors!" interrupted Brea. Either you're left sitting in the waiting area like a forgotten child or they take you back to one of the examining rooms and have you strip down and wait for yet another eternity in that little paper gown. I guess they think you're less likely to get up and leave if you've already removed your clothing. It's as if by disrobing, you've committed yourself to waiting whatever length of time they might choose to leave you there."

"Breathe Brea! Just inhale, relax, and let it go!" interjected Cassandra. She had been a huge Iyanla fan since the first time she saw her on OPRAH. "To his credit," she continued, "Dr. Howard does not overbook his appointments. It's just that his patient load is so large that the probability of having several emergency or walk-in patients on any given day is higher than most. And by the way

Brea, if your optometrist has you strip down in his examining room or any other room for that matter, I suggest you check for hidden cameras."

"Cassie, don't be so literal. You know what I'm saying here." Brea winked at Diedra who was nowhere near their conversation, and continued "I understand that you feel a sense of kinship with the members of the medical community but honey don't be so defensive. You're not even through medical school yet.

"You're incorrigible!"

"I know, but isn't that why y'all love me?" quipped Brea.

"Hardly, it's why we're the only ones who love you. Me, Diedra, and Shar; we're the only people you can't scare away."

"Well forget anyone who can't handle an intelligent black woman with a strong personality!"

Brea and Cassandra continued along on that line for several minutes. Neither one realizing that Diedra had not said a word from the moment she sat down.

Baby girl was a term that Brea generally used when she was being sarcastic or just teasing. She used the term with no specific implication intended, but today when she said those words they took Diedra back to her dream the morning of her anniversary: the one that Granddaddy and Big Daddy were in. It had all seemed so real! She felt as if she had really spoken with them and they had told her something significant, but try as she might, she just couldn't recall what it was. She felt like it was teetering at the tip of her consciousness but she just couldn't pull it in.

Twice today, someone had alluded to remarks made by Granddaddy and Big Daddy and each time she felt she was on the verge of remembering, but each time she fell short. She felt the answer to this question might possibly put her entire life into perspective. A distinct possibility given that she believed Big Daddy had told her what her life's purpose was.

Brea and Cassandra laughed and teased each other. The *four of them* looked at her in alarm as the room started spinning and everything went black!

Brea jumped into action as Diedra started to slip from her chair. "Candy! Get Dr. Howard. Now!" she screamed as she caught Diedra and gently lowered her to the floor. Cassandra grabbed Diedra's wrist to check her pulse and then Brea started rambling. "What the hell is going on with you Diedra?" She was wringing her hands and shaking her head from side to side. "Lord, I don't know what I'd do if I lost my best friend! She's family! Cassie what's wrong with her?" She cried, "You're supposed to be…"

"Okay ladies we'll take it from here." Dr. Howard and another, much younger man appeared at their side, along with a couple of nurses. The younger man kneeled down beside Diedra and began to examine her while Dr. Howard tried to calm Brea. He walked her over to a chair across the room. Cassandra cried softly and continued to hold tightly to Diedra's wrist until Candy came and led her over to Dr. Howard. "Let them take care of her Cassie. She'll be alright." She tried to reassure her.

"How do you know she'll be alright? We don't even know what's wrong with her!" Cassandra snapped." Candy just hugged her and left her with Dr. Howard and Brea.

Dr. Howard walked back over to Diedra and knelt down beside her. He and the younger man spoke quietly as they continued to examine her, then Dr. Howard returned to Brea and Cassandra while the younger man tended to Diedra.

"Why aren't you taking care of her, Dr. Howard? Aren't you supposed to be her doctor?" asked Brea "Why are you leaving her to some stranger? He doesn't know her history, he doesn't know her!" Brea was practically hysterical. She buried her head in Dr. Howard's shoulder as she cried.

In all the years they'd known each other, Cassandra had never seen Brea cry. Not even when her mother had passed. Seeing her in this state served as a stabilizer for her as she tried to pull herself together. She took a deep breath and tried to remain calm a she spoke, "She's right Dr. Howard. Diedra needs you, not some resident. You know she came here today because she had some serious concerns about her health. How can you leave her to some…?"

Dr. Howard motioned for Candy to bring Brea a box of tissues as he interrupted Cassandra. "I know you're scared and concerned for your friend. I'm concerned as well. I assure you she is in the best possible hands. Rodney is here specifically to see Diedra today. He has been fully briefed on her history. In fact we were going over her charts when we heard Brea cry out."

"Rodney? Your son?" Cassandra asked, feeling a sense of dread come over her as she watched Dr. Rodney Howard Jr. and the two nurses take Diedra to the back. "Isn't he a neurologist?" she asked, barely able to choke out the words.

"Yes, he's one of the best. And I'm not just saying that because he's my son."

"Oh I know!" said Cassandra. "I've read some of his articles and he is highly respected at UAB." She rubbed her hands across her face. "Sooo..." She was almost afraid to ask. "Did he come over here just for Diedra?" She barely breathed as she waited for his reply.

"Oh no! I'm sorry, but I don't know enough about her condition to make that kind of referral. He was in town for the weekend and I mentioned her case to him. He had a few questions that I couldn't answer, so he offered to come in and examine her today." Dr. Howard did not want to further alarm Cassandra or Brea. "You know Rodney and Reggie were always pretty close. He was just doing this as a favor. We both agreed that we could determine today whether further testing was needed or not; and if they were, he would do what he could today."

"What are you saying?" asked Cassandra. "Do you think her headaches are indicative of some sort of neurological problem?"

"That's a pretty rare phenomenon. There could be any number of explanations, but we won't be able to determine anything until we examine her. I can tell you this though. Apparently Diedra fainted. But she's coming around. I am not sure of the exact cause of her fainting and won't be until she's been further examined, but I'm sure the fainting itself is not a major crisis."

By this time Brea had calmed down considerably. She wiped her tears and spoke to Dr. Howard. "I'm sorry for losing control. Diedra's like a sister to me. She's been having these headaches for some time now." She wiped a tissue across her face. "We've been worried about her and even though she won't admit it, I know she's been worried as well. And realizing how scared she actually is has doubled my anxiety. So when I saw her falling, I panicked. I didn't know what was happening. All kinds of horrific thoughts crossed my mind. I thought she could have been having a heart attack or stroke or something." She shuddered as if the mere thought of such a thing would send her back into an emotional tailspin. "I'm glad to know it wasn't something major like that but I think you should go on and see about her," she said. And as an afterthought she added sheepishly, "or your other patients."

"Yes. I do have other patients." He agreed as he stood up. He excused himself, and headed to the back. As he opened the door, he turned and asked "Are you ladies sure you're okay?" They both nodded yes and he disappeared through the doorway.

Cassandra and Brea both sat silently for several moments, then Brea said "I'm sure she'll be alright. She didn't eat any breakfast this morning because she was so nervous. That might be why she fainted. I know I can't function if I miss a meal. I told her she's probably just pregnant." She laughed nervously. "That happens to pregnant women doesn't it? Did you ever faint when you were carrying your girls?"

"I'm sorry, I didn't hear you. I'm just sitting here trying to figure out what questions Dr. Howard had that needed to be answered by a neurologist."

"Don't all headaches have some sort of neurological origin? Maybe Rodney is here more in the capacity of a family friend, as opposed to a neurological consult."

Cassandra thought that might make sense. At least it was a possibility. No sense stressing over the unknown. They were here to get some answers and whatever they were, they would have to be strong for Diedra. She looked at Brea sitting next to her; cool, calm, and seemingly in control. No trace of the panicked, woman who'd been pacing, crying, and blubbering nonsense a few moments ago. This was Officer Breanna Thomas of the Jacksonville Police Department. Always poised and steady. From what she had heard, Brea had managed to keep her cool in some pretty hairy situations. But just now, she had practically fallen apart when she thought their friend was hurt. Cassandra was grateful that Brea's instinct took over before she fell into complete disarray. But still...! She smirked at Brea who continued talking for a moment.

"What?" Brea asked.

"I didn't say anything," she responded.

"But why are you looking at me like that?"

"I'm just wandering. If you were called to my home for an emergency would you make it there in record time, or would you be so upset that you'd forget your way to my house? Or, would you make it to my house in record time and forget all procedure once you arrived?"

Brea turned her head in an attempt to conceal her blush as she tried to recover from the barb. She laughed aloud and turned back to Cassandra. "I know you're not talking! If I come to you in labor, are you going to deliver my baby or take my pulse?"

"It's perfectly normal to check the vital signs of an individual who's fainted."

"Sure it is! What was Diedra's pulse by the time Candy pried you away from her?"

Cassandra put her hand to her face and giggled softly. "Okay, we both fell apart. But seriously Brea, I was afraid! When I saw her falling, the first thought that came to my mind was stroke. You know her granddaddy died from a stroke. What would James do with all those boys if something happened to Diedra?"

"I don't know, girl. I'm just glad she's okay for now and I hope that their examination of her brings positive news. I mean even if there's a problem, knowing what it is means they can focus on treatment."

"Yes! Now you're starting to sound like the Breanna I know and love. We have to keep a positive outlook for Diedra's sake. She could make herself that much sicker from worry and stress."

"Well I wish someone would let us know what's going on."

"I know girl."

"But Cassie," Brea leaned over and said in a conspiratorial tone.

"Yes."

"Did you see Rodney?"

"Yes I did! I can't believe I didn't recognize him. Has it been that long?"

"I don't know girl, but I'll tell you. I didn't think he could get any finer than he was when he and Reggie were in High School."

"Um! Is he still married?"

"I'm sure he is. Kayla's no fool."

"He was always crazy about her and I'm sure he still is. If it had been an option for class superlative, those two would have been voted most likely to grow old together."

"I know. They did seem like they just belonged together. I saw them a few years ago at the fireworks at Oxford Lake. You know the year you and Shawn went to visit your in-laws for the fourth. I swear they seemed more like best friends than husband and wife. But you never know. Things happen."

"I wouldn't hold my breath for that one though Brea."

"Don't get me wrong now. I'm not hoping for the demise of anyone's marriage." Brea smiled coyly. "I'm just saying…If they did happen to break-up for some reason. Whatever reason, I'd sure like to have a chance at that."

"You'd like a chance at what?"

The voice brought back a stream of high school memories. In that instant they became like a couple of giggling adolescents. Rodney Howard had not lost his touch. He still possessed the same magnetism that caused the younger girls to swoon and fall all over each other whenever he entered a room. The former All American QB was still a fine athletic specimen. He smiled down at the ladies as Brea smiled what she thought was her sexiest smile, but it turned out to be a goofy, toothy grin. Cassandra stammered and stuttered and tried to answer him until she just gave up and gave him a grin to match the one that was spread across Brea's face.

"Excuse me ladies. I didn't mean to interrupt but I thought you would want to hear some news about Diedra."

"Is she alright?" they chimed in unison.

"Yes. She'll be right out."

"What happened? Why did she faint?" asked Cassandra.

"Cassie, I'm sure you understand that I can't give you an in depth report on Diedra's case, but I'm certain she'll tell you what's going on when she comes out." Neither Cassandra nor Brea was too pleased with that response, but they realized he was right. Rodney sat in a chair across from them, "It's been a long time. How have things been going with you two? Besides worrying about Lil' Dee that is."

"Oh don't you dare let her hear you call her that!" said Brea. "She finally had to accept being called Dee, but she'll just about fight you for calling her Lil' Dee."

"You're kidding?" he asked, shaking his head and laughing softly.

"No she's not," said Cassandra. "She always felt that was an insult, especially coming from her big brother and his friends."

"I see, well thanks for the warning. We never meant any harm though. The four of you were like our own little sisters. Better actually, because we could always leave when you started getting on our nerves," he laughed, "But I'll be sure not to address her as Lil' Dee though." He reached over and tweaked Cassandra's arm. "So Cassie, I hear you've reentered Medical School. How do you like UAB?" Same old Rodney, he always seemed to make everyone feel as if he were genuinely interested in them and what was going on in their lives.

"I didn't realize you were aware that I'd been to medical school in the first place." Cassandra was surprised. It wasn't like he'd been around all these years. From the time he'd left for med school he'd never spent more than a couple weekends a year back in town. He had attended some fancy medical school, and then went on to an extraordinarily successful career in medicine. His parents were not ones to brag on their youngest son, or any of their children for that matter, so it was not easy to keep up with him. He and Diedra's older brother, Reggie were still close and that's where they got most of their news about him. Occasionally Shar would share updates from Atlanta. Apparently, he kept up with what was going on in their lives as well.

"Of course I was aware. I hated to hear that you'd decided to leave medical school. We need good minds like yours in the medical field. I was even tempted to call you when I heard the news but Kayla convinced me that it wasn't my place to interfere with your life choices. She insisted that you couldn't walk around with medicine in your heart and not eventually pursue it, and if it wasn't in your heart, you shouldn't pursue it."

"She always was a smart one, that Kayla," said Brea.

"I know that's the truth. This is one time I am more than happy to be able to say 'You were right' to her though. And what about you Ms. Breanna, how do you like Law Enforcement?"

Brea's face lit up as she spoke. "It's wild! There's always something going on. No such thing as a dull moment. Those college students are a trip. I don't believe I was ever as doe-eyed as some of them."

"I'm sure we all were." Rodney said knowingly. He had known some of them just as long as they'd known each other. He and Reggie started kindergarten together. His father left the military for private practice when he was still quite young. So when their families were overseas, his was still right there in Jacksonville. Perhaps that was why he stayed away as long as he did once he went out on his own. Even so, he and Reggie had always remained close and he had spent a great deal of time with the Daniel's family and their friends. Back in the day, Diedra and her friends were like his own pesky little sisters. He knew they had major crushes on him. Reggie teased him about it constantly.

When they became teenagers and began to mature into the beautiful young women they were destined to become, it became a little harder to view them as little sisters; until other guys would start to notice them. Then he would become as protective of them as Reggie.

Today when he looked at the ladies they had become he was as proud as if he had helped to raise them himself. Cassandra was happily married, raising a family and attending medical school. She had married some white guy she dated at Howard. He was a military brat as well, and according to Shar, they had been inseparable from the time they got together.

Brea, who'd done a stint as a teacher up north, was a police officer now. Leave it to her to do something totally unexpected. She always was unpredictable. Although he didn't meet her until she was in high school, he felt just as protective of her as the others. Things had been a little harder for Diedra than she had ever expected, but she seemed to be finding her way.

And Sharnell Jackson, Shar as they called her, was a girl after his own heart. She was a card-carrying member of overachiever's anonymous. She went off on her own to follow her career as a high-powered attorney and was doing quite well for herself. He came across her occasionally at different social or political functions in Atlanta and she always seemed to have it together.

She was actually the one who'd kept him up to date on the happenings in these ladies' lives. Shar had told him about the headaches Diedra was having and she'd asked him to come home and check her out.

Shar hadn't married yet. She didn't even appear to be on that track, but she was happy. She had a plan and so far she'd accomplished everything she'd set out to do. She was living her life to the fullest and she relished life in the city.

He, on the other hand, was worn out by the constant rush of urban life. Which was why he had decided to move back home and accept the offer from UAB to join their staff. The University of Alabama in Birmingham medical center was close enough to Jacksonville for him and his family to enjoy the best of both worlds; small town living and breakthrough medicine.

Rodney's thoughts were interrupted by the sound of Diedra's voice as she and his father approached. He looked up to see her ashen face. She still hadn't been able to digest the only certain answer they were able to divulge from the day's examinations. Who wouldn't be stunned by the morning's revelation?

CHAPTER 5

WHEN RODNEY AND THE TWO nurses, escorted Diedra back to the examining room she was still a bit disoriented. Rodney assured her that she would be fine and proceeded to examine her. He ordered some blood work and stayed with her while they waited for the results. During this time he explained to her why he was the one examining her instead of his father and they discussed her medical history.

By the time the initial lab reports came back, Rodney was convinced that his initial suspicions were correct. He took the report into his father's office and read over her lab results, which were mostly inconclusive. He read over them thoroughly, and then once again to ensure that he hadn't missed anything. After he made a few notes he went back into the room where Diedra waited, to explain the results to her.

She looked vulnerable sitting on the examining table with her legs dangling over the side. He thought about how he would begin to explain to her what was certainly ahead for her and what the other possibilities were. He decided to begin with the certainty.

"Well Mrs. Davis! He said as he pulled up a chair. "How are you feeling now?" She nodded her head and told him she felt fine.

Rodney looked at Diedra wondrously, shaking his head from side to side. He said, "It's incredible how time flies. It seems like only yesterday when you and your friends were hanging around Reggie and me, and just getting in the way."

Diedra responded, "Your memory fails you, Dr. Howard. It was you and Reggie who always seemed to be underfoot. Always hassling me and my friends."

"Never-the-less, it amazes me to see you all grown up, and raising a family of your own at that. How do you like motherhood?" He watched closely for her response to the question.

"I love being a mother," she responded. "Although I would have never dreamed that I would have five children, and all boys too! I can't imagine what my life would be like without them. They put everything into perspective."

"What do you mean?" he asked.

Diedra smiled through tired eyes. "Being around young children who still get excited by the simple things in life, and watching them meet each day expecting a new discovery, and knowing they are never disappointed is a blessing. When they are as young as the triplets are, they seem to embrace every aspect of life wholeheartedly. They react so intensely to everything, be it good or bad.

Being in a position to help guide them through all these emotions and lessons is about the biggest responsibility I could have ever taken on. Then when they get to be the twins' age and you can look at them and feel certain they are on the right track... Rodney, I can't tell you how satisfying that is."

Rodney smiled warmly at Diedra. "You really were cut out for motherhood weren't you? Do you regret not having any girls?"

"I would have loved to have had at least one little girl, but I wouldn't trade any of my sons for anything in the world. I don't guess it was meant to be."

"Why do you say that?"

Diedra chuckled at his question. "You're not serious! You know how old I am. Besides, as much as we love our sons, James and I have a hard enough time feeding and clothing five growing boys. Another child, girl or boy, would send our budget right through the roof."

Rodney understood where Diedra was coming from. He knew she and her husband had to be struggling with all those children. Even though they both worked and he assumed Derek helped, raising children was expensive. "So if you felt you could afford it, would you consider trying for that girl?" he asked.

"I don't know for sure." Diedra said slowly as she scrutinized Rodney with a piercing gaze. "Why are you asking me all these questions about children? I know you don't think I could be pregnant. Brea suggested that, but I would know if I was pregnant."

Rodney hesitated slightly before he stated. "Diedra, I've done as thorough an examination of you today as I was able.

We ran several lab tests and unfortunately, most of them were inconclusive. The only thing I know for certain now, that I didn't know before is…" He paused and took a deep breath.

"What is it Rodney? What's wrong with me? Do not keep me in suspense." Diedra said, even though she'd just realized how terrified she was of hearing the answer."

"Diedra you are pregnant, again," he announced.

Diedra nearly fell off of the examining table. She was stunned. Rodney caught her and held her elbows while she clenched the front of his lab coat tightly in both her fists. She stared past him into some distant place. Rodney continued to stand in front of her, holding her up, not wanting to let go for fear she might fall over, or worse, off of the table. After several minutes he spoke.

"Are you alright?" He asked.

"Yes, I'm fine." Diedra said softly. She continued to stare at something, someplace. Rodney didn't know what. She released his jacket with one hand, ran her palm across her face, resting it on her cheek and sighed heavily. Are you sure?" she asked. Her voice was little more than a whisper.

"Yes, this is the one thing I am certain of," he replied.

"S…S..So," she stammered. "So does this have anything to do with my headaches, and dizzy spells?" she questioned.

"It could, but I'm not certain that it's the only contributing factor. We'll have to schedule further testing, but for now, let's concentrate on your pregnancy. I'm going to get my dad so he can examine you himself and I'm sure he can answer any questions you may have about your pregnancy." He released her elbow and gently removed the corner of his jacket from the hand that still clenched it tightly. Before he turned and left, he patted her shoulder affectionately and said, "Diedra you're right you know. Motherhood is truly a blessing." Then he left to go get his father.

Diedra sat alone in the room trying to digest the news she had just received. Pregnant again! Even though Brea had teased her about the possibility, she had never thought, not even for one millisecond that it could be the case. *This had to be a mistake.* Besides, when she was pregnant before, she knew almost immediately. How could she not know it this time? She realized that no two pregnancies were exactly alike, but she knew her body. She couldn't be pregnant. How far along was she supposed to be anyway? Besides, Rodney was no OB-GYN. He could have made a mistake. He had to have! *Well, maybe this is my girl.* She smiled to herself. *Maybe I did have a girl in me after all.* Her thoughts were all over the map. *With my luck, it's probably another boy. Four this time! What is James going to say when he hears the news?* "This is crazy!" she said out loud.

The two Dr. Howards entered the room. Dr. Howard Sr. approached Diedra with his chart in hand, smiling from ear to ear. "I see we've got some exciting news. Congratulations, Mrs. Davis." Rodney excused himself and his father took over.

Dr. Howard was a wonderful physician and Diedra was glad to have him. Since Diedra's cycle appeared to have been uninterrupted, he set about trying to determine an approximate date of conception and due date. He measured her uterus and listened for a fetal heartbeat. He was quick and thorough. Upon completion of his examination, he wrote a prescription for iron and prenatal vitamins and explained to Diedra that she appeared to be approximately 18 weeks along but he would not be certain until they were able to perform an ultra-sound.

Dr. Howard instructed her to set an appointment with Candy before she left. He congratulated Diedra once more, and then left her to regroup. Diedra slowly dressed herself and gathered her things. When she walked out into the hallway she stood in front of the room for several minutes before she turned toward the checkout window. Candy gave her an appointment time for her ultra-sound along with her receipt for services. Diedra stumbled as she headed back out to the waiting area where her friends were waiting for her.

When she passed Dr. Howard, he greeted her but she failed to respond. Realizing that she was in a veritable state of shock, he turned and escorted her back to her friends. He struck up a meaningless conversation about the rain forest or some other topic that seemed light years away from the reality Diedra was being forced to comprehend at that moment. Rodney got up and gave Diedra his seat. His father bid them good day and returned to his other patients. Cassandra and Brea both noticed the expression on Diedra's face. She looked confused and disoriented. Brea was the first to speak.

"What up girl-friend?" she said teasingly. "You sure did give us a scare, falling out like that in the middle of the lobby here."

Diedra didn't respond. She made a weak attempt at smiling and wiped her hands across her face as if she was trying to wake up. Brea studied her friend. She was reminded of that afternoon nearly 16 years ago when she and Diedra sat in the dorm suite they shared at UConn. Diedra and Derek had gone to the hospital for an ultra-sound that afternoon and she had rushed in from track practice to hear if they were having a boy or girl.

When she arrived at their suite, she found Diedra alone with the same confused, scared, and awestruck expression. She remembered that Diedra was excited to learn that she was carrying twin boys but she said Derek didn't share in her excitement. Afraid she was going to be forced to choose between Derek and her babies, Diedra had tried to rationally weigh her options. Fortunately, she realized she only had one. She was going to keep her babies regardless of what Derek did. But it wouldn't be easy.

Diedra had so many conflicting emotions going on that day. She was ashamed and proud at the same time. She was anxious and excited about the prospect of becoming a mother, of twins no less, but she was scared as well. She built a wall around herself that stood fast for a very long time. Brea felt she was the only one privy to Diedra's true emotions; all of them, good and bad. Brea had her own set of issues going on at that time but she was forced to put them aside in order to become the source of support her friend needed.

Today, Brea watched her friend grapple with the same spectrum of emotions that had gripped her that day, so long ago. "Well?" she ventured cautiously. "Are you alright?" she asked, uncertain whether she wanted to hear the answer or not. Diedra tried to smile but couldn't muster one up. She really didn't know how to answer that question so she just sat for a few moments more, staring at the floor a few feet in front of her.

Cassandra placed an arm around Diedra's shoulders and assured her "Whatever the problem is, we can handle it Diedra."

Diedra looked up at Cassandra, Brea and then Rodney, "I'm alright. I'm just pregnant, again, is all." Cassandra and Brea both stared at her in surprise. Cassandra was the first to speak.

She squeezed Diedra in a big excited hug and said, "That's wonderful! You are truly blessed, Dee!" Cassandra had always wanted a house full of children. She had thoroughly enjoyed both of her pregnancies. She would have been happy to stay home and raise eight or ten babies but after Jasmine was born, she'd had some complications and was unable to conceive again. She was excited at the prospect of experiencing motherhood again, albeit vicariously, through her friend.

Brea, on the other hand, had been the one who had been with Diedra when she carried her twins and she knew first hand, how difficult a time she'd had, both physically and emotionally. She realized that was in part, due to the way things had gone with Derek.

Her second pregnancy was a different story all together. Diedra was totally happy and excited about the prospect of giving birth to James' children and he was most supportive. Although it was a high risk pregnancy, due to the multiplicity factor, it was not nearly as stressful a time for her as when she carried Adrian and Austin.

But looking at her now, Brea determined that this time Diedra was not certain of her feelings about the matter. This was understandable, given the circumstances. Any woman in her mid-thirties with five children, barring Cassandra, would be overwhelmed by the revelation that they were carrying baby number six.

Although she had no children of her own, Brea thought she could empathize with Diedra. Brea wanted a child of her own. One! But she wasn't sure if she wanted to do that at this point in her life. Have children. She kind of felt she'd missed that train. And, if by some stroke of fate, she was to find herself in a boxcar seat to motherhood, she didn't know how she would react.

She waited for Cassandra to release Diedra and said "I know this had to come as a surprise to you, but maybe this time you'll get that girl you've always wanted."

Diedra looked at Brea, realizing that she, better than anyone else, even her husband, would probably understand what she was feeling right about now.

"I wouldn't even count on it. When James and I were pregnant with the triplets, we agreed that they would be the last. We didn't believe the odds would be in favor of our next child being a girl. You know we love those boys more than anything in the world, but..." she hesitated and before she could resume speaking Brea interrupted.

"I know. It's a lot to process. We should get you home so you and your husband can discuss this and work through it together. And no matter what," She shot a warning glance over at Cassandra. "You have to know that your friends are always here for you."

Cassandra took the hint and chose not to force the issue of how lucky Diedra was to be pregnant again with what might very well turn out to be her sixth and possibly seventh child. Instead, she agreed with Brea that they should start making their way home. She suggested they grab some lunch and then call it a day.

The three women gathered up their things and headed out the door. They decided to eat at a new restaurant in Jacksonville. It was an old barn that had been converted into a restaurant called the Old Farmhouse. This was their favorite restaurant mainly because they served the most authentic German food either of them had tasted in the states. Except for that one place in Pennsylvania that Diedra and Brea had stumbled across one weekend when they were at the University of Connecticut. They were at the Penn Relays and had gone off on their own looking for a decent restaurant. They found a little place called the Jaeger Haus, in the vicinity of the track meet, that brought about serious flashbacks of their high school days in Germany. From the Bavarian décor down to the brötchen, every detail was authentic. This restaurant didn't have the Bavarian décor but their wiener schnitzel and German potato salad were on point.

Cassandra followed behind Diedra and Brea as they drove back toward Jacksonville. They headed up Quintard, which was part of the strip of road that the entire county was centered around. It was mid-afternoon and traffic was steady but not too heavy. The sky was clear and the air was cool, but it was not as nippy as it had been earlier. Diedra and Brea were both silent. By the time they passed through the light at Summeral Gate they saw a woman who appeared to be just a little older than them, working her way toward Lenlock with three shopping carts loaded to the brim with various items. They saw her stop and leave two of her carts next to a clump of bushes in the divider and then return to the cart she'd left several hundred feet behind her and push that one up to the other two. They continued to ride in silence. Diedra stared out her window until Brea spoke. "Did you see that woman?" Brea asked. "Doesn't she make you think of the city? I never would have thought we would have bona-fide street people in Calhoun County. But if anyone qualifies it would be her, cart and all."

Diedra glanced back for a final glimpse and said. "You know we had the Long Rider in Jacksonville for a long time."

"Yeah, but she wasn't really homeless. I heard she had a house."

"I hear that woman has her own home as well. But you have to wander what would motivate an individual who actually has a home to go to, to spend so much time wandering the streets, especially in this weather."

"At least she dresses accordingly. Have you seen that guy running along this same stretch of road every morning? I'm talking tank tops in the winter and sweaters in the summer, and never any shoes!"

"Yes, I've seen him, one sock on and one sock off. I believe he's wrestling with something we can't even understand." Diedra placed a hand absently across her abdomen and the other one against the window. "Haven't you ever wanted to just get up and run, and just keep going? Or get in your car and drive as far as you could go on a full tank and just see where you ended up?'

Brea glanced over at Diedra and replied lightly. "One tank of gas won't take you far, Dee."

"I know that, but sometimes I wish I could remove myself from right here for just a little while. You know no kids, no job, and no responsibilities. Just for a little while. I know that sounds selfish but sometimes I wish I could have a respite from being responsible."

"That's not selfish at all. Everyone needs a little time to concentrate on themselves. Not their family, but themselves. It's called a break, or even better, a vacation. And by the way, when was the last time you had either?" She asked, knowing full well the answer. Diedra had never been away from all her children for more than a weekend. And when she was, they were the ones who left, not her. She was usually left home to catch up on housework, or go to her job as a supervisor at the printing company.

At least James' job gave him an excuse to break away from the norm now and then. His profession allowed him to temporarily remove himself from the day-to-day grind of raising a family when he went on business trips several times a year. Diedra didn't even have that.

Now that the triplets were older and the twins were able to babysit, she and James had started discussing joining their friends on that Memorial Day cruise this year. But she was likely to let this new bit of information put a stop to that.

They continued along to the restaurant in silence, both women deep in thought. When they arrived at the Old Farmhouse they parked in a space near the main entrance and Cassandra pulled into the space beside them. The three women hurried into the building and headed for the main dining area.

## CHAPTER 6

THE OLD FARMHOUSE HAD A comfortable elegance. It offered a quiet atmosphere and it was the perfect place to relax and absorb a startling revelation such as they had received. As soon as the ladies were seated their waiter, a young college student, approached their table with water glasses, complementary brŏtchen, and menus.

As he filled their glasses he asked Brea how she was enjoying the weather and had she had an opportunity to dine at the Old Farmhouse before? Was she originally from Jacksonville or was she here to attend the university? Brea smiled politely and replied that she loved the weather, and the Old Farmhouse was her favorite restaurant. She'd lived in Jacksonville for many years now, and had even attended high school here, but she'd graduated from UCONN many years ago.

He looked at Brea appreciatively and said, "I'm sure it couldn't have been too many years ago."

Diedra and Cassandra smiled across the table at each other and Diedra took a sip from her glass mumbling "No he isn't trying to flirt," as the exchange took place.

The waiter, who looked to be no more than 19, was not put off one bit. He smiled at Brea with a full set of beautiful white teeth and said. "Well, I've always been a Husky fan. I'd love to get with you sometime and share insights on Husky-mania and its impact on the basketball fans of today."

At that, Diedra began to cough uncontrollably. Cassandra jumped up and hurriedly moved around the table to assist her as she tried to regain her composure. Cassandra patted Diedra's back vigorously as she tried unsuccess-fully to stifle her own laughter. Brea shot them a sharp glance before she re-sponded to the young waiter.

"I'm extremely flattered, um Michael, is it?" she said, reading his nametag. "But frankly, I find the whole idea of Husky-mania having any visibly lasting ef-fect on even a minute portion of society, to be grossly overstated. Now if you'd really like to get together and discuss any relevant social issues, preferably those pertinent to us here in Alabama, I'd be more than happy to get together with you and any other students who'd like to hold an open forum. That's something we did regularly back when I was in college… several years ago." She looked pointedly at him. "We found it to be both an enlightening and entertaining experience that proved to be even more beneficial when we were able to in-clude faculty members." She turned to Diedra and asked "Don't you agree Mrs. Davis?"

Diedra shook her head in agreement, coughed once more, and then she and Cassandra completely fell apart. They laughed so hard that they both nearly fell over onto the floor. They were both brought to tears. Cassandra looked at the waiter and tried to pull herself together. She wiped her eyes and sat up straight in her chair saying, "Don't mind us. It's been a terribly long day. Very stressful, and I don't even know why I'm laughing. She smiled at Diedra and tried to continue, but just shrugged her shoulders and took a long swig from her glass of water. She held her glass out to Michael and sheepishly asked, "More water please?"

Brea rested an elbow on the table and put her fist to her mouth as she bit down on her lower lip in an attempt to cover her own smile. Then she smiled wryly at her friends and turned to Michael. "Please forgive my friends," she said as lightly as she was able. "It really has been a stressful day. If you'll give us a moment, we'll be ready to order shortly."

With that, the young man excused himself and the three ladies watched him walk across the room.

"I see you've still got it, Brea!" Cassandra said as she leaned over and watched Michael disappear behind the swinging doors that led to the kitchen. Brea smiled coyly and asked. "What are you talking about Cassie?"

"She's talking about the way you can't go anywhere without someone hitting on you. I swear Brea! You probably couldn't even walk through a monastery without someone slipping you their phone number."

Diedra laughed and Cassandra joined in with, "At least in that instance, odds are, they'd probably be legal. Junior over there can't be a day over 18, if that. Brea, they seem to get younger and younger."

"Oh Cassie, don't hate!" replied Brea. "All he did was pour us water, but you have to admit the boy is fine."

"Sure he is, in a juvenile sort of way," said Cassandra.

Diedra had to disagree. "Please! Girl, he is a young man, but the operative word here is man!" She said to Cassandra. "Do you think he was wearing contacts? A dark skinned man with green eyes! Ooh!" and then to Brea she said. "And no point in denying it, I saw the way you looked at him. You'll see him again."

"Sure I will," said Brea. "He'll be back to get our orders shortly."

"Whatever. You don't have to front for us. We know you like your men young." Diedra and Cassandra both knew that Brea didn't really center her attention on one particular age bracket when it came to her social life, but she seemed to especially enjoy the company of younger men. She didn't deny that she liked younger men. She liked men in general. Beyond her friends Diedra, Cassandra, and Shar, she really didn't seem to bond at all with women. She was single and she liked to socialize. And she had no shortage of 'friends'.

Brea reached into the bread basket and selected one of the brŏtchen. She held the perfectly crusted roll in front of her and inhaled the enticing aroma that always flooded her senses with memories of Germany. She smiled across the room at Michael who was headed back toward their table, and spoke to her friends. "I don't know about you two, but I'm hungry, so can you please let the man take our orders without anyone falling out of their chair into the middle of the floor?"

"Sure thing," they both said in unison. The waiter came and took their orders and returned shortly with their food. They each had ordered the Wiener schnitzel and pom-fritz; breaded veal and French fries. Michael set the plates before them and asked if there was anything else he could get for them before he moved on. They all thanked him and turned their attention to their plates. The day's events had stirred up healthy appetites among the three women. All three of them ate in silence and as they finished their meals they began to joke with each other.

Both Diedra and Cassandra swore that Michael had favored Brea's plate with double portions of everything. They continued with more good-natured teasing about cradle-robbing and the like. Brea took it all in stride. By the time someone realized it was after 4:00, they decided it was time to go home. Diedra and Cassandra excused themselves to the lady's room, and Brea stayed at the table to pick up the check.

Michael handed the bill to Brea and smiled flirtatiously at her. She returned his smile and asked him how old he was anyway. He stood over her and looked into her eyes in a way that communicated to her that he was definitely not some schoolboy with a crush. And just in case she didn't get the message visually, he said "Oh I assure you that I am definitely legal. Even if the thoughts I've had since you walked in here may not have been. But if it will ease your mind at all, I am 25 years old and in my last year of grad school."

Brea laughed, releasing a sigh of relief. She was glad to know that the thoughts she'd had ever since he approached their table earlier had not been focused on a minor. "Do you have any idea how old I am?" she asked even though she knew it wouldn't matter. She handed him her credit card along with the bill.

"I'm quite sure you're old enough," he said before he headed toward the cash register with her payment.

She watched him walk halfway across the room and then dug into her purse for one of her calling cards with her phone number and email address already printed on it. When Michael returned to the table he returned her credit card and receipt and she handed him her business card folded inside a ten dollar bill. "It was a pleasure meeting you. My friends call me Brea," she said observing his surprised expression as she got up to leave.

"Yes, and it was nice meeting you as well. Don't you lose that receipt now." He smiled and winked at her as he moved on to his next table. She put the receipt in her purse and smiled when she realized that Michael's name and telephone number were boldly scrawled across the back.

"What's that goofy grin about?" asked Cassandra as she and Diedra met her at the door.

"I guess I just look that way," her smile broadened as she headed out into the afternoon air replacing her sunglasses. The three women said goodbye as they got into the two cars. Cassandra promised to call Diedra that evening and drove off. Brea drove Diedra back to her home in Mecca Woods and went home to her townhouse on Francis Street. Diedra reflected on how blessed she was to have such caring friends.

## CHAPTER 7

DIEDRA WAS GLAD TO SEE the house was empty when she arrived home. She would have a minute to gather her thoughts and pull herself together before she was hit with a barrage of questions from her husband. There was so much information to process. The message light on the phone flashed in the dark as she took her boots off and hung her coat up in the hall closet. She would check that in a while.

Diedra retrieved her slippers from her bedroom and went to the kitchen to make sure there was something to feed her family. *Pregnant again! How could that be? How? How? How?* She stood in front of the open freezer door for several minutes before she realized that she was in no mood to cook anything. She decided to call James and have him grab something on his way home. She walked across the room to the wall phone, grabbed the receiver and dialed James' number.

"Hello! Diedra! Is that you?" It was James. She was surprised to hear his voice before the phone even rang.

"Yes James, it's me. What are you doing on the phone? I didn't even hear it ring. What time are you leaving work?"

"I was calling you." He laughed at the coincidence and continued. "I guess you didn't get my message. I'm in the car on my way to your parents' house and after I pick the boys up we'll stop and get some carryout. Any suggestions?"

"It really doesn't matter much to me. I'm not hungry at all. Whatever you and the boys decide will be fine. I'm just glad I don't have to cook. I'm really not up for it tonight."

"Well you just sit down and relax and I will see you real soon. Okay?"

"Thank you dear." She hung up the phone and went to her bathroom to run herself a hot bubble bath.

This was another room that James had fixed to her taste. If he wanted to, he could give Bob Villa a run for his money. James had spent most of his summers as a teenager working construction for his uncle who was a contractor. In the process, he'd learned his way around a hammer and nail. When he first showed this house to Diedra she was not thrilled, but it was within their budget and the location was ideal. Diedra had to admit that the large double lot was perfect; but this was an older home with only three bedrooms for the seven of them.

James knew Diedra would have preferred to have a large new home in Brittany Downs where Cassandra lived, but something like that would have overstretched their budget. This was a good, solid house in a nice, family oriented neighborhood. The house was going to need some work but he promised her this was a place where he could give her and their children the kind of home he'd always dreamt of. After he walked Diedra through it and allowed her to see his dream through her own eyes, she was sold. Especially after he promised his first projects would be to remodel the kitchen and master bath to her specifications.

His cousin Huey, who had followed in his father's footsteps, had promised to supply the materials as a belated wedding gift. The bathroom was the easy part. She had shown him a picture of her dream bathroom. She'd told him if she could have that bathroom she wouldn't care what the rest of the house looked like because she'd hardly ever see it. By the time James and his cousins finished the room, it was more beautiful than the one in Diedra's picture.

Whenever she entered her bathroom, Diedra felt she had stepped into a fantasy. They had knocked out a wall and extended the space to the point that it was about as large as the bedroom itself. The walls and the heated floor were granite, and the color scheme was soft and soothing. It featured a jetted garden tub with a large beveled glass window to let in plenty of sunlight. The ceiling over the tub was vaulted, with a skylight that displayed a stained glass design in the center, and at the foot of the tub, was a gas fireplace. Another window boasted a garden seat with decorative pillows and a magazine rack. There was a separate walk-in shower and his and her sinks with granite countertops.

The pewter framed mirror was centered between a pair of delicate sconces. The cabinet beneath the double sinks was mahogany with pewter hardware. Across the room was a dressing table for Diedra. The natural perfume of the flowers interspersed around the room with candles helped to keep the air fresh and inviting. They'd considered putting a phone in, but decided that time spent in here should be time sheltered from the outside world.

Diedra took some scented bath beads from the decanter and placed them in her soap dish. Then she looked through her selection of bubble baths to find a scent that would complement the sweet scent of the beads, and she picked up the body oil and carried it all to the bathtub. She turned the radio on to WENN, flipped the light switch to soft lighting and sighed in anticipation of the feeling of total relaxation she derived from a luxurious soak in her bathtub. She turned the water on as hot as she could stand it, allowing the water to trickle through her fingers as she affirmed the jet streams were at the correct pressure. Next she poured in the bubble bath. Once the water started bubbling up effectively, she broke the beads underneath the running water and let them dissolve through her fingers.

She walked across the room into her closet and slipped out of her clothes. She placed them in a hamper, and as she turned back toward the tub she caught a glimpse of herself in the full-length mirror. She stood there a moment, inspecting her relatively flat abdomen from each angle. She sighed and shook her head from side to side before she walked back out and over to the bathtub.

Just before she entered the tub, she poured the bath oil into the water and stuck her left foot into the water to test the temperature, swirling the water around with her toe. Then she stepped into the tub and gently lowered herself into the foamy bubbles to be swept away on the gentle currents of the warm, scented water. Her head rested on the neck support as she leaned back and closed her eyes. It had been a taxing day, and the soft music that poured over her body along with the silky water, was just what she needed to help soothe her senses.

Diedra was floating on a raft along a tropical waterway in crystal clear water that reflected a topaz blue sky above her. The beaches on either side were filled with the whitest sand she had ever seen; with pebbles that sparkled so brightly that she was sure they were diamonds. Palm trees lined the beach up and down the waterway, swaying gently in the breeze. Occasionally she would notice an exotic fruit tree with colors so vivid that they looked as if they had sprung from the pages of an enhanced travel brochure.

She was in a place she'd been many times before. It was a peaceful place far away from any trouble or pain. A place she liked to go to whenever she had problems that seemed to be bigger than she was. She was able to accomplish anything she chose here. There were no barriers. Everything she wanted was well within her reach. This was where she went to get ideas for some of her best stories. Sometimes she was able to get answers to troubling questions, and sometimes she just gained perspective. But most of her time spent here in this fantasy was spent with her characters, whose problems always had solutions and whose questions always had answers.

Diedra continued to drift along the waterway, occasionally waving at a young couple running along the beach or a couple of kids building sandcastles. Then she noticed two figures walking toward the water. She could see that they were coming toward her but she didn't recognize them.

They stood on the edge of the beach waving at her and one of them reached up into one of the trees picking one of its fruit, and reached out across the water and handed her a plum. *A plum!* Diedra was surprised at that. She hadn't eaten any plums since she was a little girl and Big Daddy would pick them for her from the trees in his back yard. "How did plums get on my island? And how did they get out here to the middle of the stream so quickly?" She asked herself.

She turned to see who had handed her the plum. She looked up to see Big Daddy, who was still standing on the beach and yet, standing over her as if he was right next to her. Granddaddy stood next to him and they smiled tenderly at her.

Big Daddy spoke first. "Hi there, Baby girl! Your granddaddy and I want to tell you something." Diedra looked at them and waited in silence to hear what they had to say. As she waited, she noticed the clouds in the bright blue sky above them. Although she was certain the sky had been cloudless before, she now noticed that there were exactly seven perfect clouds in the entire sky; two large ones and five smaller ones. All of them perfectly shaped. The sky was beautiful and peaceful and the clouds gently rolled along in sync. Then a gentle rain started pouring from the two larger clouds, which were still white and perfectly shaped. She realized they were situated a little higher than the other five clouds, which seemed to grow a little from the water they absorbed from the two larger clouds.

As she watched the clouds, she felt a sense of peace come over her, and then the two larger clouds drew together and combined into one enormous cloud right before her eyes. The gigantic cloud split and two smaller clouds broke off from it. Then there were eight clouds all together. The oversized cloud hovering over seven smaller clouds, all floating gently through the sky in perfect harmony. She continued to watch the clouds as she drifted along with the water gently lapping over her, and suddenly she knew. She knew what Big Daddy and Granddaddy wanted her to know without having heard a word they said. She also knew that it was good. She shivered as she felt the cool water gently lap over the sides of the inner tube and over her breasts.

"Wake up Babe." James whispered softly into Diedra's ear as he gently washed her chest with the cloth he'd taken from the side of the bathtub. He dipped the cloth back into the water and let the cool water trickle over her breasts. "Come on sleepyhead. It's time to come back from dream land," he whispered to her. Then he kissed her gently on her forehead.

Diedra woke up and smiled dreamily at James. "Hey there," she said as he kissed her on her forehead again and continued to bathe her. "Where are my babies?" she asked. Then she stretched her arms and rested them across her abdomen.

"They're in the kitchen eating dinner," he told her. "The million dollar question is 'Where were you just now?' To look at you, one would think you didn't have a care in the world." Diedra sighed softly and continued to smile.

"There are no troubles in Dreamland" she whispered.

"Yeah, well you can take me there anytime," he replied as he kissed her gently along her neckline.

Later that night after he had bathed the triplets, put them to bed, and cleaned the kitchen, James tiptoed into his and Diedra's bedroom where she was already sleeping. He turned the TV on and turned the volume down as low as possible in order to keep from waking his wife. He hadn't had a chance to ask her about her doctor's visit. She didn't seem as if she'd been given any heavy news, but he knew her well enough to know that he couldn't assume anything. He would just have to ask her in the morning. She needed her rest, and right at that moment she seemed to be resting better than she had in months.

He reached over and gently caressed her cheek. There was no sign of tension on her face. He had to find solace in that. He crawled into the bed, sat with his back against the headboard and pulled the covers across his legs. He turned his attention away from the television and thought about his wife, the woman he loved more than anything on this planet. He was really beginning to worry about her. Those headaches of hers had become more common and her mood swings were practically unbearable, not to mention, totally unpredictable. He wondered if her headaches had anything to do with that.

"Lord, she has been through enough pain in her life. I wish..." he faltered as he involuntarily reached out and touched her face again.

Diedra's eyes opened and she tried to focus on her husband. "You wish what?" she asked sleepily. James reached his hand around and cupped her head as he leaned down to kiss his wife on her forehead. She smiled and asked, "What was that for?"

He looked into her eyes with a look that seemed to see all the way down into the depths of her soul. His eyes told her that he liked what he saw there. He loved her completely and unconditionally. She reached up, grabbed his neck in her hands and pulled him back down to her and kissed him gently, showering feathery kisses on the corners of his lips and on his cheeks. She kissed him softly on his forehead and nipped at his ear; and then she returned to his lips where she kissed him, tenderly at first, gently slipping her tongue between his lips, searching hesitantly.

James tried to restrain himself. He let his wife lead him down the exquisitely gentle path to passion. But when her tongue met with his, the sensation of that first contact was so electrical that he felt as if he would burst. He wrapped his arms around her and pulled her in to him.

As she sensed his response, her kiss became more urgent. She squeezed him tightly and pressed into him. She wouldn't be satisfied until there was no space between the two of them. She wanted to be connected to him. She wanted to be one with him.

James felt the same urgency. By the time he and Diedra had spent every last bit of energy their bodies possessed and they laid in each other's arms content and exhausted, trying to catch their breath, they couldn't even remember how his pajama pants and her nightshirt ended up hanging from the headboard.

James was the first to speak. He ran his fingers through her hair as she rested her head across his chest. "Do you know how incredible you are?" he asked.

"Yes," she replied matter-of-factly, without even looking up.

"Excuse me! Ms. Modesty," he teased.

"That's not immodest," she responded. "James, for someone as wonderful as you are to love me as much as you do, I have to be an incredible person. I must have done something right somewhere along the line. And you are my reward. I…"

James interrupted her at that point.

"Dee, do you know that I thank God every day for bringing you into my life. You have brought me so many blessings. Before I met you I was beginning to think there might not be a single woman who could give me everything I needed. But then you came into my life and brought along more than I'd ever dreamed. Babe, I didn't have a clue!"

"But James, I know I haven't been the wife you deserve. I just feel like, as a wife, I've been lacking. It seems as if I'm always asking you for something; to give something, or to accept something, or even to change something."

"That's a part of being a husband I would never change. I married you because I want to give you everything. I accept all that is you, or a part of you. And I am willing to change whatever doesn't work in our lives."

"I'm glad to hear you say that," she said. "Because we're about to be in for some big changes,"

"What? Are you pregnant or something?" he quipped.

# CHAPTER 8

JAMES JUMPED OUT OF THE bed before the alarm clock had even gone off. They had all slipped back into their regular routines after the holidays. The twins had arrived back from their trip with their father, and returned to school for their second semester. The triplets were back in daycare. And since Diedra had worked last night, it was his responsibility to get them all up and on their way. Fortunately, she already had breakfast warming and ready for them before she climbed into bed.

This was the regular routine, but today was different. Today, after he dropped the boys off at school and daycare he would return to wake Diedra up so they could go to her doctor's appointment with Dr. Howard. He was still struggling with the information Diedra had divulged to him last Monday night. He loved their children and truly believed that all children are a gift from God. But he just didn't know how they were going to manage to care for six children, and with Diedra's history, possibly more.

Hopefully, today they would at least learn for certain if she was carrying a single or multiples. They were looking for some other answers this morning as well. Diedra had explained to him that the two doctors were not certain the headaches were symptomatic of her pregnancy, and after the ob. appointment they would have a neurological consult with Dr. Howard Jr. Both doctors would decide how to proceed, taking into consideration her pregnancy.

When James returned from dropping off the boys, he found Diedra up and ready. She was sitting on the chaise lounge reading her Bible. "What are you reading babe?" he asked.

"I don't know, I guess I was just searching for some reassurance," she replied.

James sat down beside Diedra, put his arm around her and pulled her next to him. "May I?" he asked. She handed him the Bible and he turned to 'The 27th Psalm' and began reading aloud to her. After he finished reading, he began to speak. "Do you find comfort in that?" he asked. She nodded her head and he continued. "You know babe, Pastor Mckinney and I were talking after the Men's Bible study last night. He said something in the meeting that really hit home for me and I wanted to ask him about it."

"What did he say?" she asked. He shifted a little and pulled her closer to him as he shared. "Well, during the meeting he stated that we as men are charged to be the priests of our households. He said we have a responsibility to lead our families in worship and prayer. When Jesus charged us as Christians to go out and tell the world about him he intended for us to start at home.

This doesn't mean that as the head of our households we are to rule over our families like tyrants. We should lead by example and practice servant leadership. We are not only to pray for our families in our quiet time, but we should also pray with our families and start speaking over them using scripture. He also said that it was important for our families to worship together at church.

Babe, I realize that sometimes I'm guilty of using the Word as a weapon rather than as a tool to uplift and encourage you. I want to apologize to you for that and I promise you I'm going to do better."

"Uummhm," she said, and then, "So are you supposed to drag me to church now? I don't need to go prove…"

"Hold on now!" He said softly. "Just let me continue, please."

"So, continue."

"Okay, so afterward, I approached him and asked him to pray for us and our situation. He did pray with me and he directed me to that scripture I just read to you. Then he asked how you were holding up under everything. I told him how strong you are and how much I admire you as a woman. But then he asked me about your faith and mentioned that he hadn't seen you in church lately. I explained to him that even before the headaches you seemed to be exhausted all the time, and when you did come to church you would always fall asleep."

"James why would you tell him that?"

"Because it's the truth. But then he said something that might surprise you."

"What was that?"

"He said New Kingdom might not be the place for us."

"What?" Diedra asked as she sat up and looked at James. "Is he trying to kick you out of the church because of me?"

"No not at all. Diedra, have you ever noticed how many churches we have in Jacksonville? I mean, there are three churches in Eastwood alone. Pastor Mckinney made a very astute observation. He said there are many different churches that come in various sizes with different styles of worship and even preaching. That is by design, because there are many different people with different needs. Perhaps New Kingdom is not giving you what you need."

"Are you serious?" Diedra asked with an incredulous look. "He actually stated that his church may not provide what a member needs?"

"Yes, that's exactly what he said."

"Incredible!"

"He said that we should pray about it, together, and maybe start visiting other churches. And I responded by saying, 'But Pastor, I'm a Deacon.' And he said 'What's more important, your position in the church or your position in your family? Your family is your primary responsibility.' Diedra, he just blew me away. I've been thinking and praying about this all night. I mean, with all that we have going on in our lives right now, it is so important that we as a couple have a strong spiritual foundation. We are going to have to draw closer to God and really lean on him and make him the cornerstone of our marriage. You know, a three-fold cord is not easily broken." There was a tangible excitement in James' voice.

"Would you really consider changing churches, James?"

"I am telling you now that I am ready to find a church home that will serve the needs of our entire family," he replied. "Diedra if this is what our family needs, then this is what we'll do. Are you willing to come with me to visit other churches?"

"Yes, we can do that, James."

James drew Diedra back into his arms, squeezed her tightly and spoke a soft prayer over her. Then they prepared to head out for the day's appointments.

At Dr. Howard's office James and Diedra sat silently in the waiting room as they waited for her name to be called. James stared across the room at the television while Diedra rested her head on his shoulder, drifting in and out of sleep. Finally, Candy called them to the back. After the preliminary assessment they entered the examination room and waited for Dr. Howard.

"Do you think we'll learn the sex of the baby today?" He asked.

"I'm not sure, 19 weeks, that's almost 5 months. They might possibly be able to tell, but I doubt it. I just hope that whatever it is, it's just one."

"If it should happen to be another set of multiples, we'll handle it. You're an amazing mother."

"But James, how can we even afford to raise one more child? What about our dreams of seeing all of our children graduate from college? What about my dream of one day returning to college? This is just going to push my dreams further back." She slumped over and dropped her head. Her arms hung at her sides as she said, "I am so, so tired."

"I know babe, but you've got this. I've got you and God's got us. And we know that all things work together for good to them that love the Lord and are called according to his purpose."

"Purpose? Is it my purpose to keep popping out babies?"

"Obviously that's part of it, but I'm sure that God has much more in store for you than motherhood. You are a gifted lady and I'm sure He wants you to use your gifts or he wouldn't have blessed you with them."

Diedra gave James a quizzical look and said, "Just one conversation with Pastor Mckinney, huh?"

James smiled and replied, "He has been praying, studying and counseling with me for a few months now. I know you don't really appreciate his style of preaching, but he's the real deal." He leaned over and kissed her lightly on her forehead. "But perhaps he and New Kingdom are not what our family needs for this season of our lives. I've come to consider Pastor Mckinney a friend and I will keep in contact with him. Who knows, after all is said and done, God just might lead us right back to New Kingdom."

Just then both Dr. Howard's entered the room. "How are we doing today?" asked Dr. Howard Sr.

"You tell us, Doc," replied James.

"All your levels look good, Diedra. Your weight is good. You are only slightly anemic but the prenatal vitamins and iron I prescribed will correct that." He turned to James and congratulated him and then asked, "Are we ready to get a look at the little one?"

"Yes sir!" The couple said in unison.

"First let's take a listen to the heartbeat and then we'll see if we can find an image." The younger Dr. Howard stuck his head out the door and signaled for the ultrasound tech to bring the equipment in. She wheeled the machine in and began to connect the unit. While they waited for the tech to set up, James held Diedra's hand and she squeezed tightly while he soothed her with words of comfort.

Once the equipment was set up and Diedra was prepped, Dr. Howard took over. He gently glided the transducer across her abdomen for several seconds and then stopped. "Listen." He whispered. "Before I formed you in your mother's womb, I knew you. Before you were born, I sanctified you." Dr. Howard spoke those same words over all his patients the first time he heard their heartbeat. "There it is; the most beautiful sound on earth, the sound of a new life. Do you hear that? God has chosen the two of you to care for this new soul while it is here on this earth, both a blessing and a responsibility. Congratulations once again. Now let's find that image."

He shifted the transducer over a little and said, "There she is! That's your little girl." Diedra looked up at James and saw that he was in tears. She reached up and stroked his cheek and he grabbed her hand and kissed it, holding it next to his lips as he whispered a prayer of thanks.

Diedra asked, "Are you certain it's a girl?"

"Yes I am," replied Dr. Howard. "Just look at her, a perfectly formed little girl, one of God's greatest miracles."

"Amen," said James who was a bucket of water by this time. Diedra was crying softly as well. Dr. Rodney allowed them to bask in the revelation for a while before he interjected.

"Ok, so we do have this other issue to address." He conducted a neurological assessment and then asked her a few questions about the frequency of her headaches and her sleep patterns. James asked what he thought might be causing the headaches.

Dr. Rodney said, "I don't want to alarm you but I am concerned. We definitely need to conduct more extensive testing but with Diedra being pregnant there are some limitations on what we can do."

"You mean X-ray?" asked James.

"Right," said Dr. Rodney. "We do not want to administer any radiation or contrasts. But we do need to get a look at Diedra's brain."

"Can't we wait until after I have the baby in June?"

"I wouldn't recommend it, Diedra. We need to do the imaging so we can get a definitive answer as to the source of your headaches. When you had your episode in here Monday, It appears that you had a minor seizure and if that is a regular occurrence, it could be harmful to your unborn child."

"Seizure!" James said in alarm. "Episode? What are you talking about, Doc?" His eyes on Diedra the entire time.

"When I was here Monday, I fainted. I thought it was because I hadn't eaten breakfast, being pregnant and all. I didn't think it was worth mentioning."

"Babe, everything concerning you and this baby is worth mentioning. Ok?"

"You're right." Diedra answered, remorsefully.

Dr. Rodney informed them that he had made an appointment for them at the Kirklin clinic at UAB, for that afternoon, if they could make it. They would do an MRI without contrast and he would meet with them Monday morning back here at his father's office, they would go over the results and the four of them would discuss treatment if necessary.

Diedra called and made arrangements for Cassandra to pick the triplets up from daycare in case they were late returning from Birmingham. They stopped at Brad's before they hit the highway. Diedra ordered a side of fried green tomatoes with hot sauce, jalapeno poppers, and a sweet tea. James ordered a large pulled pork sandwich along with fries and an extra-large tea. He recalled that Diedra seemed to crave spicy foods when she was pregnant with the triplets. The drive to Birmingham was fairly quiet, both of them engulfed in thought. James made a couple of attempts at small talk, but he was just as distracted as Diedra, so he just allowed the silence to envelope the vehicle for a while.

By the time they reached Lincoln, which was the halfway point, Diedra had fallen asleep. James was surprised she had lasted that long after working a twelve hour shift the night before. He was grateful her rotation was over and she would be off for the next four nights. He would try to make sure she got plenty of rest from now on. He wandered if she would be able to maintain this schedule throughout this pregnancy. He also wandered what the doctors were looking for on this MRI.

"Lord, take care of my wife and protect her from dangers seen and unseen. I would prefer that the doctors find nothing on the MRI, but if there is something there, allow them to find it, identify it and treat it. In Jesus name I pray. Amen." he whispered softly.

He reached over and turned the radio on to Immanuel Broadcasting, a Christian radio station, and allowed the music to minister to his spirit. They arrived at the Kirklin clinic just in time for Diedra's appointment.

They were solemn as they entered the building; walking from the parking garage to the elevator. As they stood on the elevator waiting to arrive at their floor, James reached over and grabbed Diedra's hand, gripping it tightly. When the elevator stopped to load and unload passengers a clean shaven little girl with big bright eyes and a smile just as bright, bounced into the elevator. When she noticed the people already on board she stopped and looked around apprehensively. Her mother and father came in right behind her and she shrunk back, placing her thumb in her mouth as she attempted to hide behind her father's leg. She looked around the group shyly and when someone would make eye contact with her and speak to her, she would hide her face in her father's pants leg.

"She is gorgeous!" Diedra said to her mother. "How old is she?"

"Thank you, she's eighteen months," responded the child's mother. She was a beautiful young woman, who looked to be no more than 24 years old. She smiled at Diedra through eyes that appeared to carry a weariness that was well beyond her years. Both she and her husband seemed to be straining under the weight of some unseen burden. Diedra sensed a false bravado as they interacted with their little girl.

The elevator stopped and Diedra and James stepped out behind the child and her parents and the little girl ran across the room to the receptionist's desk. They were surprised to see the young family proceed to the same waiting area they were directed to. They watched as the sprightly young child climbed up on the chair and worked her way from parent to parent. "She certainly is a bundle of energy, and she seems to be right at home here," Diedra stated.

"UAB and Children's have been her home away from home since she was nine months old," her mother replied. Her head dropped slightly before she continued in a hesitant whisper, as if she feared saying the words out loud would bring forth some physical manifestation of the turmoil her family had faced for the last nine months. "It has been an endless rollercoaster ride since she was diagnosed with cancer." She smiled at her daughter. "She's a trooper though. Some days she is so sick she can barely move, then there are days like today, when she is bouncing around like any healthy child."

"I am so sorry she has to go through that," Diedra told her. "I know that as a mother, it has to be hard for you to watch your daughter suffer through such a thing."

Just then they heard Diedra's name called and she and James got up from their seats and went to the back for her tests. She had her MRI and afterward James took her to dinner at The Fish Market, one of her favorite restaurants. Before they headed home they went by the Cheesecake Factory and ordered cheesecakes to take to the boys.

Once on I-20 headed back East, James asked, "So, have you thought about where you want to go Sunday?"

"You mean church? No, not really. My mind has been on other things today. I'll go wherever you choose this week. James, I just can't stop thinking about that precious little girl. I didn't even get her name."

"It's Maura. Her father asked that we pray for her. Why don't we visit your parent's church? We haven't been there in a while."

"I'm sure they'll love for us to come to Friendship. And I'll be glad to pray for that precious girl."

They rode along in silence and Diedra drifted off to sleep again. Shortly after they passed the Talladega Super Speedway, James noticed that the SUV in the left lane was moving over into the right lane where he was. He swerved a little to his right to avoid them, and then straightened up as the SUV did the same. Then the vehicle moved over into his lane again and he swerved once again, and blew his horn. The vehicle came over a third time and this time he swerved a little harder and went off onto the shoulder. When he attempted to straighten back up, his minivan continued turning to the left and went over into the left lane. After several unsuccessful attempts to straighten the wheel, which resulted in him swerving back and forth across both lanes, the mini-van started spinning in circles.

Diedra woke up on the final spin, and as they began to tilt on two wheels, she saw an image of the van rolling over in the divider and she screamed out, "Lord Jesus please! Help us now!" And right at that moment, the van came back down on all four wheels, landing as softly as if it was on a bed of clouds, and stopped. They sat in the right lane of I-20 facing a line of traffic behind them that had come to a complete stop as well.

James turned and looked incredulously at Diedra and she looked at him, eyes wide as saucers. "Babe, are you okay?" James finally asked Diedra.

"Yes, how about you?"

"I'm okay."

"What happened?"

"I don't know. Some fool practically ran us off the road, then I just lost control. I could not straighten back out."

Just then a short, stocky guy in a State Trooper's uniform came and tapped on their window. He had been in the line of traffic behind them and had pulled over into the divider when he saw them spinning. "Is everybody alright?" He asked.

James rolled down his window and responded. "Yes, we are both okay. Just a little shaken, but we'll be alright."

The Trooper said, "Great! Can I get you to back up completely off the pavement? Then you can sit here as long as you need to."

James backed up onto the divider, placed the van in park, and turned the ignition off. The Trooper walked back up to the window and asked, "Are you sure you're okay? If I hadn't seen it for myself, I wouldn't have believed it. I have to say, you handled your vehicle pretty well. That could've had a disastrous outcome. It's a good thing you had your seat belts on," he observed.

James looked at Diedra knowingly and said, "But God! We are fine, we're going to head on home now."

"Amen, brother! Y'all have a great day" and then he went and climbed back into his vehicle and drove off.

James started the vehicle, merged back into traffic, and continued on. When they reached the next exit, Diedra asked him if he wanted to pull over and get out of the van for a few minutes. They drove down the windy road until they reached a large church. He pulled over into the parking lot and stopped. Once he turned the ignition off he began to tremble uncontrollably. Diedra reached over and hugged him and he held her so tightly, she could barely breathe. They sat like that for several minutes before they stepped out of the van. They stood in the front, leaning against the vehicle, holding hands and staring out into space, not saying a word. A car rode slowly by them and the occupant waved. They absent-mindedly waved back. The vehicle got to the end of the parking lot, circled around and came back. The driver rolled down his window, revealing a handsome face beneath a shock of black hair peppered with grey, and asked, "Y'all ok?"

James replied, "Yes."

"You don't look ok? Are you sure nothing's wrong?"

Finally, James admitted that they had just had a scare on the interstate.

"Would you like to come in and have a cup of coffee before you get back on the road? It might help calm your nerves. You don't look fit to drive right now."

Diedra looked at James and said "That might be a good idea. You're still pretty shaken, and I know I am."

The gentleman led them inside the building to a lounge area and invited them to sit while he poured them some coffee. "None for me," said Diedra. "I would prefer tea if you have it?"

He looked at her quizzically and asked "Are you expecting? Or you just don't like coffee?" he laughed, his eyes twinkling. Diedra laughed nervously, and James replied

"Both. She doesn't like coffee and we just found out last week that we are expecting."

"That's a blessing." he replied. "Are you excited?"

"Yes, and anxious; this will be our sixth child. We just learned today it will be our first girl," replied Diedra.

"What are you anxious about?" he asked.

Diedra looked at James and sighed. She didn't know why she felt compelled to share her personal business with this complete stranger but she did.

"Well, I just found out I'm nearly five months pregnant with my sixth child, who is my first girl. My other children were multiples, by the way, twins, then triplets. I've been having severe headaches and," she glanced at James, "apparently seizures. And we don't know the cause. Due to my pregnancy, testing options are limited. But we are on our way home from having an MRI, and we won't learn the results until Monday."

"You could hear a pin drop. The man looked at Diedra contemplatively for a moment, and then turned to James, "So what happened on the interstate? If you don't mind me asking." James recounted the entire incident, from the first moment the other vehicle came over into his lane, to when they spun out of control and Diedra woke up and cried out to Jesus, to when they pulled over into this parking lot.

"Why did you stop here?" he asked.

"I don't know," replied James, "We just decided to pull over so I could get my bearings and calm down before we continued on."

"Yes, but you could have stopped at the Service Station right at the exit or you could have pulled into the parking lot of the church across the street. Why did you stop here?"

"Were we trespassing or something?" asked James. He was a little annoyed by the barrage of questions.

"Not at all. You are welcome here. As a matter of fact, I would like to say a prayer with you if you don't mind."

"We need all the prayer we can get," sighed James.

They all three joined hands and he began,

"Jesus! Jesus! Jesus! If I know no other words to pray, I say Jesus. There is power in that name. The one who knows all, who hears all, and sees all. Jesus you know what we need before we do. You have already fixed this situation. Though we may not see it in the natural, I trust and believe this natural situation is not the final word or the finished product. You said in your word, that whatever we bind on earth will be bound in heaven and whatever is loosed in heaven will be loosed on earth. I bind the enemy and all of its attacks against this family and I loose favor, mercy and blessings over them. Let thy will be done on earth as it is in heaven. In Jesus' holy name we pray,

Amen, Amen and Amen."

As he prayed, James began trembling uncontrollably and tears were streaming down Diedra's face. When the man finished praying, he hugged them both and told them to be blessed.  They left feeling as if a heavy cloud they hadn't even perceived, had been lifted from around them.

Back at the car, Diedra asked James if he wanted her to drive the rest of the way home.

"No, I've got it."

"Are you sure?" she asked. "The way you were trembling in there…Are you sure you're able to drive after all that's happened this afternoon?"

"Steady as a rock." He said as he held up his hand to show her. "I don't know why, but I feel a sense of calm like I haven't felt in a long while."

"Yes, I do too."

# CHAPTER 9

Sunday morning James jumped out of bed bright and early, before the rest of the household, as usual. He went into the kitchen and prepared a light breakfast before he woke everyone.

Even though he loved New Kingdom, the prospect of visiting a brand new church was rather exciting to him. He and Diedra had decided to go back to the church off the interstate. After the basketball game Saturday, they had spoken with their friends about the prospect of finding a new church home. As it turn out, Cassandra and Shawn had visited this new church a few weeks earlier and really enjoyed it. They said they felt a sense of genuine acceptance they didn't always get at other churches.

Brea and Michael, who had been inseparable, these past couple of weeks, said they would probably go as well. Oddly enough, those two seemed to have a real connection.

James went back into his room to wake Diedra so they could get their morning started, have breakfast together as a family, and get ready for church. When he saw her laying in the bed sleeping with a slight frown line on her brow, he was taken back to that day 10 years ago, when he first saw her sleeping, in the back of her parent's Ford Bronco with Adrian and Austin snuggled up against her. At first he had thought she was their older sister rather than their mother. He smiled softly as he kissed her gently on her forehead and whispered "Wake up Sleeping Beauty."

She smiled sleepily at him and said, "I haven't heard that in a while."

"I know I don't say it, but I am still as blown away by you as I was when I first saw you," he said. Diedra blushed just like he knew she would. "Why are you so uncomfortable receiving compliments?" he asked. "Don't you know by now that you deserve that and more?"

"Sometimes I wonder why you chose me when you had women falling over themselves to get with you."

"The Bible says he who finds a wife finds a good thing. I found you; you didn't find me. Although I really wasn't used to it, I enjoyed courting you, and still do, Mrs. Davis."

"I am certainly glad you did, Mr. Davis."

"Let's get this party started, shall we?" he said as he pulled her up out of the bed.

The family arrived at the church thirty minutes early for the morning worship service. James hopped out of the vehicle, eagerly went around to open Diedra's door, and gave her a quick peck on her forehead as he helped her out of the car. He was excited. Adrian and Austin climbed out on the driver's side as he and Diedra helped the triplets out from the passenger's side. James proudly surveyed his family as they walked to the building. Travis, Trevor, and Tremaine, all held hands between Adrian and Austin, who held the hands of the boys on each end. They were all neatly dressed and well groomed, fine young boys, and well-mannered as well. And Diedra! The most attractive thing about his wife was that she had no idea how beautiful she actually was. Yes, he was a blessed man, and he knew it.

Once they arrived at the church door, they were met by a couple of greeters. They hugged them and enthusiastically welcomed them to their church. "Is this your first time visiting with us?" the gentleman asked. They told him that it was. "We are glad to have you!" they both said enthusiastically. The lady informed them that there was a children's church across the vestibule, down the hallway to their left.

Fortunately, they had arrived early enough to sign in and come back to the sanctuary and get a good seat. As the family continued on, they couldn't help but notice the energy that seemed to fill the place. The members looked to be genuinely happy and glad to be there. The volunteers in the triplets' classroom were pleasant, and appeared to be engaged with the children. As they headed back toward the main sanctuary, they each observed their surroundings and took in the sights, the sounds, and the people. Austin said, "This place is awesome!"

James and Diedra smiled at each other, and James said. "There seems to be a good energy here, but let's see what the Pastor has to say."

As they approached the sanctuary doors, they could hear the praise and worship team getting warmed up inside. Diedra cocked her head to one side and listened intently. "That sounds just like Sherry Michaels, John's wife. Is this the church he has been telling me about?" she wondered aloud.

"Could be," James replied. When they arrived at the sanctuary doors, they met another set of greeters/ushers.

"Welcome, welcome, they said as they reached out and hugged them. "Would you like to sit in the front, middle or back?" asked the gentleman, as Diedra and James looked around the large sanctuary.

"How about the back of the front?" James asked as he surveyed the room. The pulpit sat in the middle of a large stage. The seating was divided into nine sections, three across and three from front to back. He noticed there was a balcony in the back. There was a platform in the center of the rear section that held a media station. He was going to keep an open mind, but the whole production seemed to be a bit much to him. But, if the members were as genuine as the fellow they had met Friday appeared to be, it might just be alright.

"We can certainly do that," the usher said as he led them to find seats. As they moved into their seats near the back of the front center section, directly in front of the pulpit, they saw Shawn and Cassandra sitting in the next section over. Since their row was practically empty, Diedra motioned for them to come join them.

"Good morning!" James and Shaun shook hands as Diedra and Cassandra hugged each other.

"Cassandra where are the girls? Have you seen Brea?"

"Jasmine is in children's church, and Nicholette is in the balcony with her friends. And I actually, have not seen Brea yet."

"She must not be coming because Brea is never late for anything. But let's just hold a seat for her just in case."

As they settled into their seats to listen to the praise team, they noticed several people throughout the sanctuary engaged in various forms of worship. Some were standing and waving their hands in the air. Some jumped up and down. While others just stood quietly with their hands folded together in front of their chest. There were also those who chose to stay in their seats and wave or clap their hands.

The praise team was excellent. And yes, that was Sherry Michaels up there. Diedra always loved to hear her sing. Even if this really wasn't the style of music she preferred. The praise songs were a little radical but the worship songs seemed to do just what they were designed to do. Something was stirring in the atmosphere. During the last song, the Pastor came out on the stage and joined in worship. Once the music died down, he encouraged the congregants to hug and greet their neighbors. During the greeting session, James and Diedra ventured out into the aisle to greet a few people they recognized in the next section. James noticed Brea and Michael walking across the front of the church to a seat in the second row from the front. He pointed them out to Diedra, and they walked over to speak. When they returned to their seats they gave Cassandra and Shawn a final hug before they sat down. Cassandra informed Diedra that they had seen Rodney and Kayla sitting near the front of their section. Diedra and James shared that Brea and Michael were in the front of the next section on their other side. They each waved and then turned their attention to the pastor, who to Diedra and James' surprise, turned out to be the gentleman they had met Friday evening.

The pastor did not get immediately into his sermon as they had expected. He explained to the congregation that he felt the Holy Spirit moving mightily in the sanctuary that morning, and he felt led to do something a little extraordinary. He said he was going to say a prayer, and then they would have an altar call, and anyone who had a need for prayer was welcome to come.

The pastor prayed and welcomed the Holy Spirit to remain in the sanctuary. He asked that the Holy Spirit would direct them as they prayed this morning and that the power of God would manifest not only in this service but in the lives of these people.

Once he finished his prayer he invited all who needed personal prayer to come down to the front. If they were in need of salvation, healing, deliverance, whatever the need, they were welcome to come down. At this time, members of the ministerial staff lined up in front of the stage: a diverse group of people, dressed in an array of styles from suits and dresses to blue jeans. They were comprised of men and women of various ages.

A crowd of approximately thirty people approached the stage. The pastor smiled and said "Praise God! Is there anyone else?" Then he surveyed the group and asked, "How many of you are here for salvation, raise your hand?" He addressed the entire congregation and asked, "Do you understand what I mean when I ask that? If you have never accepted Christ as your savior, or you have before, and you have back-slid, or perhaps you're just not sure if you are saved, then we will corporately pray the prayer of salvation with you today." He looked around and asked, "Now, is there anyone else who would like to come down? I feel like there is someone else who is hesitating. We don't want to leave anyone out."

At that time a few more people trickled down, including Brea, who for some unfathomable reason, had been squirming in her seat the entire time she had been there. During praise and worship, she had been so uncomfortable that she felt compelled to stand up, but then when she would stand up, she had the unnerving feeling that everyone was watching her, so then she would sit back down, until she jumped up again.

By the time of the altar call, she had begun to feel that God was trying to tell her something, but she had no clue what it was. She felt like her life was just spinning around with no clear direction, and she didn't know where to go. When the pastor gave the altar call she didn't move. To her surprise, Michael, who was a member, turned and asked if she would like for him to go to the altar with her. She shook her head no, and immediately regretted the response, but her stubbornness would not allow her to recant. But when the pastor repeated the altar call, she moved without giving herself a chance to really think about it.

"Wow! God is awesome isn't he?" asked the pastor. He looked at the group of people standing in front of him and asked, "How many of you came down for salvation?" Brea raised her hand, to her own surprise. She had been baptized when she was a teen-ager and she had grown up in church. She tried to be fair and honest with others. She prayed nightly. She even spoke in tongues that one time. Didn't that mean she was saved?

The pastor said, "It's okay to seek reassurance of your salvation. We should all know that we know that we know that we are saved and going to heaven, without question. The word of God says 'That if thou shall confess with thy mouth the Lord Jesus, and shall believe in thine heart that God has raised Him from the dead, thou shalt be saved.' I want those of you seeking the prayer of salvation to step forward and move in toward the center." This move placed Brea directly in front of the pastor as he continued, "And I want the entire congregation to reach out your hands toward them as we pray in agreement the prayer of salvation." The prayer came up on the monitor and the entire congregation began to pray,

"Dear God

I come to You in the name of Jesus. I acknowledge to You that I am a sinner. I repent for my sins and the life I have lived. Father, I need your forgiveness.

I believe that Your son Jesus died on the cross for me and I am willing to turn from my sin.

I believe You raised Jesus from the dead and I invite him into my heart as the Lord of my life. I accept Jesus as my own personal savior and according to Your word, I believe that I am saved.

Amen, Amen, and Amen"

As they were praying, tears began streaming down Brea's cheeks. She didn't understand it but she let it flow. Waves of peace washed over her as she prayed. After they finished the corporate prayer she stood with her eyes still closed and hands still in the air speaking softly in tongues for a few moments.

The pastor observed the group, some of who were crying softly, some who had expressions of peace and relaxation spread across their faces. He stated softly, "That's the power of The Holy Spirit. If you do not require further prayer you may return to your seats."

A woman on the ministerial team walked over to Brea and asked her name. She told her, and then the woman said. "I keep hearing Tamar." Diedra sat up in her seat when she heard that.  The woman continued, "God says today he has delivered you from that spirit of rejection and shame that has tormented you for years.  He has allowed you to experience hurt and rejection so that you may be a shelter and an encourager to other daughters of Tamar who have experienced these things. But today, God says he will be your comfort and he will be your strong tower. God wants you to know that He loves you and he forgives you. Time out for playing church! It's time for you to step in to the purpose that God has designed you for. You are blessed and highly favored and you will be a blessing to many."

Diedra didn't understand why she was so strongly affected by what this woman was saying to her friend. But by the time she had finished speaking Diedra was crying profusely. She barely heard the rest of the prayers. Cassandra noticed her demeanor and reached over and hugged her as she fed her tissue after tissue. After the people in front of the stage were prayed for, the pastor preached his sermon which was entitled "God's people are called into a holy priesthood." He reminded them that the last thing Jesus said to his disciples was to go into all the world and spread the gospel.

James felt that his sermon was confirmation of what Pastor Mckinney had told him at the men's prayer group the prior week. His style of preaching was a lot different from what he was used to, but he did get his message across in an engaging manner. Most importantly, everything he spoke about was backed up with scripture. He didn't feel there was any personal agenda infused in the message. Furthermore, Diedra stayed awake and attentive the entire time. He noticed she would nod in agreement with some things and laugh at his corny jokes. She seemed to enjoy the message. But to his surprise, the pastor was not finished after the sermon.

Pastor Vaughn walked back to the pulpit and leaned over and rested his forearms across the top as he spoke. "I just want to share one thing with you all before we leave this morning.-" He looked down in the congregation and gestured toward Rodney and Kayla. "I want you all to meet my friends Rodney and Kayla Howard. Dr. Rodney Howard is an old college buddy of mine that I met during a summer program at Oxford. He has moved his neurology practice from Emory Hospital in Atlanta to UAB. Rodney and Kayla are living in Jacksonville and they are going to be an integral part of our team here at our church." Once Rodney and Kayla were standing beside him, he began speaking again.

"I want to share with you all an encounter I had Friday. It just illustrates some of the ways we can walk out Jesus' direction. It's not about nagging people to come to church. It's about allowing them to see Jesus in you, maybe praying for them, or with them, if they allow it." He went on to describe how he had been at the church Friday afternoon for a counseling session and the person never showed up, but he felt compelled to wait around. As he was leaving, he decided to drive around the building to make sure they were not at one of the locked entrances or just pulling up into one of the parking lots. As he drove through the front parking lot, he passed a couple standing in front of a mini-van holding hands. He waved at them and continued on but the Holy Spirit told him to go back. So he circled around and drove up to them.

He proceeded to explain what happened between him and the couple that afternoon. How they had described the experience on the interstate that resulted in them stopping there, the pregnancy and the woman's headaches and seizures. He told the congregation that he felt that this couple, whoever they were, had arrived there at that time by divine appointment and that they were under spiritual attack. He wanted Rodney, Kayla and the rest of the congregation to join him and stand in the gap for this couple in prayer.

"Woohoo! Come on Jesus!" Kayla literally jumped as she shouted out loud.

The pastor said. "That's what I'm talking about. She's excited about praying."

Rodney said, "You don't even know. Pastor, we're pretty sure we know the couple you're referring to. We know them well, and the woman is a patient of mine and my father's."

"Wow! Look at God!" said the pastor.

"Oh, it's even better than that!" said Kayla. "They're here this morning."

"What, where are they?" he asked, peering out into the congregation. At that point James and Diedra stood up and the pastor jumped down from the stage and practically ran over to them. He gave them both a hug and then reached out and shook their hands. "May I ask your names?"

James answered "James and Diedra Davis. And these are our sons, Adrian and Austin."

"Did Rodney and Kayla invite you this morning?"

"We didn't even realize they would be here."

"I am so glad to meet you, again. I'm Pastor Vaughn." He was so excited that he just had to hug them once again. Then he got serious. "I know some of you here today may not realize it, but the Holy Spirit is so real and he is constantly moving in our lives, whether we realize it or not. Which of us could have conceived the order of circumstances that have occurred here? Look at this; Dr. Howard, a successful neurologist leaves a prosperous practice in Atlanta to move to Jacksonville, Alabama and start a practice at UAB at the same time his friend discovers that she is in need of a neurologist. James and Diedra have this harrowing experience on their way home from her neurological tests, which leads them to stop in our church parking lot. My appointment doesn't show up, so I decide to ride around the building at the precise time they are sitting in the parking lot. We fellowship and pray together about her health and they show up today along with her neurologist who happens to be a friend of mine. Wow! Talk about divine appointments and intervention. Church, I believe all this has happened for a reason."

He turned to James and Diedra and asked, "Is it alright with you if we pray for you and your family."

By this time, tears were streaming down all of their cheeks, and James' was trembling. "Yes sir," he said to the pastor,

Pastor Vaughn said to James and Diedra "Your entire family is under attack." He saw the expression that registered across their faces. "Don't be alarmed. God has a plan for you that the enemy doesn't want to see come to fruition, and that is why it seems like at every turn the enemy is coming after you. I am sure it has seemed that whenever you take two steps forward you get pushed three steps back, sometimes four." Diedra nodded her head in agreement. "I know, it seems like your running backwards sometimes, doesn't it? But remember, delay is not necessarily denial. God has a distinct purpose for you and no attack of the enemy is going to stop God's plans from coming to pass. Just remember, that for every demonic force assigned against you, God has just as many, if not more, angels assigned to protect you. Those that are for you are greater than those that are against you, because greater is he that is in you than he that is in the world, says the Lord. I want you to know that I have been praying for you since I met you.

Today, I want you to know that even in the darkest of situations God is in control. For we wrestle not against flesh and blood, but against principalities, against powers, against the rulers of darkness in this world, against spiritual wickedness in high places. This battle is not yours, but God's, and even when it looks like the devil is winning in the natural, just remember that God has already won.

You may feel like giving up, but you need to gird up your spiritual armor, arm yourselves with your spiritual weapon, the word, and speak out against the enemy at every opportunity. James and Diedra, start speaking over your children daily, especially your unborn child. Instead of talking about what you see in the natural start talking about what God can do. God, who forgives all your sins, heals ALL of your diseases. He delivers you from all of your afflictions. His plans for you are to give you a future and a hope.

I want you to search your Bible daily for a word to hold on to and pick a verse. Keep quoting that one scripture all day. When you start thinking about what's going on, recognize it for what it is; a spiritual attack. Stand your ground and tell the devil that he has no power in your life. He is a liar, he is not in control. 'You have a God of restoration and redemption and it is never too late for him."

"Glory!" Kayla just couldn't contain her excitement. Then a wave of praise spread through the sanctuary. People were shouting, praising God, and clapping their hands.

"Now that's a word!" said Pastor Vaughn. "Please join me as I pray." He laid hands on each of the family members as he prayed, and by the time he finished, the power of the Holy Spirit had fallen on them. James and Adrian were speaking in tongues and it seemed that Austin was interpreting, and Diedra... She started laughing uncontrollably. Then Pastor Vaughn, Rodney, and Kayla started laughing. The laughter spread through the church like a wave. After a few minutes, Pastor Vaughn gestured for the group to return to their seats, and headed back toward the front of the church to close the service. "He will fill your mouth with laughter and your lips with shouting." He said as he approached the pulpit.

After the service, Diedra practically ran into John Michaels, literally. They were in the vestibule walking toward the lounge area to wait for Adrian and Austin to return with the triplets. He gave her a warm hug and then hugged James as well. "I am so, so glad that you finally came. "Ain't God good?"

"Yes he is," replied James.

"That was such an awesome move of the spirit today. I don't want you to think it's like that every time though."

"No, but that is the expectation each week, isn't it?" said Rodney as he and Kayla approached.

Cassandra and Shawn, and Brea and Michael, joined them shortly, and they all decided to meet up at The Top of The River, a seafood restaurant in Anniston, for dinner.

When they arrived at the restaurant the line outside was long, as usual, but they were all willing to wait. They enjoyed animated conversation and fellowship as they waited for seating for their large group. Before they knew it, their party was called inside. While at dinner, Rodney and Kayla informed them that they were starting a small group at their home in Heritage Highlands and invited them all to join.

"I truly believe God has brought us together for a powerful purpose, and this will be an amazing experience for all of us. We'll get together each week, have a little Bible study, and just let the spirit move." They were all eager to begin, so they agreed they would start that same week on Thursday night.

## CHAPTER 10

ON MONDAY MORNING, DIEDRA AND James went through their regular routine and got all the boys off to school before they headed to Dr. Howard's office. They were going to meet with him and Dr. Rodney Howard Jr. for her results. The drive to Anniston was quiet because they were both deep in thought. They had no idea what the possibilities were. The doctors refused to speculate. They said they didn't want them to worry unnecessarily, not realizing it was inevitable. James and Diedra were left to their own imaginations and that was vivid enough.

They had derived some peace from the prayers of their friends, as well as the members from the church in Coldwater. This morning as they travelled down highway 21, Diedra read her Bible and James prayed silently. They were both thankful they would get some answers once and for all, and they would finally know just what they were facing.

As Diedra attempted to read her Bible, the words seemed to swim across the page as her mind raced through several scenarios, some of which ended with her own funeral. She kept reminding herself of the common message she had heard throughout the weekend. "God is in control." She thought about her sons and this unborn daughter, who she now feared she may not see grow up. She heard a voice in her head say **God's going to move you out the way so someone else can do a better job of raising them.** Diedra gasped sharply.

"You okay babe?" James asked. He could sense her uneasiness increasing the closer they got to the doctor's office.

"I guess so. I mean, I'll feel better once we get some answers."

"Well, that's what we're going in here for. In the meantime, try not to dwell on it. Just focus on the fact that we're going to have a beautiful baby girl, who's going to be spoiled by you and all the men in our house."

"Yes" In spite of herself, Diedra smiled softly as she envisioned a little girl with her daddy's trademark dimple. "We'll finally have to get rid of this old Maxima and get another mini-van or at least an SUV."

"Never!" He said emphatically. "This car is paid for, and besides, it's lucky,"

"What do you mean lucky?"

"I met you the very first time I took it on a road trip." He winked at her and continued driving, smiling the rest of the way.

When they arrived at Dr. Howard's office James found a parking space directly in front of the door. He went around to help Diedra out on her side of the car, leaned down and gave her a hug, and kissed her on the cheek as soon as she stepped out. He closed the door, checked the locks, and proceeded to walk her into the building. Upon entering the building, he led her to a seat where he helped her off with her coat. Then he went to hang both their coats as she went to sign in with the receptionist.

Once they were situated in their seats, James turned his attention to the television across the room, as Diedra settled into the chair next to him with her head resting on his shoulder. She wasn't really sleepy; she just wanted the comfort she derived from leaning on her husband's strong shoulder. She knew James would protect her with his life if he had to. Unfortunately, he could not protect her from what she was facing now. But she was so grateful that she had him to support her. He was her covering, her comfort, and her soul mate. Diedra didn't know why James loved her the way he did, but she never doubted that he did. He truly did love her like Christ loved the Church. She believed that she was able to experience God's love through her husband. She and her children were blessed to have him. She wondered if he felt the same way about her. She knew he loved her unconditionally. But did he know that she loved him the same way? Was he able to feel God's love through her?

"Diedra Davis?" the nurse was summoning them to the back. They rose slowly from their seats and followed the nurse. Since they were there for a consultation, she led them directly to Dr. Howard's office. As they walked through the hallway, Diedra observed all the pictures of newborns plastered on the walls, some with and some without Dr. Howard.

Inside his office, Diedra and her family were on the "legacy" wall. There was a picture of herself as an infant at Fort McClellan Hospital with a much younger Dr. Howard, right next to a snapshot of her, Dr. Howard, and the triplets. There was also a picture of her entire family; James, Diedra, the twins, and the newborn triplets. Diedra made sure to select a seat where her visual focus would remain on the pictures. James pulled his chair close to hers and put his arm around her while they waited for the doctors to enter.

The door opened slowly and the couple turned to see both doctors enter the room. Dr. Howard greeted the couple as he walked around his large desk to his chair and took a seat, while Dr. Rodney leaned up against the wall next to him with a file in his hand. Dr. Howard spoke first.

"So, just to recap what we told you Friday, your pregnancy is going great in spite of the late revelation. The baby's weight is good, as well as yours, her heartbeat is strong, and we found no issues with your blood work."

"With all due respect, doctor" James interrupted. "We are aware of all that. I want to know what is causing my wife's headaches... and seizures?" He was still having difficulty wrapping his head around the fact that she had fainted and didn't mention it to him.

Dr. Rodney responded. "James, we know you are anxious about Diedra's condition, but we just wanted to be sure you understand that your baby is not in any danger."

"Danger!" Exclaimed James. "Danger from what?" Diedra reached up and placed her hand over his hand in an attempt to calm him. She'd had more time to process all of this than he had.

"Let them talk, honey." She said as her eyes remained focused on the picture of their family displayed on the wall.

Rodney began to speak, "Yes, well Diedra, the results from your MRI indicate that you have anaplastic astrocytoma, as indicated by the presence of a glioma in the right temporal-parietal lobe of your brain."

"English please," said James.

"He's saying I have brain cancer." Diedra said. And to the doctors she said. "I assume a glioma is a tumor?"

"That is correct," replied Dr. Howard. "But don't be discouraged. We have come a long way with cancer treatment. A cancer diagnosis no longer serves as the impending death sentence it once did. Survival rates are steadily improving as we learn more. And God always has the final say."

"So how are you going to treat this, chemo, surgery, radiation?" asked James.

"They can't do radiation or chemo." Diedra reminded James. "Because of our daughter," She turned her attention away from the collage of pictures and looked into his eyes to see a look of hopelessness she had never seen there before. They were glassed over with moisture, and his lower lip was quivering as he attempted to speak.

"Does that mean she'll have to have surgery?" he asked, staring back into her eyes. He looked as if he was ready to flinch as if the answer to that question would come in the form of an actual, physical blow.

"Uhhgh." Dr. Rodney coughed as he quickly swiped a hand across his eye. "Yes, well fortunately we did find it early. I believe the increased blood flow due to the pregnancy, accelerated some of the symptoms, such as the headaches and seizure. But Diedra, I don't recommend any type of surgery during your pregnancy unless it is completely unavoidable."

"So what are we going to do?" asked Diedra softly, unaware that she had started squeezing James' hand.

"You know you are welcome to a second opinion, but we have consulted with a Neurosurgeon and a neuro-oncologist, and we have concluded that the best course of treatment will be to meticulously monitor your pregnancy. We will place you on anti-seizure medication and keep a very close watch over your progress. We will schedule bi-weekly ob. appointments for fetal monitoring, alternated with appointments at the Kirklin clinic for neurological evaluations. Which means either my father or myself will see you at least once a week. I will be partnering with the neuro-oncologist at the Kirklin clinic, and he will be available to you throughout your treatment, if you like. Then after you deliver the baby we will schedule surgery, followed by radiation. You have approximately four to five months to go in your pregnancy, and I believe the prognosis for a complete recovery is good, if you follow doctor's orders, and don't overextend yourself. In other words, you have to allow others to help you."

Unbeknownst to Diedra, her grip had tightened on James' hand to the point that her fingernails were digging into his skin. He didn't even feel it. They sat there in their chairs, him with his arm around her, and she holding onto his hand as if it were a life-line keeping her from falling into a gaping abyss of depression.

He wandered how much a single individual could take? She had been through so much, but she always came through. Was this it? Was this the breaking point? Was he going to be able to help her through this? He didn't even know what to say to her. He looked into her eyes and saw that distant hint of sadness that had rested just beneath the surface when he first met her. It seemed to seep out from her eyes and cover her entire countenance right before his eyes. Was that defeat he saw? Not Diedra! She was the strongest person he knew.

He forgot about the other two people in the room. His focus was on his wife. He pulled her over into his chair, right there in the doctor's office, and sat her in his lap. He let her rest her head against his chest while he spoke.

"Babe, remember what I said. I've got you, and God's got us. It's going to be okay. We will get through this one day at a time. We will follow the directions of the doctors, and we will keep all of our appointments. We will get through this. We will pray, and we will pray, and we will pray. And like Dr. Howard said; God's got the final word on this. And someday, I believe you will even write a book about it."

By the time he finished speaking, he realized that Diedra was crying softly, and he continued to hold her and rock her in his arms in silence for a few minutes before Dr. Howard spoke.

"That is exactly right, James. We have a solid game plan for treatment, but the most important prescription we can give you is prayer. You and Diedra keep praying and studying the word, and know that God is still in control. Even when it looks like things are bad in the natural, He has already won. Rodney and I will definitely be praying for you."

Dr. Rodney asked if they had any questions about anything they had discussed. "Now you know if you have any questions about anything at all, you can feel free to call me anytime, day or night. I am here for you. I believe Pastor Vaughn was right. I was brought back here for such a time as this." He stopped and smiled at Diedra before he continued, "See, God was working this thing out before we even knew there was anything to work out."

"For whom he foreknew, he also predestined." James whispered.

"That's right!" both doctors agreed.

Before the doctors left the room, Dr. Howard advised Diedra and James that they could remain in the office as long as they needed, and Candy would have their recurring appointments entered and ready for them by the time they were ready to leave. Someone from the Kirklin clinic would be calling to set them up on a recurring schedule as well. The doctors excused themselves and eased out of the office.

# CHAPTER 11

As James was driving home from work, he reflected on the events that had taken place thus far in this new year they were not even a full month into yet. He and Diedra had been slammed from several directions at once, but in the midst of it all, there had been some blessings and breakthroughs as well.

Before New Year's Eve, he felt that the chasm between him and his wife might have become too wide to cross. He could feel her slipping away from him. Or so he thought. Turns out that what he thought was indifference from his wife was symptomatic of her struggle to simply hang on through all the mental, emotional, and physical, not to mention hormonal, turmoil, her body was going through. His own idiosyncratic viewpoint did not allow him to discern that she was suffering. He could only see how it was impacting him.

Not only did they learn that she was pregnant with their sixth child, but she was diagnosed with brain cancer as well. He didn't think she was going to be able to continue working under the circumstances, but she insisted she could. It was up to him to convince her that they didn't need the money. If that meant taking on overtime or finding a part-time job even, then that was what he would have to do.

James maneuvered around a bicycle as he pulled his car into the driveway. He observed another bike leaned up against the basketball goal on the side of the driveway, as he parked next to the side door. He didn't bother to pull into the garage, since he and Diedra would be going to Rodney and Kayla's house as soon as they got the boys situated. He was rather excited to be going to their small group for the first time. They had missed the last week because Diedra worked that night. But last night was the final night of her rotation. Tonight she was off and they would finally join the group.

They had decided to join the church in Coldwater and he really felt that was where they were supposed to be at this time in their lives. The way things had come together with Rodney and Kayla, Pastor Vaughn, even his former Pastor, and Diedra's co-worker, John; right now, it seemed this is where they belonged. Diedra seemed to be fully engaged as well. She was also excited about going to group.

James was disconcerted by what he saw when he walked into the kitchen. Diedra was sitting at the kitchen table in her housecoat, talking on the phone while she was chopping vegetables. The sink was full of the day's dishes, and there was a trail of toys leading from the kitchen to the den.

He surveyed the disaster that was their kitchen, and considered his wife as she sat there, shakily dicing the onions into fine pieces. Tears were streaming down her cheeks as she worked on her task. Three tomatoes, one bell pepper, a bowl of mushrooms, and a clove of garlic were on the table next to the cutting board. There was also a dish of boiled chicken strips waiting to be diced.

James walked across the room, picking up toys as he went, and headed to the living room. He stopped in front of the closet, took his coat off, and placed it inside, along with his brief case. He returned to the kitchen to find that Diedra was off the phone and had moved on to the bell peppers. Her face was still wet with tears. He walked around behind her and placed his hands on her shoulders as he gave her a kiss on the cheek. He walked over to the sink and rolled up his sleeves before he picked up the dish washing liquid, turned the water on and began to wash his hands under the running water. Once his hands were thoroughly cleaned and dried he reached under the sink and retrieved another cutting board. He grabbed a knife from the butcher's block and returned to the table where he took a seat next to Diedra and began to cut the chicken.

"I gather we're having chicken spaghetti tonight."

She nodded her head and continued chopping. "So, who was on the phone?" He asked.

"Shar."

"Shar? You haven't talked to her since Christmas have you?"

She shook her head.

"Is she doing okay?"

She nodded. He realized that she had not made direct eye contact with him since he arrived home. She was probably waiting for him to say something about the state of the house or why she was just now cooking when they were supposed to leave in less than two hours, *But I don't care about this house. I care about you. I want to know what's going on with you. Are you okay, are you sick? Talk to me Babe!*

Out loud he said "Were you able to get any sleep today?"

"A little. I kept waking up. My mind kept racing through different scenarios and I had the worst headache. Before I knew it, it was time for the triplets to come home. Fortunately, I didn't have to go get them. Cassandra picked them up along with Jasmine. She brought them just a little while ago. They said they wanted spaghetti tonight so, that is what we're having. I don't know if we'll be able to sit down with them though."

"You still planning to go to group?"

"I feel like I have to."

"You don't have to."

"I mean, I feel like I need to. James, I feel like I'm drowning in the fear of the unknown. I just have to get out and get around some positive people."

"You know I'm here for you, right?"

"Yes, but you are going through the same thing I am. I don't want to add my emotional burdens to yours. How can I support you if I'm weighing you down with my own load?"

"We can carry a lot more together than we can individually."

When he said that, Diedra was reminded of the dream she had when the two large clouds combined into one. What was that James had said after his conversation with Pastor Mckinney? "A threefold cord is not easily broken."

"James."

"Yes."

"I love you"

"If I know anything at all, I do know that." He replied with that grin she adored. "Babe, you can go ahead and get ready for Group, and I'll finish the spaghetti."

"Are you sure?"

"Absolutely, just don't tell Adrian and Tremaine I made it," he said with a wink.

"Silly."

Diedra told James about her conversation with Shar on the way to Group. She was doing fantastic as usual. She was jetting between Atlanta and Los Angeles on a regular basis. She seemed to be spending more time around Derek in recent years. Especially, since she had started representing some of his clients.

It all seemed complicated to Diedra. Most of Derek's clients had their own attorney's to represent their interests in contract negotiations with Derek and other entities as well, but Shar would handle other legal matters such as law-suits or even brokering the original contracts. For example if Derek was representing a player who signed with the Atlanta Hawks, Shar would draft the paperwork for the deal Derek negotiated with the team regarding sign-on bonuses, annual salary and the number of years the commitment was for. The client's personal attorney would negotiate specifics such as percentages paid to Shar and Derek. It all worked out pretty well for all parties involved and Shar and Derek both were garnering a lot of respect in their fields.

When they were all younger, Shar and Derek had always gotten along because they were so much alike. But now Diedra wondered if their relationship was more than professional.

"What if it is? Romantic, I mean." asked James. "Would you have a problem with that? I can see how that would be weird."

"I don't know. I guess he's going to have to settle down some day. Who with, has absolutely nothing to do with me and my life. That chapter of my life was closed many years ago. At least if he were with one of my friends I wouldn't have to worry about someone mistreating my children."

"Did I ever send him a Thank You card?"

"For what?"

"For being such a fool."

Even though it was dark, he knew she was blushing, and he loved it. As they crept up the steep hill toward Heritage Highlands, they both observed the large homes lining either side of 11th street. "I figure we'll be ready to move by the time the baby is two at the latest." James said.

"Let's take one step at a time why don't we?"

"I'm just saying. We have to start looking ahead. You know I'm all about planning. Did you know my cousin Huey has some property up here?"

"Okay, so can we first plan to deliver a healthy baby and get me cured of cancer?"

"Oh we got that! Babe we just have to trust and believe in God's word. You know, we keep asking God for a sign to let us know he hears our prayers, or a sign to show us his answer. We keep looking for reassurance, when he has already given it to us. Jesus said with faith the size of a mustard seed we can move mountains. Our Father cares for the flowers in the field. How much more does he care for us and our needs. Jesus told Thomas 'Because you have seen me, now you believe, but blessed are they that have not seen, and yet have believed.' I am claiming all of God's promises for us, right now!"

As they reached Heritage Highlands the houses were much newer and much larger, and as they came around the curve at the top of the hill they saw the number they were looking for on a mailbox, on the side of the street. They looked beyond the mailbox, across the yard that sloped up to a palatial brick home set off by grand white arches, amid a large circular portico with stately columns.

"It's like that?" asked James.

"Apparently so. I know Kayla said they were able to get a lot more house for their money, than what they were paying for in Atlanta, but wow!"

They pulled up into the driveway and James parked his ten year old Maxima alongside Brea's new Land Rover. The Land Rover had been her vehicle of choice since college. Whenever they had a model change she would trade hers in for the latest model. Even though she owned a brand new BMW, she still enjoyed driving her Land Rover. James opened his door and climbed out of the car. He gazed at the house for a moment before he walked around to Diedra's door and helped her out of the car.

"You really like that don't you?" he asked, gesturing toward the house.

"Why do you ask that?"

"Because I know how much you love houses. And frankly, I'm impressed by this one myself. It is remarkable."

"Yes it is, but I'm not admiring it in a covetous way. I just appreciate beautiful style and architecture, whether it's in a grand home like this, or if it's a modest home like ours. Because I want you to know, that our house does have some very unique features, thanks to you."

James picked Diedra up into a bear hug and swung her around before he kissed her. They were so lost in each other that they didn't notice John and Sherry's Cadillac as it pulled into the driveway. Or when the couple got out of their vehicle and headed up the driveway.

"Uhhm. Uh, excuse me; there will be none of that out here kids."

James set Diedra back down on the ground, and looked up to see John and Sherry grinning at them. "Oh I'm sorry. I thought you were a couple of teenagers out here." John joked. "Carry on, Ma'am, sir," and he and Sherry headed for the door.

"Wait for us." Diedra said as they followed behind the couple arm in arm.

John handed Kayla a covered cake plate as she welcomed them all to her home. "Is this one of Sherry's creations?" she asked.

It was; a red velvet cake with cream cheese icing shaped in the form of a cross. There was a three dimensional palm tree in the center. Sherry had a gift for baking and decorating cakes. It was a hobby that had developed into a lucrative business.

"We are going to be doubly blessed tonight. We will be both spiritually and naturally fed. Rodney always welcomes any excuse to fire up 'Big Bertha', so he has smoked some hens for us. I made some macaroni and cheese, green beans and potato salad to accompany the chicken, and Sherry's cake will round out the meal nicely," she said as she placed the dish on the table in the dining room. "And of course, I am sure John is going to have a wonderful word for us tonight."

As Kayla spoke, they noticed that Brea and Cassandra, were already sitting directly in front of them, in the spacious living room with the cathedral ceiling. The backdrop of the panoramic view, peeping through the two story windows was breathtaking. The low hanging moon was suspended over the town, like a watchman overseeing his charge.

"You have a beautiful home Kayla. And that view is stunning!" Diedra said before she turned to greet Cassandra and Brea.

"Thank you, Diedra. We love it." To John and James she said, "Gentlemen, you can go into the kitchen where Rodney is finishing up the last touches on his birds he is so proud of. Then we will all meet up in the living room where we'll pray, and John will share with us. After that, we'll eat dinner. I hope you're all hungry, because there's plenty."

"That sounds like a plan, Kayla," James' responded. "Brea, is Michael in the kitchen?" Diedra tried to bump him slyly with her hip, but they all noticed. "What? Did I say something wrong? I thought you two were inseparable. Did another one bite the dust?" He jokingly asked.

Diedra noticed this was one of those extremely rare occasions when Brea did not have a snappy comeback. She realized that she hadn't heard her mention Michael since that day they all met up at church and went to the Top of The River together. She didn't pry into her friends affairs. Brea would tell her and Cassandra what was going on when she was ready.

As the men removed themselves to the kitchen, the ladies assembled in the living room and engaged in small talk about work, family and relationships. Diedra attempted to apologize to Brea for James' tactlessness.

"Don't even worry about it? If he hadn't asked, I would have been uncomfortable because I knew he was thinking it." Before any of the ladies could ask Brea what had actually taken place between her and Michael, they heard the doorbell. To their surprise, it was Michael.

"What are you doing here?" asked Brea.

"I believe I was invited."

"Are you serious?"

"I definitely am."

"It's so good to see you again, Michael," said Kayla. "You always bring such insight to our discussions. Come on in," she said as she ushered him into her home. She took his coat and sent him into the kitchen with the rest of the men."

"Brea, I'm going to need you to behave," she whispered as he left the room. "What's going on with you two anyway? I'm with James. I thought you two were getting along great. Did he do something?"

"No, he's a perfect gentleman, but I can't continue like I have been. That word I received from that woman at church has resonated with me ever since. I have got to make some changes in my life. I don't know what God's plan is for me, but I know he wants me to do better. I have to stop jumping from one relationship to the next." Brea's shoulders seemed to slump under the weight of her thoughts. She sighed deeply before she said, "Don't you think I want to be married someday?"

Just then, all the men returned to the room. After the husbands sat next to their wives the only seat left in the room was next to Brea on the Love Seat. "May I?" Michael asked her.

"Do I really have a choice?"

"You always have a choice. Just say the word and I'll stand all night."

"You don't have to do that," interjected Kayla. "Rodney honey, bring Michael a chair out of the other room, please."

"That won't be necessary. There's plenty of room here." Brea reluctantly stated, waving a hand at the empty space beside her.

As Michael took his seat next to Brea, John stood up at the podium Rodney had placed in front of the expansive window. He stood tall and erect as he looked around the room. "First I'd like to thank Rodney and Kayla for allowing me to share with the group tonight." He drew a handkerchief from his pocket and wiped his glasses before he placed them on the tip of his nose. He led them all in a short prayer, and then he began.

"I'm going to speak to you today from the Book of Genesis, chapters 37-42. I believe the story of Joseph speaks to me more strongly than any other story in the Bible. It reminds me that delay is not denial. Joseph knew from his youth that he was destined for greatness, He didn't know when and he didn't know how, but he knew that somehow God was going to set him up in a place of honor.

Joseph's brothers were so jealous of him that they hated him. When Jacob gave Joseph his coat of many colors their hatred was fueled all the more. They weren't jealous of that beautiful coat their father had given him. They were jealous of the favor it represented. When they sold him into slavery they still hadn't stripped him of his favor.

As the years went by and they thought they had "got over", little did they know… They went about their business, eating, drinking, raising families, and even thanking God for blessing them with plenty.

Then the famine came. And after they had gone through everything they had, their entire tribe was on the brink of extinction. The only man in the entire world, as they knew it, who was in a position to help them was… You guessed it! Joseph! God had lifted him up out of the dungeon and placed him in a position of power second only to Pharaoh.

What do you suppose Joseph did during those years in slavery, and then in the dungeon? Do you suppose he kept replaying in his mind the events of that last day at home? What he could have said differently, or done differently to avoid ending up in chains? Do you suppose he spent his days whining and crying to God? No! The Bible says Joseph was the best servant in the house of Potiphar. Then he was the best slave in the dungeon, honing the skills he would later use as a ruler over Egypt.

Pay attention! God is doing a work right now that no man can take credit for. Keep your eyes on Him. As He says in His word: Look to the hills from whence comes your help. Not to the left nor to the right. Not even within your own might. God has a plan for you, and it is to give you a future and a hope. It's already done. Worrying and stressing will not change a thing. Stay focused and trust in Him, because we are not of those who turn back to perdition, but we continue on to the saving of our souls. Amen" John looked around the room as "Amen" and "Thank you Jesus" reverberated throughout the room.

"Now that's a good word for somebody!" said Rodney excitedly. He walked up to John and gave him a quick hug coupled with a handshake as he replaced him at the podium.

"Can anyone think of anything they've been waiting on, or believing God for?"

James was the first to speak. "I really needed to hear that on so many levels John. I have been waiting for years to move up to the next level in my profession at the depot. Lately, I have become frustrated with the entire process and I have actually considered going out to the Honda plant they're talking about building in Lincoln." Diedra shot him a surprised look. This was the first she'd heard of that.

"Your words have been enlightening and encouraging to me tonight." he said as he returned Diedra's glance with a self-conscious smile. He reached out and placed his hand on her knee as he continued. "When I married Diedra it was with the intention of giving her the world and I still want to do that, especially now. She shouldn't have to work so hard. I just want her to stay home and focus on raising our sons, getting well, and delivering a healthy baby. And even though we are in the midst of a struggle right now, I do believe our greater is coming. Thank you for reminding me of that."

"Well I've been in the dungeon, and this is not it," Diedra asserted. "When I was in that apartment in Hartford with Adrian and Austin, I used to constantly question why I was there, in that position. I thought I was being punished for having children out of wedlock...yes I really did. So I determined to be the best mother to them I could be. By the time I met James, I had resigned myself to the idea that it was going to be me and the twins forever, which was why I had such a hard time allowing him to break through the shell I had placed around myself. But I believe I went through everything I did to prepare me to be his wife. I know what I have in a husband, and I am grateful for him and the life we have right now."

James gently squeezed Diedra's knee as she absentmindedly caressed his large hand.

"That's what I want!" blurted Brea. "I want to marry someone who will love me just like that. I don't believe God intended for me to be alone for the rest of my life. But sometimes I feel like I am being punished as well."

"She's looking so hard, she can't even see what's right in front of her." Michael said softly.

"Excuse me."

"You will never find what you're looking for, as long as you keep running scared. You have a man right here, who wants to love you, and you don't even know how to accept it."

"It wasn't going to last anyway," she scoffed.

"How do you know? You didn't even give us a chance."

"She's probably right," said John to everyone's surprise. "Can I ask you two a personal question?"

"Yes, the answer is yes," replied Brea.

"You haven't even heard the question, Brea." said Kayla.

"I already know the question. Yes, we have been intimate. And I have been dealing with that ever since I went to the altar for prayer. I want to get right with God and I can't be a hypocrite. I know he is not pleased."

"So this right here," she said as she gestured her arms between her and Michael. "It has to be over."

"It doesn't have to be completely over," said John. "It is never too late for God. Just because you started out wrong, doesn't mean you can't repent and change what you're doing."

"That's exactly what I'm trying to do." Brea blurted out. "Michael is like no other man I have ever met, but I don't believe God will honor this relationship as it has been."

"Don't I get a say in this?"

"No!"

This time Sherry spoke. "Brea, be careful you don't throw the baby out with the bath water."

"What do you mean?"

"We can all see that there is a connection between the two of you that goes beyond the physical. How far beyond, is for you to determine. Do you really feel you have to sever the entire relationship in order to eliminate the aspect that you feel is not pleasing to God?"

"Well, I'm pretty sure he won't…"

"Please don't attempt to speak for me," Michael interrupted. "I want you in my life, and my desire is much deeper than physical."

"Okay, sounds like you two have a lot to talk about…in private!" said Cassandra. "Medical school would be the thing that I had to wait for. I gladly put school on hold to follow Shawn as he pursued his military career. But even after we settled back in Jacksonville, it seemed like the responsibilities of being both a JSU faculty member's wife and an officer's wife, along with being a full-time mother, left no time for school. I began to lose sight of my lifelong goal of becoming a physician. But God is faithful! I am back in school and Shawn has been great, and it's all working out."

"Amen. God is good! Does anyone else have anything they want to share?" asked Rodney. Since no one responded he closed that portion of the meeting. "Thank you so much for sharing tonight John. Next week we will hear from a female perspective. How about you Diedra? Would you like to speak next week?"

"I pass."

"Come on babe, you will be great." James nudged.

"Uhh… no. I don't mind giving feedback from the peanut gallery, but I'm not ready to stand in front of the group."

"I'll go next," Cassandra volunteered. "Can I pick any topic I want?"

"As long as it comes from the Bible." Rodney said as he began to put away the podium. "Who else is hungry? Let's bless the food and then you ladies go be seated in the dining room and tonight we will serve you." Rodney said grace, and all the men got up and headed for the kitchen.

"Wow! That was pretty awesome tonight," said Cassandra as the ladies gathered at the table. "I'm so glad you and Rodney started this group."

"Thank you. I think God's going to do some powerful things, and I'm glad to be a part of it." Kayla replied. "So what are you going to talk about next week, Cassie?"

"I'm not absolutely sure, but I have a few things tossing around in my head." she stated, as she eyed the cross shaped cake with the palm tree in the middle of it. The men entered the room one by one. After all the other ladies' husbands had set their plates on the table before them and sat down next to them. Brea, who was feeling a little uncomfortable, got up and went into the kitchen."

James smiled after her, and chuckled as she walked away.

"What are you laughing at? That's not even funny," whispered Diedra. "Why do you give her such a hard time?" James just continued grinning as he placed a fork full of potato salad in his mouth, and then gave Diedra a peck on the forehead.

Brea entered the kitchen to find Michael garnishing a baked potato with butter and sour cream. He knew Brea did not like potato salad so he had asked Rodney for a potato to bake for her in the microwave.

"What are you doing in here?" he asked.

"When you didn't return with a plate for me, I thought I was going to have to get my own."

"You really underestimate me don't you?" he asked. "Brea, I am for real, and I believe what we have is special. Give us a chance."

"We'll talk." she said as she walked around the island to see what else he had placed on her plate. A leg, a thigh and a wing, a generous helping of macaroni and cheese, green beans, and a roll, to go with her baked potato. *He did pay attention didn't he?* she thought.

"Where's your plate?" she asked, as she reached for an empty plate off the island.

"You heard what the man said. We are serving the ladies. You just sit right there on that stool and allow me to take care of you. Next week you can reciprocate."

"Yes sir," she said, through an acquiescent smile. Michael arranged her potato on her plate with the rest of her food and then quickly fixed his own. He would not allow her to carry anything as they returned to the dining room.

When Diedra saw him place the plate in front of Brea she gave James a playful nudge as she realized what he had been grinning about.

After dinner the group gathered back in the living room for prayer. They prayed for James and Diedra and their family. They prayed for Brea and Michael. They prayed for Cassandra and Shawn as she pursued her medical degree, and they asked that God would guide Cassandra and provide her with a timely message for their next meeting. They prayed that God would continue to watch over them all as they went about their daily lives. As they gathered their coats and prepared to go back out into the night, Kayla announced that next week Rodney would smoke some baby back ribs.

In the car on the way home, "James, I didn't know you were frustrated to the point of leaving your job."

"Babe, you know I've been at the Depot for 13 years now. I know it's a good job, and I am grateful for it, but I should be a senior engineer or a Division

Manager by now." As he maneuvered the vehicle back down 11<sup>th</sup> St, he continued to speak.

"I'm beginning to feel that not having a military background has hindered my progress and kept me from promoting as high as I should have. But even so, John's words tonight reminded me that no man can keep God's blessings from me."

"You are going to be fine James."

"We are."

# CHAPTER 12

THINGS CONTINUED ON RATHER SMOOTHLY. James and Diedra continued their daily routine; get the kids to school, go to work, get the kids settled in for the evenings, go to work, and repeat. They attended Diedra's doctor's appointments, and so far her pregnancy was progressing smoothly, and the tumor was being rigorously monitored. She had not had any other issues beyond the headaches and nausea. The anti-seizure medication seemed to be doing what it was prescribed to do.

By the time they returned to Rodney and Kayla's home for their small group, they were excited for the outlet. With so much going on in their lives, they had not had much time for anyone outside of their immediate families. Once they learned of Diedra's health situation, both their mothers had taken it upon themselves to start delivering meals on occasion. Diedra's mother would even come over once a week and clean the house for her. That was a hard one to get Diedra to accept, but to James' delight, she did.

James worried that Diedra was still not getting the rest she needed, so he was even more prone to cook. Even Adrian and Tremaine ate his meals without complaint. Although he was a talented cook, he had three main go-to meals; spaghetti, chili, and hamburgers and fries. He liked to experiment with the spaghetti and chili, and it didn't always come out as intended. But they always ate it without complaint. Except for that one time, he himself, insisted on throwing the entire pot of spaghetti out. What possessed him to put nutmeg in the sauce, no one knew. He swore he had read that somewhere. Maybe he had used too much, but ugh, never again. Tonight they would eat at Rodney and Kayla's, and the boys were having pizza.

They were the last to arrive at the house. They noticed that Brea and Michael were sitting next to each other on the love seat. Cassandra, Shawn, Sherry, and John were on the couch, Rodney and Kayla had the large overstuffed chair on one end of the room and the other one was waiting for James and Diedra. By this time, Diedra was nearly six months along, and her petite frame had begun to betray her condition to the observant eye. Her breasts strained against the top of her over-sized sweater and the slightest silhouette of a mound curved underneath.

"Oh look at mama!" Cassandra exclaimed as she and Brea raced over to their friend. "Has she started kicking yet?" They both reached out and laid a hand on Diedra's abdomen. No one else could have gotten away with that, other than James and the boys of course.

"Oh yes! She is a strong one."

"Like her mother," they chimed in unison.

"Just like her mother." James agreed.

Brea returned to her seat and Cassandra approached the podium in front of the large window. She gazed out at the spectacular view for a moment before she whispered softly "Look at God!" And then she turned her attention to the group. She began by praying and thanking God for placing their group together and allowing them to pour into each other's lives. She thanked God for allowing her to have the insight to share what she was about to share with them, and then she began.

"I think this is especially for Diedra and Brea. I'm sure we can all benefit from it, but especially you two ladies. I kept thinking about you as I studied. Do you remember what you told me about that night you decided to leave Hartford and come back home? I believe even then, God was trying to tell you something...I want to talk about Tamar in the Bible. Do you know who Tamar was?"

Diedra and Brea both shook their heads no and Michael said, "Wasn't that Judah's daughter in law, who tricked him into laying with her and later gave birth to twins?"

"I thought that was David's daughter. The one who was raped by her brother." said Shawn.

"You are both right."

Brea looked over at Diedra and asked out of the side of her mouth, "Now what exactly is she trying to say?"

"Hang on, hang on!" Cassandra said to Brea. Then she continued, "Both of these ladies' names were Tamar and they both experienced rejection. They both experienced redemption as well." Cassandra leaned over on the podium as she began. She had always been an eloquent speaker. In high school and college, Shar had tried to convince her to go to law school with her and one day practice together, but her passion had always been science.

"Tamar's husband died before they had conceived a child, so…as was the custom back then, his father Judah, gave her to his second son to provide an heir for his older brother. But he didn't want to bring a child into this world that he would have no claim to, so he made sure that it didn't happen. If you know what I mean. Then he died as well. So she was twice widowed, with no heir. Judah then sent her to her father's house to remain a widow until his third son became of age. But when the third son was of age, Judah failed to send for Tamar, for fear that his last son would die as well. Rejection.

As Michael stated, Tamar, who was not content to remain a childless widow, deceived Judah and they came together and conceived twins, Perez and Zerah. Initially, when her pregnancy was discovered, Judah had condemned her to be burned. Rejection. But once it was revealed that he was a party to her acts, she was pardoned for her trespass. Tamar and Judah were later listed in the lineage of Jesus through Perez. Redemption. You can read the details in Genesis chapter 38.

Now, the second Tamar mentioned in the Bible was David's daughter. Tamar was a beautiful young virgin, and her half-brother, Amnon, had such a strong desire for her that it made him ill. The Bible says he loved her. He was so consumed by his lust for her that he didn't even consider if his feelings were right or wrong. He just wanted what he wanted.

His cousin devised a plan of seduction for him. And once Amnon had lured Tamar to his personal quarters by feigning illness, he proceeded to sexually assault her… his sister. She begged and pleaded with him and even suggested that her father would give her to him in marriage, rather than allow them both to be shamed by this act. He didn't listen, because he wasn't concerned with the consequences of his behavior.

As soon as the act was done, his feelings toward his sister altered from love/lust to hatred/disgust. He couldn't even bear to look at her.

I personally believe this was a result of guilt and shame at the realization of what had transpired, and he somehow blamed her.

Nevertheless, after he had committed this abominable act, which not only destroyed his sister's innocence, but had stolen her future from her: she would never marry, nor have children, and she would never be the princess or queen she had been bred to become; he sent her away with her shame. Treating her as if she was the one who had committed the trespass in that situation… Rejection. When her full brother, Absalom, learned of what had taken place, he took her into his home and provided a covering for her; protection from further physical abuse, defense from ostracism, and shelter from the outside world in general.

Tamar was ruined. Defiled by her own brother. She could never take her rightful place in society because her older brother who was supposed to be her protector, had been her greatest nightmare come to life. But fortunately, she had another brother who was her protector, her shield, her strong tower.

Absalom showed her that regardless of the abuse and heartache she had been subjected to, she was still worthy to be loved. And in the most genuine, purest sense of the word, he loved his sister enough to see beyond her circumstances and remember who she was as a person, his sister. He even named his own daughter Tamar. Redemption. You can read 2 Samuel 13 for this story.

I believe there is a spirit of rejection that was assigned to those two ladies and it is still roaming around today. Its purpose was to destroy them, but God's purpose was greater.

I want you to remember that God is not a man that he can lie, and his promises will come to pass. Regardless of the attacks of the enemy, we have this treasure in earthen vessels that the excellency of the power may be of God and not of us. We are troubled on every side, yet not distressed; we are perplexed but not in despair; persecuted but not forsaken, cast down but not destroyed; always bearing about in the body, the dying of the Lord Jesus, that the life also of Jesus might be manifest in our bodies." By this point, Cassandra had gotten so excited that they thought she was going to hoop. She paused and took a deep breath.

"My point today is that regardless of what has happened in your lives, whether to you or by you, you have a redeemer, who is ready to wash the past away, and take you in, and love you and protect you. You may feel bombarded by the attacks of the enemy, but he can't stop God's plan for your life. Everything you have gone through in your lives has helped to prepare you to receive God's promises: everything, every mistake, every hurt, every setback, and every rejection."

As she closed her lesson they gave her a standing ovation and they rushed to her and hugged her and patted her on the shoulder.

"Wow Cassie!" Kayla said through a stream of tears. "I believe that was for me."

"What do you mean?"

"Well, my father left my mother when I was five years old and I always experienced feelings of abandonment. For years I believed it was my fault. My mother wasn't much comfort, because she was hanging on by a thread herself. Working two, sometimes three jobs at a time, just to make ends meet.

Fortunately, Rodney and I became friends at a young age and thanks to the love and support I received from him and his family, I survived. His father was like my own father, which was why he walked me down the aisle at our wedding."

"I had no idea." replied Cassandra.

"I know. You ladies are several years younger than us, so I wouldn't expect you to really know, but my life could have turned out much differently, if it hadn't been for my husband and my in-laws. I was angry, bitter, and rebellious, but they loved me right through it.

This is why this is so powerful. I have been talking with Rodney for years about my dream of starting a women's ministry focused on helping women get beyond the pain of rejection and live to their fullest potential. I want to be a mentor to younger women in the church and the community at large, and maybe help them avoid some of life's pitfalls.

Cassie, I think your lesson today would serve as the perfect cornerstone for such a group, and I believe you ladies would each have something to contribute to make this a powerful ministry. We could call it Daughters of Tamar. "

"I feel like you're on to something, and I'm in. I felt really strongly about this message as I was studying. You know rejection can come in many forms. When Shawn and I got together, we faced all kinds of rejection. Fortunately, coming from military families, we received great support from our immediate families. I have to tell you, it hurt not having all of my friends there to stand up with me at my wedding. On some levels I understood but on other levels... it still felt like rejection." She paused and smiled as she said, "But you won't believe what other little nugget I discovered while I was studying!"

"What was that?" asked Diedra.

"For he shall be like a tree planted by the waters, and spreads out her roots by the river, and shall not see when heat comes, but her leaf shall be green, and it will not be anxious in a year of drought nor cease to yield fruit. Jeremiah 17:8."

"Alright now."

"Oh you don't get it yet. But you will. That tree by the water is referring to a palm tree. Do you know what palm tree means in Hebrew?"

"I never really thought about it," replied Diedra.

"Wait for it... It means Tamar. In Christianity, the palm tree has been used as the symbol for victory of the faithful over enemies of the soul."

"My God! My God!" exclaimed Brea in wonder. "Did you hear that Diedra? I receive every bit of that."

"I know right. That was pertinent on so many levels." Diedra was awestruck.

They were all excited about the message and how it fit into each of their lives. They talked a little more before the group dispersed, men to the kitchen, and women to the dining room. The men had decided they would continue to serve the women each week.

As they gathered at the table, Cassandra noticed that Sherry's cake was another cross with a palm tree in the middle. "Is that another red velvet cake, Sherry? How did you come up with the design?"

"Actually, this one is a key lime cake. The cross was an obvious choice, but the palm tree…that was just something I added to give it a little color. I figured I could keep the design and surprise you all with the flavor each week. How fitting is that?"

"That is so wonderful. You have such a gift."

"Thank you, Cassie."

Brea sat down next to Diedra who was absentmindedly rubbing her hand across her abdomen. "Hey Lady, what's on your mind?"

"You know Brea; it had been years since I even thought about that night with Mike and Ike until that woman spoke over you at church a few weeks ago. Then Cassie brings that whole incident up again tonight."

"Yes, they've been on my mind a lot since that day."

"When was the last time you heard from them?"

"Ike and his wife sent me a Christmas card."

"Yeah, we received one as well. But it wasn't until that Sunday, that I really couldn't get them out of my head."

"Let's call them!"

"Now?"

"Why not? They're only an hour ahead of us. Kayla, do you mind if I use your phone to make a call? To Connecticut. I'll pay for it."

"Sure, don't worry about it. It's no extra charge to us."

"Mike and Ike?" she asked Diedra.

"Yeah, apparently their mothers' were so close, people would say they were closer than Mike and Ike, the candy."

"Who are they?"

"They were a couple of friends of ours in Hartford and New Haven, who turned out to be more like guardian angels. I think it was their influence that led Brea into Law Enforcement."

She and Brea walked across the room to the phone, and she stood beside her as she picked up the receiver. Brea dialed Ike's number and to her surprise, it was picked up on the first ring. "Hello. This is Breanna Thomas. May I speak to Ike?"

"Brea? Is that you? Where have you been? I have left you several messages tonight."

"Really? I'm out with some friends. Diedra and I were just talking about you and Mike and we decided to give you a call."

"Diedra's with you?"

"Yes, we're at a small group meeting with some friends from our church."

"Are you serious?"

"Well, Yeah."

"I am really in need of the assistance of some strong prayer warriors right now."

"What's wrong?"

"It's Mike."

"Mike?"

"How is Big Mike anyway?" asked Diedra.

"Brea, you wouldn't happen to be on a speaker phone would you?"

"As a matter of fact, I am."

"Put me on speaker please. Because I don't think I can bear to say this more than once."

"Okay Ike, but you are making me nervous." she said as she depressed the speaker button.

"I am sorry for that. Do you have me on speaker yet?"

"Yes you are. And hello Ike. This is Diedra. Our friend Cassie, who you met at my wedding, is here along with Kayla and Sherry, two more friends of ours. Now please tell us what's going on with Mike."

"Hello everyone."

"Okay? About Mike?"

"He was shot today."

"Shot! What do you mean shot?" asked Brea.

"He was at work. At the jailhouse. There was an altercation involving one of the inmates. He wasn't even involved. He just happened to walk in the room when the inmate got one of the deputy's gun and shot him... He just shot him!"

"Is he ..."

"He's alive, but still in critical condition. He's out of surgery, and it's just a waiting game now. The doctors say all we can do is pray. So we've been calling everyone we know who cares about Mike. He has got to pull through! He's like a brother to me."

Diedra felt as if someone had knocked the wind out of her. She leaned over the phone stand and grabbed her chest, as she tried to breathe. She stared down at the phone as if she was waiting for Ike to come through the line and tell her it was all a misunderstanding; that the man who had practically saved her life all those years ago was not now fighting for his. Her mind flashed back to those last two weeks in Connecticut when he spent every night sleeping on her couch as her self-appointed guardian, just in case Desmond had not heeded his warning to stay away from her.

"Who... Who... did this?" she asked between breaths. She could barely speak.

"I think she's hyperventilating!" Kayla said as she ran in the kitchen to get Rodney and James. Sherry led Diedra to the nearest chair and Cassandra stood next to Brea with an arm around her shoulder.

"It was Desmond. He's been in and out of jail for petty crimes for the past ten years. But this time, he's going down for good!"

James and Rodney rushed in to the room and went straight to Diedra, who was leaning over in her chair, one hand resting on her abdomen and the other clutching her chest, as she gasped for air.

"What is going on?" asked James as he kneeled down in front of his wife. "Is it the baby?"

She shook her head no.

"Kayla was right, James. She's hyperventilating, or having a panic attack. Will someone please tell me what's going on? And who is that on the phone?"

"Ike, I am so sorry to hear about Mike. I promise you we're going to pray for him, but we have to see about Diedra. I'll call you back when I get home. Okay?" Brea exclaimed through tears and rushed off the phone.

"Sure, I'm sorry. I didn't mean to upset her."

"You have nothing to apologize for. She wouldn't be upset if she didn't care."

Rodney and James were focused on Diedra. "James, I need you to help her to calm down. This is not good for the baby or her."

"Look at me, Babe. Relax and breathe slowly. It is all good. I've got you. Come on. Slow and easy."

"That's right. Slow and easy. Diedra, close your mouth and try breathing through your nose. Keep your eyes on James but answer my questions okay?" Diedra stared into James' eyes as she responded to Rodney.

"Are you having any pain, anywhere?" he asked.

She shook her head no. "Good." He exclaimed. "Keep breathing."

Her breathing gradually slowed. "Any feelings of indigestion or nausea?"

She shook her head no. "Great! Now I need you to answer me out loud."

She breathed slowly as she waited for his question.

"Look into your husband's eyes and tell me. Are you in love with the man in front of you?"

Diedra smiled without hesitation and said, "Yes."

James drew her into his arms and hugged her close to him as he asked what had sent her into such a state. She explained to him that she and Brea had decided to give Mike and Ike a call because they were the first ones to tell them about Tamar. Brea called Ike, who told them that Mike had been shot that very day by Desmond, the man who had attacked her years ago. She told him that she wanted him to lead the group in a prayer for Mike. James was more than happy to.

They gathered around the table, held hands, and prayed, in earnest for Diedra and Brea's friend. James started it off, but they all joined in praying in the spirit, some speaking in tongues, some speaking out affirmative words, some crying, and some laughing. They all prayed until they felt the heaviness that Ike's news had brought was lifted from the room. By the time they'd finished praying it was late, and they all decided to pack up their food and take it with them.

While James and Diedra were in the car headed home, they continued to pray silently for Mike. Once they arrived home they sat in the car for a few minutes, before they went into the house. James reached across the vehicle and pulled his wife close to him and held her for a moment.

"Thank you." she said.

"For what."

"For being you. For allowing me to feel God's love through you. For praying with me and for me." Just then she winced and sat up straight in an attempt to elongate her abdomen.

"What's wrong? Is it the baby?"

Diedra laughed and said, "It's okay. I believe she's just stretching. It feels like she has a foot lodged in the top of my rib cage."

"She's already spoiled you know? She is the first to have that room all to herself. The others all had either double or triple occupancy. She'll probably be the largest one of all as well."

"You're silly."

"Sometimes." He leaned over and placed his head lightly over her abdomen. Is this uncomfortable for you?"

"Surprisingly no. Maybe she'll take after the women in my family and be a small baby."

"Sorry, not at the rate she's growing. Which is a good thing. She's going to need every advantage in order to continue to thrive if your tumor should decide to rear its ugly head."

"You're right."

"Are you ready to go in?"

"Sure."

He jumped out of the car and went around to her door, and opened it. "My Lady, allow me to escort you to the manor." He said with a sweeping bow as extended a hand to her. She reached out her hand and placed it in his, and after she stepped out of the car, he swooped her up in his arms and carried her to the front door. Diedra rested her head on James' shoulder and enjoyed the ride. When they arrived at the front door, Austin, who had been looking out for them, opened the door. "Is Mom okay?" he asked.

"I'm fine baby. I'm just tired," she reassured him.

James carried Diedra into the house, across the living room and down the hall, to their bedroom. Once they arrived in their room they found Travis asleep in their bed. James gently laid Diedra across the foot of the bed and walked around to the front to get Travis. He picked his son up and carried him into his bedroom, and placed him in his own bed.

Once he returned to their room he found Diedra fast asleep. He gently undressed her and placed her underneath the covers.

"Good night Sleeping Beauty," he said as he kissed her on her forehead, before he went to shower.

# CHAPTER 13

Fortunately, Diedra was off work the next few nights, and she was able to utilize that time to get some much needed rest. Brea kept her updated on news about Mike. The doctors didn't understand why he was still in a coma. They said his surgery had gone well and they had removed the bullet with no added complications. All they could do now was monitor him… and wait. Brea informed Mike's wife that they were praying for him and they would continue to pray for him and her as well.

On her last day off from work, Diedra's mother and her mother-in-law came and took her shopping for baby furniture.

"I don't know why you insist on buying baby furniture. Do you think James and I need charity or something?" she asked them both as they rode along in her mother's silver Mercedes.

Lee Beverly responded, "This is not charity Diedra. We just want to do something for our granddaughter. And since you haven't purchased anything at all, we figured we would help you with the furniture. That way, you can coordinate everything else."

"Right," added Mrs. Davis. "I know you don't want to have a hodge-podge of mix-matched furniture and accessories. Not for your little girl."

"I still think it's much too soon to make such major purchases," she insisted.

"Child, when you were pregnant with the triplets you had their entire room furnished and decorated before you reached five months. You're six months along and have not purchased anything for this baby," Ruth Davis observed.

"I was already practically five months when I learned about this pregnancy."

"Which would lead me to think you would be anxious to get things together." Lee Beverly eyed her daughter through the rearview mirror. She was always a hard one to read. "Diedra," she said gently. There are no guarantees in life. Even a so-called normal pregnancy, with no complications, has its risks. You have to trust God and believe that everything is going to be okay. You cannot expect the worst."

"I know Ma, but what if…"

"No what ifs! You are pregnant with a beautiful baby girl and we're all going to spoil her; starting with the most gorgeous crib and dressing table we can find."

"Yes ma'am," she replied. Then she rode in silence as the two elder ladies chattered excitedly about how they would spoil the little miracle that would be their latest granddaughter.

She was not excited though. She was afraid this was a mistake. If she had her way, she would not buy anything other than a bassinet and a car seat before she actually held her daughter in her arms. What if the unmentionable happened? Then James and the boys would be left with this monstrous display as a reminder of their loss. That would not be fair to any of them. She couldn't say that though. She couldn't admit to the fears that haunted her thoughts daily and her dreams nightly. What would they all say if they knew she was having these thoughts? She was just trying to be realistic and accept the very real possibility that this time bomb ticking inside her head might have devastating consequences to her and her unborn child.

She rode along in silence as they headed to the Baby Boutique; and she followed along while they excitedly shopped for baby furniture. They did have some beautiful pieces there. Mrs. Davis found a light oak crib that looked as if it was made to go with her and James' bedroom furniture. It was a perfect match. She had to admit the matching dressing table was perfect as well. When she reached out to turn the tag over and look at the price, her mother snatched it out of her hand.

"Don't you worry about that!" she said. "This is a gift, remember?"

The three of them continued through the store, picking out items for her gift registry; and by the time they finished shopping, her enthusiasm had surpassed theirs, and she even purchased a beautiful bedding set, decorated with pink fluffy lambs.

After shopping, they took her to the Victoria for lunch. She loved the old southern charm and elegance of this venue. The chicken salad was light and tasty. She expressed her gratitude to them for insisting on the outing. It did her a world of good. Once she returned home she sat on the chaise lounge in her bedroom, cherishing the moment.

*James will have to move this out of here to make room for the baby furniture. We are busting out at the seams. He's right. We do need to start planning to upsize. But how are we going to afford a larger home?* She began to feel that now familiar throbbing in her head and she laid across the chair and closed her eyes, attempting to relax. She woke up to see Adrian and Austin sitting on the floor in front of her bed playing a video game. She had no idea which system they had connected to her TV. They had them all. Whenever a new system would come out, Derek would send it almost as soon as they learned of its existence.

"What time is it?"

"Five o'clock. And Dad's on his way with Travis, Trevor, and Tremaine," replied Austin, as he maneuvered his controller to manipulate the character on the screen.

"Yeah, and we already took grandma's lasagna out of the freezer," added Adrian. "Score!" he exclaimed excitedly as he high-fived Austin.

Diedra stretched out and positioned herself on her side to watch her two oldest sons as they played the video game. "What no homework?" she asked.

"Nope," they said in unison.

"No tests to study for either?"

"We had a test today and we turned in our history reports. We're good."

"If you say so." She knew they took their education as seriously as she and their fathers did, if not more so.

"How do you think you did on your test?"

"I'm pretty sure I got a perfect score, but Austin… Sometimes I think he overthinks the essay questions and he goes way beyond what the teacher is looking for."

"I know, I know, but I think Ms. Keith gets me. She says I always keep her on her toes."

Diedra smiled to herself. Ms. Keith was one of her favorite teachers when she was in high school. What she said was, she almost always had to do extra research whenever she graded Austin's papers. She continued to watch her sons play the game as they waited for the rest of the family to arrive.

When Diedra returned to work, she arrived fifteen minutes early as usual. She stopped by the manager's office to pick up her work orders before she went to her station. Fortunately, she had a huge order so the one job would last most of her shift. Regrettably, one of her operators was out and she would have to run the worst printer in the shop. She went to her computer, entered her warehouse orders, and assign tasks to the nine men who would arrive shortly. Next, she would begin her routine maintenance on her printer. To her surprise, she found John was already crouched down at one of the printer doors with his head inside. She walked over to him and asked, "What's going on?"

"I think I finally figured out why this tray keeps jamming. It gave me the blues last night. I thought I'd give this a try before you got here. Hopefully, it will run smoothly for you tonight. If not, I'll be on that one right across from you."

"Sure, experiment on my night, why don't you?" she teased. She knew John was better at troubleshooting these machines than some of the manufacturer's technicians. Diedra enjoyed the nights when she and John worked together. They ensured that both of their crews worked together as a team and the entire shop ran like a well-oiled machine.

"Hey, you know I got this. I would have done it last night, but I was the only supervisor here. On top of that we had a bunch of small jobs."

"Sounds rough."

"It was, but I handled it."

"Naturally."

Once their team arrived, they held a short meeting at the front of the shop and gave out their assignments for the night. When the crew got situated and settled into work, Diedra and John returned to their printers at the back of the shop. Ordinarily they would sit at the desks in the front and monitor the progress of the crew, pulling more jobs if need be. But they had been short-handed lately, which meant they had to operate the additional two printers. Since they were only on one each, they chose to operate the last two, which were also the worst two.

There were twenty printers in all, which meant twenty tasks should be going at all times. Sometimes one printer would have one job and other times, like tonight, one job would be split between several printers. The job tonight would utilize all twenty printers, and it would run through most of the shift. It was important that Diedra and John monitored the proceedings closely to ensure that all aspects were coordinated and delivered to the collating area in perfect alignment, with no errors or damages. They were a good team. The operators took pride in their work and they were consistently, the most productive crew in the company.

How long do you think you'll be able to do this?" John asked as he pulled a stool up to the counter between the two printers for her.

"As long as I need to. Why? Are you trying to get rid of me?"

"No, not at all. No one else can run this shop like you and I do, but I'm just concerned about your health."

"I believe that, and I thank you for your concern, but I'm okay."

"You say that… but…You just have to take care of yourself. I don't want you going in to labor here at the shop," he said with a nervous laugh.

Diedra was the first and only female to work in the printing shop and once they became aware of her pregnancy, all of the men there had become overly protective of her. When she had the triplets, she went out on leave early in the pregnancy due to it being a high risk pregnancy. John didn't understand why this wasn't designated as a high risk pregnancy with the brain tumor and all. But, he was no doctor and it wasn't his call. "So, is everything going alright?"

"So far, so good."

"How's your friend doing? Mike, wasn't it?"

"I don't know. He's still comatose and they don't know why. I wish Rodney could go up there."

"He's not the only competent neurologist in the world, you know?"

"I know, but I trust him."

"Which is why he needs to stay here and see about you."

"I know." Diedra said as she walked over to clear a paper jam in her printer. She shot John the side-eye as she opened the exact same door he had worked on just a little earlier.

"What? I didn't say they stopped completely. Give it a chance to warm up though."

"Sure John." She pulled out her maintenance log and notated the time and location of the jam. Thankfully, both printers ran pretty smoothly the rest of the night, which gave John an opportunity to broach a subject he'd been wanting to discuss since the first time Diedra and her family had come to church. He knew his friend was saved but he sensed that she was missing something in her spiritual walk.

"I'm glad you finally came out to visit our church. What do you think about it?" he asked.

"I think it's great. So far, Pastor Vaughn has been right on the money every time."

"What do you mean?"

"I always feel as if he's speaking directly into my life and my marriage, but I don't feel like he's beating us up. He's always encouraging. And we learn something new each week. Group is the same way, but on a more direct level."

"Well I'm glad! I thought you might get spooked after that first Sunday, especially James. He always seemed like more of a traditional Baptist."

"He is to an extent, but he's more concerned with what the scriptures say than by-laws or covenants. As long as the message is biblical, he's good. Trust me. If he doesn't recognize it, he will do his research."

"That's good. You should do that too. The Word says to study to show yourself approved unto God, a workman that needeth not to be ashamed, rightly dividing the word of truth."

"I do, just not as in depth as him. James reads his Bible daily anyway.

"You don't?"

"To be honest with you, I always seem to get sleepy when I try to read my Bible. Unless I'm trying to find something to make a point with him," she laughed. "Lately though, he's been sharing with me and reading out loud to me, especially after group. He will always find something to add to the topic that really pinpoints its relevance to us."

"With all you've got going on, I'd think you would study more for yourself."

"What makes you say that?"

"Diedra, don't you know there is power in the Word of God. For the Word of God is quick, and powerful, sharper than any two-edged sword... Do you understand what I mean?"

"I'm not really sure."

"First, let me qualify what I am about to say. Diedra, I don't question that you're saved. I know you have accepted Jesus into your life as Lord and Savior. I've even witnessed the presence of the Holy Spirit in your life. What I'm sensing is, that you're not walking in the fullness of all that God has promised to his children, through his son Jesus Christ."

"What do you mean?"

"Before Jesus even hung on the cross for us he said he would leave us a Comforter and he would leave us his peace. The Comforter is the Holy Spirit that dwells in us. You have access to his comfort and his peace. The more you study your Bible, the more you will become aware of the gifts that are available to you, Diedra, as a spirit filled child of God."

"If these gifts are so readily available then why don't all Christians have them?"

"Let's see what the Bible says about that." he said as he reached in his bag and pulled out his Bible. He flipped through until he found what he was looking for. "My people perish from a lack of knowledge, Hosea 4:6... and you have not because you ask not, James 4:3. Those two scriptures tell me that many people just like you, are unaware of what is available to them so they don't know what to ask for. Or, they don't use those gifts that are already dwelling in them because they aren't aware that they have them. Then again, there are many who don't desire spiritual gifts or see a need for them in today's world."

"Gifts?"

"Yes, gifts. In the book of Acts, when the Holy Spirit first came down and filled the inhabitants of the upper room they were all given spiritual gifts, including the gifts of tongues, prophesy, and healing."

"James and Brea didn't even ask to speak in tongues, but they received it. So why didn't I?"

"I can't really tell you why you didn't spontaneously speak in tongues, but I do believe it's available to you. I think as you study and pray and open your heart up to the Holy Spirit and allow him to work in you, he will start to reveal your gifts to you. The least of which is speaking in tongues... according to Paul. And remember that wisdom is the principle thing. Therefore, get wisdom and in all your getting, get understanding. My prayer for you is that you develop a deeper relationship with Jesus and that you invite him and his Holy Spirit into your prayer life." He gestured toward his Bible and said, "That all begins by learning what the Word says for yourself. Why don't you start with the first four chapters of Acts?"

"You have given me a lot to think about."

They didn't talk much for the rest of the night. Diedra thought long and hard about what her friend had said. Peace was one thing she desperately needed right now. She felt like she needed a prayer language as well. She determined right then that she would start studying her Bible more. She said a silent prayer, asking God to give her a deeper understanding of his Word and to help her to pray, as she prayed for her health, her family, and her friends.

## CHAPTER 14

VALENTINE'S DAY WAS ON A Sunday this year, so they were celebrating on Friday and Saturday. The high school would have a formal Dance on Friday night and the adults would celebrate on Saturday. James could not determine if Diedra was thrilled or apprehensive at the prospect of her sons going out on their first date. She would bustle about like a mother hen making sure they had just the right accessories to coordinate with their date's dresses.

Austin was going with Cassandra and Shawn's daughter, Nicholette, and Adrian would be taking Kayla and Rodney's daughter, Victoria. Rodney III was driving them all. He and his date, Bianca, were both juniors and his father had insisted that the only other alternative Victoria had was for him to drive her himself. Nicholette was the youngest of them all, but because her date was Austin, Shawn and Cassandra agreed to allow her to ride with the group. Besides, they would be chaperones at the Dance anyway. Both of the girls' fathers insisted on having the young men over for heart to hearts before the big night. James and Diedra reminded them of the behavior that was expected of them as well.

On the night of the Dance you would have thought it was prom night the way the parents acted. The group had to stop by each of their homes for pictures on the way out, and the girls were showered with flowers, chocolates and teddy bears.

"I can't believe my babies are going out on a date. Just yesterday I was giving them piggy back rides and reading bedtime stories with them." Diedra said softly as she and James watched Adrian and Austin complete the finishing touches of their hair and make final adjustments to their ties. They were using the full length mirror in James and Diedra's room.

"They are growing up, Babe. They've got their learner's permits, and soon they'll be driving their dates themselves."

"I don't want to think about it."

"Why not? You've raised them right. They are responsible young men. I, for one, am proud of them."

"I am, as well. But I feel like they're slipping away from me. Next will be prom, then they will graduate and go to college, and then what?"

"The sky's the limit! And that's a good thing."

"I know it is, but..." She sighed deeply and walked across the room. "Let me get that," she said as she reached out to adjust Austin's pink tie. Austin observed the glassy shine in his mother's eye and he reached out and hugged her.

"You will always be my number one girl," he said. Adrian joined in and hugged her saying. "Mine too, Mom." Then the flood started.

"You guys! I am so proud of you. My two handsome, sensitive and caring men. You have a great time tonight," she sobbed.

"We will."

Meanwhile, James was capturing the moment with Kodak. "Okay, everyone turn and face the camera."

"James you haven't been taking pictures the entire time have you?"

"You'll thank me one day," he said with a wink.

Trevor and Tremaine came running into the room yelling, "Somebody's at the door!"

"Where's Travis?" asked James.

"Playing the game."

"Of course." James went to the front door to let Rodney and Bianca in. "Hello, come on in. Ms. Bianca, you are looking mighty lovely tonight. I am sure Mason is one proud father."

"Thank you sir," she blushed.

It was still pretty early, but in order to maneuver the operations of getting the boys to their dates and back to their own home for pictures, and then making it to the Dance on time, they'd had to allow for extra time. Adrian and Austin came out of the room and headed for the door. James reached into the closet and handed them their overcoats as they headed out. To Rodney he said, "You drive carefully, you hear?"

"Yes sir."

The group arrived at Cassandra and Shawn's house first. "Okay Austin, you're up!" Rodney told him as he pulled up into the driveway. "Don't be long now. We still have to go pick up my sister and then stop back by your house."

Austin looked out the window, across the yard to the front door. A door he had sauntered through many times since he was almost as young as the triplets. "You coming Adrian?" he asked.

"No he's not," replied Bianca. "Nicholette is your date. You go up and ring the bell and ask for her like a gentleman. We'll be right here."

Austin looked around the car. Adrian just sort of shrugged, and Rodney smiled at him encouragingly. "Go get'em tiger."

He slowly opened his door and climbed out of the car. He reached back in and picked up the flowers, chocolates and teddy bear he had for Nicholette, and turned toward the house. *I never noticed how big their yard was.* He thought to himself. *What am I nervous about? Nickey and I have been friends since I was in kindergarten. That's right! I have been over here a thousand times.* His thoughts were racing as he approached the large, double front doors. He reached out and timidly knocked on the door and then he rang the doorbell.

"Who is it?" He had never noticed how deep Major Smith's voice was.

"Uh. It's me. Austin Daniels, sir," he said.

Shawn opened the door and glared at Austin, who was taken aback at first. "Uh, good evening, sir. Is Nickey...I mean Nicholette ready?"

"Come on in. She will be out in a moment." Shawn said as he eyed Austin closely. He stood there in his foyer observing Austin as Austin's attention switched from the ceiling to the floor to the top of his shoes.

Finally, Austin spoke. "Thank you for allowing Nickey... uh Nicholette to accompany me to the Dance tonight, sir."

Shawn continued glaring at Austin as he spoke. "Well, I'm sure you know Nicholette is my princess. I cherish that little girl in there. And to be quite frank with you..." He said as he continued to glare at Austin. "To be quite frank... The only reason I'm allowing her to go on this so-called date..." He hesitated and it seemed as if all of the air in the room was held up by his pause. "Is because it's with you."

"Excuse me?" Austin breathed in a large gulp of air.

Shawn burst out laughing and said, "Boy, I've known you since you were practically Jasmine's age. I know you're a good kid and I know you respect Nicholette. Have a seat and relax. She's just like her Mother. She'll be a minute."

"Shawn, I hope you haven't traumatized the young man." Cassandra said as she entered the room putting on an earring and carrying a camera. "Hello Austin. You look handsome tonight."

"Thanks ma'am."

"Where's your brother?"

"He's in the car with Rodney and Bianca." Just then, they heard a knock on the door. Cassandra went to let the others in. She insisted Rodney and Bianca take off their coats so she could take pictures of them. When Nicholette entered the room, Austin completely lost his composure.

"Wow!" Was all he said as he stood up from his chair and stared across the room. She looked like a vision in pink standing under the archway at the entrance to the room.

After a few moments of awkward silence she spoke. "Are those for me?"

"Oh yes. I made sure to get your favorite chocolates… turtles," he said as he walked across the room to her.

Cassandra wiped a tear from her eye. "I thought I was through with all that," she sniffed as she handed the camera to Shawn. "Let's get a picture of the two of you under the archway and then we'll get the rest of the group." Nicholette's dress fit her neat figure perfectly. Her long blond hair was swept up in a French roll with a cascade of curls falling down to the small of her back. Like her mother, her hair had never been cut. She wore just a dab of pink lipstick, and she was perfect. Austin's tie and handkerchief in his grey suit matched her dress perfectly. They made a stunning couple Shawn took numerous pictures of the group, including Cassandra and Jasmine in some. They sent the young people on to Rodney and Kayla's home and they headed on out to the high school, dropping Jasmine off at James and Diedra's home.

While in the car, Austin chided Rodney and Bianca about sending him into the inquisition alone.

"That's a rite of passage." Rodney replied. "But you survived. Now it's your turn, Adrian."

"I ain't scurred!"Adrian said confidently.

"You better be just a little intimidated. You're going to my house to take my little sister on her first date. When it comes to Victoria, my Dad ain't no joke."

"I respect that. I think Victoria is nice… real nice. But so am I. I wouldn't do anything to hurt her. I think she's going to be my girl."

"Oh you do."

"Yes I do."

"We'll see about that, young player." When he pulled his father's Navigator up to his house, Rodney intentionally parked at the end of the long driveway. "You're up, Adrian!"

"This is your house?" asked Austin. Adrian had been there previously to ask Rodney if he could take Victoria to the Dance.

"Yes it is," replied Rodney. To his and Bianca's surprise, Adrian hopped out of the car without hesitation, grabbed his gifts, and walked confidently toward the door.

"What?" Rodney and Bianca looked at each other with mouths wide open.

"That's Adrian. Even if he's nervous, he won't let you see it," explained Austin.

"That is so true," agreed Nicholette.

Adrian went right up to the front door and rang the bell before he gave himself an opportunity to have any second thoughts. Rodney answered the door and invited him in to the sitting room. He offered Adrian a seat and he sat down across from him, staring directly into his eyes. He knew he came from a good family. He liked and respected Diedra and James, but what did he know about this young man he was entrusting his baby girl to for the evening?

"So, this is the big night Adrian, is this your first date?"

"No sir."

"No?" Rodney was surprised by that response.

"Well, this is the first time I actually came and picked a girl up at her house and took her out. I have been on group dates, where we met at the movies or the skating rink, or even basketball games."

"So, have you had many girlfriends?" he asked.

"I wouldn't say many. I've had a couple. Mostly, just friends though."

"So what are your intentions toward Victoria? You know she's not to be toyed with."

"I would never do anything to intentionally hurt anyone, but Victoria... She's special. I really like her."

"You really like her?"

"Yes sir, I like her, and I respect her. I hope you will allow me to see her again after tonight... if she's willing."

Rodney peered intently at Adrian and said, "We'll see." By that time, Rodney III, Bianca, Nicholette and Austin all came tumbling into the house. They all went into the living room to take pictures in front of the backdrop of the cathedral windows. Adrian was the first to spot Victoria as she entered. He rushed to her side and took her hand to escort her into the room. She was gorgeous. She had her hair swept up into a French roll with ringlets dropping around her face, and her sleeveless coral gown, with its high neck, coordinated perfectly with his tie and handkerchief he wore with his blue suit.

"You look nice," he said softly.

"Nice?" she asked.

"Really nice. You are beautiful, you know?"

"Nice save. Thank you."

"These are for you." He said, as he handed her the gifts he had for her. "Sweets for the sweet, a single rose because there is no one like you, and a teddy bear to make you think of me."

"Adrian, you are so corny," she giggled softly. "That's what I like about you though. Thank you so much." she said as she gave him a quick peck on the cheek, just as they saw the flash of the camera and heard the shutter click. They looked around and saw that everyone's attention had turned to them. Adrian grabbed Victoria's hand as he made a sweeping bow, and Victoria curtsied to the room.

"Oh my goodness, he's just like her." Kayla said dramatically as she slapped the palm of her hand to her forehead. "A mess." Everyone laughed heartily, they finished taking pictures and the group headed back to Diedra and James' house where they took their last set of pictures before they went off to the Valentine's Dance.

Saturday morning, Diedra woke up to find a trail of rose petals leading from her side of the bed, across the floor, into the master bath, up to the bathtub filled with warm sudsy water. The scented candles surrounding the tub were lit, and soft music wafted in from the stereo. Hanging from the vanity mirror above her sink was a note directing her to enjoy the warm bubble bath that was drawn according to her preference and as soon as she was ready, breakfast would be served in bed. *Just ring the bell*, the note said. *and your every wish will be provided. This morning is all about you.*

Diedra brushed her teeth and washed her face before she walked over to the bathtub. She slipped out of her gown and slid gently into the water, releasing a deep sigh of satisfaction as the warm silky water enveloped her body. "I just love that man," she said out loud. She laid back on the head rest at the end of her bathtub and closed her eyes allowing her senses to fully appreciate all of the sensations being lavished upon her body right then; the warm, silky water gently lapping against her skin, the subtle sweet scent of roses tickling her nostrils, and the soft, soothing music, playing across her ears along with the light crackle of the gas logs.

She lounged there thinking about the evening she and her friends had planned, a stretch limousine ride to Atlanta, followed by dinner at the Sun Dial Restaurant. It was a tradition they had started a few years before, and the group seemed to grow a little each year. The ladies handled all the arrangements and planning for the night out. That was their gift to their men who only had to show up. They had made some special memories. And the men always managed to do something special for their wives that day as well. This bubble bath was perfect and she knew the breakfast would be also.

Once she completed her bath, she dried herself and returned to her bed wrapped in her luxuriously plush micro-fleece robe to find a single rose and a dove chocolate on her pillow. A cup of French vanilla cappuccino sat on the nightstand next to her bed. As she climbed into the bed she heard a knock on the door. She slowly sipped her cappuccino as James entered the room, followed by their five sons.

James entered with a tray carrying two covered dishes. Austin brought in two bed trays, followed by Adrian with a chilled bottle of sparkling grape juice and two champagne glasses. Travis had a bowl of mixed fruit and Trevor and Tremaine followed with sugar and whipped cream. Diedra sat up in the bed and Austin set a tray down across her lap. James set the dishes on the tray and climbed into the bed next to her. Austin gave James the other tray and he and Adrian proceeded to set the meal out for James and Diedra. Once they had things situated, the boys wished them a Happy Valentine's Day, excused themselves, and left Diedra and James to enjoy their breakfast alone.

Diedra surveyed the meal spread before them; French toast coated with confectioner's sugar and dripping with strawberry preserves, crispy bacon, and scattered hash browns, a bowl of fresh fruit consisting of strawberries, black-berries and banana slices, and the sparkling grape juice, along with a small glass of milk. James knew just what she liked, and what she needed.

Diedra inhaled the sweet aroma of the cappuccino. "There sure is a lot to drink here," she noted.

"We wanted you to have a choice," he said. "We know you need your milk, but we also know you love your cappuccino and your grape juice as well."

"Thank you," she said as she leaned over and kissed him.

"My pleasure," he responded as he fed her a strawberry dipped in whipped cream. They enjoyed their breakfast in the private retreat of their bedroom. Feeding each other and teasing each other, forgetting about the outside world for a few special moments. By the time they were both full, Diedra rang the bell she had found in the bathroom, summoning Austin and Adrian who came and retrieved their dishes. The triplets all tumbled into the room and climbed on to the bed bearing gifts for their mother.

Once Adrian and Austin returned from cleaning the kitchen, Diedra proceeded to give them all their traditional Valentine Hearts with their favorite chocolates. And to the delight of them all, especially Diedra, James gave Diedra her customary gift of jewelry. This year it was pearls, her favorite. He had found a beautiful teardrop set of earrings and matching necklace. It would go perfectly with the Queen Anne neckline on the dress she was wearing to dinner that night.

When the limousine arrived at their home that evening they were ready and waiting, since they were the last stop. They made a striking couple. James in his black tux with tie and cummerbund to match Diedra's pink gown with the afore-mentioned Queen Anne neckline and tight pleating in the front that belied any hint of pregnancy. They climbed into the limo and greeted their friends who were all dressed to the nines. The ladies especially enjoyed this opportunity to don their formal attire and enjoy a night out on the town with their friends.

The bar and fridge were stocked with champagne and sparkling grape juice, along with fresh strawberries and shrimp cocktails. Smooth jazz music played over the sound system, and the drive into Atlanta was just as enjoyable as the night of dinner and dancing above the city.

The Sun Dial Restaurant was a three tier establishment 71 stories high atop the Westin Peachtree Plaza Hotel and the view was spectacular as the restaurant slowly revolved, revealing a variable panoramic view of the Atlanta skyline. The music was enchanting and the food was delicious. Shar had recommended the hotel to Shawn one year when he wanted to surprise Cassandra for their anniversary and James had proposed to Diedra there. When Cassandra, Brea and Diedra were trying to come up with something for Valentine's Day a few years earlier, they decided on the observatory level of the restaurant on the 72nd floor as a party location and it had been a hit. Usually Shar would be there but this year she was in California on business.

When the limousine pulled up in front of the hotel the couples peeled out one at a time to greet the cool, clear night. They took a few pictures in front of the water fountain before they entered the building. Diedra turned her back to the window and kept her attention focused on James as the others quietly took in the breathtaking view while the exterior elevator soared to the 72$^{nd}$ floor.

Once they arrived at the restaurant they removed their outer garments to fully reveal their splendid attire, Diedra and James in their black and pink, followed by Kayla and Rodney in black and red, next were Cassandra and Shawn in black and blush, a pale shade of pink, and after them, John and Sherry followed in black and fuchsia. The last two to step out of the elevator were Brea and Michael, dressed in white and white. He wore a white and silver tuxedo that matched her white fitted, backless gown with a plunging neckline embroidered with silver threading and long sheer sleeves. Her ears were dripping diamonds. Brea always looked phenomenal. But tonight, her date, Michael, was right there with her. They made a stunning couple, but she was the first to notice Diedra's new jewelry.

"Pearls!" She said excitedly. "They are gorgeous, Dee! James, you do have excellent taste."

"Thank you. Brea, I picked Diedra didn't I? She's the most perfect jewel I could have found."

"Ohh!"

"Would you two stop?" Diedra blushed, to everyone's amusement.

They each checked their coats before the maître d' led them to their party station. They had a large booth right at the window that would easily accommodate 20 people. There was plenty of room for movement as the group enjoyed each other's company along with the beautiful view. Before they ever sat down, James took Diedra by the hand, twirled her around into his arms, and they started swaying to the smooth music that was playing.

"Really?" asked Cassandra.

"Hey, that's what we're here for right? Dinner and dancing," said Shawn. He led Cassandra to the floor and then they began to waltz.

"Oh it's like that?" James asked as he looked over Diedra's head across the floor.

"You know it!" replied Shawn as he twirled Cassandra around in front of him. They glided elegantly across the floor. Her long sleeved, high necked, a-lined gown fell neatly over her curvaceous figure and her posture was perfect. Shawn, a former heavy-weight boxer was surprisingly light on his feet.

James looked down at Diedra and said, "I think that's a challenge."

Diedra smiled up at James and nodded. She placed her hands in position and allowed him to lead her around the floor. This was the way they always started the evening every year, James and Diedra and Shawn and Cassandra on the floor, ballroom dancing. The men enjoyed it as much as the ladies. Shortly, the rest of the group would join in. If a member of their party did not know any ballroom dances, they were sure to learn before the next time. It was kind of the unspoken point. Tonight, all of the couples were prepared. Michael was involved in a dance club at JSU and he and Brea gave Cassandra and Shawn a run for their money. When they did the rumba they looked as if they'd been dancing together for years.

They had observed that some of the other parties around them had adapted to their theme over the years. The restaurant itself did not require formal attire, but Valentine's Day presented an excellent opportunity to anyone who wished to dress out in black tie and gowns. And the setting was perfect. Diedra smiled as she noticed the group to their right dressed in tuxedos and evening gowns, dancing and enjoying the music.

After the first song ended James led Diedra over to a seat across the table from the window. Although she loved the view up there, she would get uncomfortable if her proximity to the window became too close. "I don't want you to overdo it, Babe. Let's take a seat."

"Thank you. I think I'd like to just sit back and enjoy your company along with the food and music this evening," she said softly.

"What's on the menu tonight anyway?"

"Well, dessert is the usual. One strawberry shortcake and one chocolate mound cake."

"That is the most important part of the meal," he chuckled, "But what is the entrée?"

"Truthfully, Cassandra and Kayla handled the menu this year. I told them to surprise me. Cassandra knows what we like."

"Ok, as long as you didn't leave it to Breanna. She would have us eating squid or octopus eggs, or some other outlandish dish."

"That may be an option," Diedra laughed, "But I'm sure there will be something to suit your taste, dear."

The ladies had done an excellent job. This year they decided to set up a buffet with several options. The wait staff rolled in the long table and quickly set the table up for them. One waiter remained to keep their bread baskets full and their champagne and sparkling grape juice flowing throughout the evening.

There was something for every palate. Starting out with a mixed green salad, spicy garlic shrimp and creamy carrot bisque, followed by roasted filet of beef, wild mushroom ravioli, and butter poached lobster. For their sides they had smoked potatoes, broccolini, bleu cheese mac n cheese, and Swiss chard.

Cassandra and Shawn stood in front of the table and she announced, "Dinner is served. Now please don't be shy. We decided to try the buffet this year so some of you, James, might slip out of your comfort zones just a little." She nodded and winked toward Diedra and James as she continued. There is plenty of food and it is already paid for, so what we don't eat, we'll have to pack up with us." she threatened, good-naturedly. "So as soon as my husband says grace, we can all get started."

Shawn blessed the food and they headed for the buffet. As James stood, he noticed that Diedra remained seated. "Are you okay?" he asked her.

"Yes, I'll just wait. I don't want to stand in line. I probably shouldn't have worn heels," she said extending a shoe in front of her.

"You don't have to stand in line. I've got you." He went to stand in the back of the group and they all ushered him to the front. He selected two mixed green salads along with some spicy garlic shrimp and returned to their table. Before they finished their salads Brea and Cassandra arrived with their main course; the filet of beef for James and the poached lobster for Diedra along with a sampling of all the sides.

"You didn't have to do that, ladies."

"We know we didn't have to, but we wanted to. We appreciate the way you take care of our friend and we want you to know it." Brea smiled at James as she went around the table to sit next to Michael in front of the window.

"What she said," agreed Cassandra, gesturing toward Brea as she sat down between Diedra and Shawn.

The food was excellent and they enjoyed themselves thoroughly. By the time the cakes were rolled out, all of the ladies were too full to even taste them. Except for Brea, who had a slice of each. The men enjoyed the cake as well. The server sliced the rest of the cake and packed up servings to take home.

Diedra was the first to start fading but she didn't want to put a damper on the evening so she and James found a quiet spot in a corner of the room and cuddled quietly as they enjoyed the view. He gently stroked her hair and sang along with Luther and Jeffrey, as she fell asleep. She loved to hear her husband sing, he sounded just like Jeffrey Osborne.

By the time they were back in the limo and headed for home, they were all exhausted but content, ready to close out another memorable Valentine's Day. They had church in the morning, and they didn't want to miss that. They rode along in silence listening to love songs playing on the sound system. No one said anything until they reached the stretch of interstate between Villa Rica and Waco, Ga.

"The luckiest stretch of highway in the country!" James said out loud.

"You think so?" asked Michael. Do they have a record for winning lottery tickets along this stretch or something?"

"That's right! You haven't heard the story, have you?" said Brea.

"Well let me tell you," said James. "It was a warm, spring, Sunday afternoon in March. The last day of Freaknik and I was driving the Maxima home with a group of friends when I saw a vehicle with Alabama tags have a blowout up in front of me. Against the wishes of some of my passengers, David and I stopped to help. Turned out it was one of my co-workers, a Sergeant Major from the Depot. When I saw his daughter sleeping in the back seat with her twin boys I made the mistake of waking her up. I'm sure you've heard that expression: Don't poke the bear."

"Yes"

"Well that little Mama Bear was fierce. The way she grabbed on to those boys…Well, even when she was yelling at me I knew she was the one who would wear the ring."

"The ring?"

"Yes, the ring. I bought that three carat diamond you see on my wife's finger with money I earned working construction for my uncle a couple of summers during high school. I saw it when I was out shopping with my sisters one day and I determined to have it. It was an odd size and it could not be re-sized. It was a special order, one of a kind ring that someone had decided not to purchase, so the price was drastically reduced."

James held up Diedra's hand as he continued, "my sisters thought I was insane to buy it, but I knew, even then, that this was the ring my wife would wear one day. So I gathered up my pennies and I purchased it. I had my mother place it in a safe deposit box for me and I went on about my life."

"So you looked for a wife to fit the ring?"

"I didn't even understand ring sizing when I purchased the ring. I just knew this was the one my wife would someday wear. And to be honest with you… I had never even had a girlfriend for real. I dated lots of girls, but nothing serious. I was just having fun. I never mislead anyone and I never mistreated anyone. I was just a young single guy who was out there.

When I tell you that I knew that first day that she was the one, I am not exaggerating. When I got back to Anniston that evening after I met her, I called my mother and asked if she could get the ring out of her safe deposit box so I could have it cleaned.

It took a few years to convince Diedra that I was for real, but three years later I placed that engagement ring on her finger and it fit perfectly. Then two years after that, on New Year's Eve, right after the stroke of midnight, on January 1st we were married."

"That is some story."

"That is sweet," said Kayla. "I hadn't heard that before either."

"How did you convince her to give you a chance?" asked Michael.

"Persistence and prayer, I was convinced that she was my 'good thing' but I had to prove myself to her. She had been hurt before and I had to show her that I was here for the long haul.  I am still proving my love daily, and so does she."

"How do you do that?"

"It's in the little things. Like this. She used to love to hear me sing this song to her." He said as he leaned over to turn the stereo up and joined Jeffrey Osborne in singing 'Stranger' followed by 'Love Ballad'. He filled the car with his smooth voice. The lyrics poured out of his mouth like butter. When Con Funk Shun's, 'Love's Train' came on Brea suddenly reached over and turned the system off.

"Can we listen to something else?" she asked.

"The struggle is real," chuckled Sherry as she replaced the cd with BeBe and CeCe Wynans' cd.

"I know it is, but it's worth it," said James. "I was by no means a virgin when I met Diedra and neither was she. But we were celibate from the day we met until our wedding night, five and a half years later. It really was a struggle but I'm glad I waited for her."

"I hear you man. After we had our son, Kobe, Sherry and I both got saved, and we made the decision to abstain until marriage."

"Kayla and I got married right out of high school. We were both virgins and didn't know what we were missing, so it wasn't as big a struggle as it would have been otherwise but it was a struggle nonetheless. But I believe God has honored that in our marriage."

"Well, Cassie and I lived together our last year in college and we had our wedding right after I got commissioned. We've had a few struggles, being an interracial couple not the least of them, but overall, we've been blessed. We have learned over the years that God's way is always better for us, but even when we made choices that were not his will for us, he protected us and kept us. That's why I always thank Him for his mercy and his grace. I heard someone say once, that his grace is when we get what we don't deserve and his mercy is when we don't get what we deserve."

"I like that," said Diedra. "When I think about how God has kept me, and I consider the people he has placed in my life, at just the right times… wow!  I mean, by the time I met James I didn't think I could ever trust another man to love me. I kept pushing him away, but fortunately, he kept pulling me toward him."

Bebe and Cece's, 'Close To You' started playing and James and Sherry sang along to the delight of the rest of the passengers.

"You two should sing something at church." Diedra told them.

"Yes James, why don't you join the praise team?" asked Sherry.

"I don't know. I haven't sung in a choir since I was at Jax State."

"You should really consider it, James. You have a beautiful voice," said Kayla.

"I'll think about it."

The rest of the ride home was fairly quiet. They rode along listening to the music, each couple engaged in their own private interactions. Diedra could not get comfortable in her seat. She kept squirming and shifting position, but she could not stay in one position for long. She wasn't in pain. She could only describe the feeling as discomfort.

Once they arrived home, she took a warm bath and climbed into the bed. She drifted in and out of sleep throughout the night. She would find herself drifting along the familiar waterway, but it was dark, with torrential winds and the raft rocked violently back and forth. It would rock so violently that she would be startled awake.

The next morning when James woke her up for church he could tell that she had not slept well. He suggested that she stay home, but to his surprise she insisted on going to church with the family.

The church service was good, as always. Pastor Vaughn spoke about God's ordainment of marriage and how marriage was a ministry in and of itself. They all went down to the altar to pray for Mike, who was still comatose. Afterwards they had a luncheon in the Connections Center.

# CHAPTER 15

DIEDRA WAS SCHEDULED TO WORK Tuesday night. She had been restless all day and by the time James came home, she was visibly exhausted. He insisted that she stay home, noting that she had not rested well for the past three days and that was not good for their daughter. She reluctantly agreed and called in to work for the night.

James made hamburgers topped with onion rings and coleslaw, French fries and cheese sticks for him and the boys. Diedra had a light dinner of soup and crackers along with half a grilled ham and cheese sandwich. Afterwards, she sat on the couch with her feet propped up, reading to the triplets while James helped the twins with their chemistry. Once Adrian and Austin finished their homework, James popped The Lion King video into the vhs player and Diedra sipped on a warm glass of milk as they all watched the movie together. After the movie, she got the triplets ready for bed as James and the twins cleaned the kitchen and put the den back in order.

By the time Diedra and James climbed into the bed they were both fatigued, but he insisted that they discuss her work situation. He was concerned for not only her health, but the baby's as well.

He reached over and placed a hand across her abdomen as he spoke. "Babe, you have to get your rest. This is not good for you or the baby."

"James, it's not the job. I don't know why, but I have had this persistent feeling of uneasiness for the past few days." She arched her back and continued. "I just can't seem to get comfortable."

"Are you in pain?"

"No, not really. I don't know how to explain it to you. I have difficulty falling asleep, and when I do get to sleep I keep getting shook awake."

"What do you mean, shook awake?"

"I mean shook awake, like someone, or something physically shook me, and I was startled awake."

"Was it something in your dreams?"

"Sometimes, but other times I don't even remember what I was dreaming about."

"Maybe you just need to relax. Lay over on your side and let me see if I can help you."

"Seriously James?" she asked incredulously.

"Seriously," he replied. "I just want to try one of the relaxation techniques we used when you were further along with the triplets. Now turn over and let me see about you."

She giggled softly as she turned over on her side. He began to gently massage the small of her back as he crooned Larry Graham's, 'One In A Million' softly in her ear,

"Ooh why didn't you think of this three days ago?" she said as she drifted off to sleep. He continued massaging her back until he felt the tension leave her body; then he turned over and said a prayer before he went to sleep.

The raft was rocking fiercely as it moved Diedra along the waterway, engulfed in darkness. Powerful gusts of wind beat against the palm trees along the beach, rocking them violently back and forth with such force that each one seemed perilously on the verge of breaking. Each gust of wind seemed to carry a voice through the night air. She couldn't understand what the voice was saying. She strained to hear and understand the voice above the roaring wind. Then she realized the voice was the wind. What was it saying?

**The power of life and death is in the tongue! Your friend is gone. Your baby will not make it.** She looked around as she heard the words carried through the wind. **The power of life and death is in the tongue! Someone else will raise your sons.** She saw the palm trees rocking violently in the wind as they withstood the force of the words. She noticed several shadowy figures behind the trees. Two in particular that seemed to stand out were that of a large man and a small child crawling along behind the trees. As they crawled along, she noticed that whenever they got between the trees they both seemed to be on the verge of blowing away. But when they were tucked safely behind a tree they seemed to relax and rest. The words of the wind continued to bombard the trees. **The power of life and death is in the tongue. No one survives brain cancer.**

The raft rocked violently as she heard a voice saying. "Child, the Word of God is sharper than any two-edged sword." Big Daddy and Granddaddy were both rowing against the wind. Their words seemed to cut through the wind as they spoke.

"Speak life, child!"

"Baby Girl there is life in the word. You've got to speak it!"

As they reached the edge of the water, Big Daddy got out of the raft and pulled it up on to the beach. Diedra's granddaddy lifted her up out of the raft and carried her across the beach, bracing himself against the words of the wind. He told her, "Baby Girl, you've got to speak the word against the attacks of the enemy. You shall live and you shall not die."

"Say it!" said Big Daddy.

"You shall live and you shall not die!" repeated Granddaddy. He carried her across the beach to the shadowy figures and told her to keep repeating. "They shall live and they shall not die."

They went up and down the beach, speaking over the shadowy figures. "He shall live and shall not die, or she shall live and shall not die."

When they came across the man and the child crawling behind the trees, Big Daddy said, "Child! You have to speak the words! Say it out loud. They shall live and they shall not die!" There seemed to be an urgency in his voice that she had not noticed earlier.

"Speak child! He shall live and he shall not die and…"

"She shall live and she shall not die!" Diedra shouted as she sat up in the bed.

"Babe, what's wrong?" James asked as he was startled awake.

"James, I think there's something wrong with the baby." she said worriedly.

"What is it? Are you in pain?"

"I don't know. I think we need to go to the hospital…now."

James immediately sprang into action. He jumped out of the bed, grabbed some sweat pants out of the dresser drawer, and retrieved a sweat suit for Diedra. He handed her the clothes and went to find a sweatshirt for himself, as she began to change. She sat in the bed and pulled her night clothes off and then pulled her sweatshirt on over her head. She pulled on her pants and stood up to get her shoes and coat from the closet. James quickly put his shoes on and was rushing around the room looking for his keys and wallet when he heard her weakly call his name.

"James…" she said, as she turned toward him and kept going; knocking the floor lamp over as she reeled toward the floor, her head barely missing the bedpost. James caught her and swooped her up into his arms.

He carried her to the door and called, "Austin, Adrian, somebody call 911."

"I've already got them on the line," said Austin, who had been awakened and alarmed when he heard Diedra cry out. Then he'd rushed to the phone when he heard the lamp fall.

"What's wrong with mom?"

"I don't know! She says she thinks something's wrong with the baby. But she's right. They will live and they shall not die!" he declared. Right then he began to pray earnestly over his wife and his unborn daughter and he kept praying until the emergency medical technicians arrived. When the EMT's arrived, James was sitting on the chaise lounge in his bedroom cradling Diedra's head in his lap.

Once they took over, he moved out of the way and went to get the phone.

"We've already called the grandparents," said Austin as he handed James the phone. "They're on their way."

Just then they heard a knock on the door. "That was quick," said James. "When did you call your grandparents?" he asked.

"Right after we called the ambulance, but they couldn't be here this quickly," said Adrian as he walked to the door. It was Brea. She had heard the dispatch and rushed right over.

"What's going on?" she asked.

"We don't know. She woke up screaming and then she said she thought something was wrong with the baby and we needed to go to the hospital. While we were getting ready to leave, she fainted."

"Sir, your wife is asking for you," said one of the EMT's as he led James back into the room.

"Babe! Are you okay?" he asked as he went back to her side.

"I am a tree that is planted by the waters. The wind blows, and I bend but I do not break." She said smiling weakly.

"What?" asked Brea.

"I don't know what she's talking about I'm just glad she's talking." replied James.

"Sir, we're going to need to take her to the hospital. You may want to call her OB doctor and let him know we're on our way."

"He's already on his way." said Brea. "Cassie too. Kayla and Sherry have started a prayer line."

James looked at Breanna.

She shrugged and said, "What? I didn't know what was going on. I just heard ambulance, pregnant female, possible fetal distress."

He turned to the EMT and asked "What's wrong with her?"

"We're not really sure. I don't think the fetus is in distress. But the blood pressure seems to be low for mom and child's heartrate is a little slow. We'll keep monitoring them until we get to the emergency room."

"Let's go!"

"James." Diedra said softly.

"Yes babe."

"Can you bring my Bible please?"

"Certainly," he said as he grabbed the book off of the night stand. He followed behind, giving directions to the boys as the EMT's rolled Diedra out on the gurney.

"Don't worry about the boys. I'll stay with them." Brea said as she comforted the little ones who had been awakened by all the commotion.

On the ride to the hospital James prayed and spoke more words of encouragement over Diedra. As she listened to him quoting scriptures, she continued to process what her grandfathers had told her in her dream. It was good that she had a praying husband, praying parents and praying friends, but she had to start speaking into her own life. If she was going to win this battle she had to be armed with the word of God. She understood that the words in the wind in her dream were the attacks of the enemy: her doubts, her fears, and even her insecurities.

Faith comes by hearing and hearing by the word of God, she remembered. "The Word of God is sharper than any two-edged sword," she whispered.

"What's that?"

"James, could you find that scripture for me?"

"Sure babe," he said as he opened her Bible and began to search. "I think that's in Hebrews."

"The Word of God is living and powerful, and sharper than any two-edged sword, piercing even to the division of soul and spirit, and of joint and marrow, and is a discerner of the thoughts and intents of the heart. Hebrews 4:12," said the EMT softly. "In this line of work, it helps when one can rely heavily on the word of God," he shrugged and told them.

Dr. Howard and Dr. Rodney were both waiting for them at the emergency room. They immediately took them up to obstetrics for examination and quickly discerned that she had suffered placental abruption and both she and the fetus were indeed in distress. They admitted her so she and the baby could be monitored through the night.

In the still of the night, after her parents and in-laws had come and left, and she and James were alone in the room, Diedra realized that she was calmer than she had been at any point since she had learned of her pregnancy and her cancer. She really did feel a sense of peace that surpassed all understanding.

She read through her Bible, highlighting scriptures and reading them aloud, stating them in the first person.

"The battle is not mine but God's."

"For the weapons of my warfare are not carnal, but mighty through God to the pulling down of strongholds."

"No weapon formed against me shall prosper, and every tongue which rises against me in judgment I shall condemn."

"Though I walk in the midst of trouble you will revive me. You will stretch out your hand against the wrath of my enemies and your right hand will save me."

"Many are the afflictions of the righteous but the Lord delivers me from them all."

"The Lord my God has given me rest on every side. There is neither adversary nor misfortune."

She continued on, reading, highlighting and speaking out loud, the living Word of God. The last thing she read was the 27th Psalm and then she closed her Bible and said, "I choose life." When she closed her eyes and went to sleep the waters were calm, the sun was shining, the Palm trees were standing firm, and the raft gently drifted along the waterway, slowly rocking side to side. She saw the figures darting in and out from behind the trees. She saw Granddaddy and Big Daddy walking along with a little girl between them. Out of the corner of her eye she thought she saw Big Mike. She woke up startled, and then she smiled and went back to sleep.

"Most assuredly, I say to you, he who believes in Me, the works that I do he will do also: and greater works than these he will do, because I go to my Father."

# CHAPTER 16

"COME ON BABE! WAKE UP sleeping Beauty. I need you to wake up." James pleaded tearfully. "I need you to come home so we can spoil you and that little miracle you're carrying."

Diedra opened her eyes to see James, Austin and Adrian sitting around her bed. Her parents and her in-laws were in the room along with Brea and Cassandra.

"She's awake!" Exclaimed Austin as James pulled Diedra's hand up to his lips and cried silent tears of joy. He looked to the ceiling and said a silent prayer of thanks as he continued to hold on to her hand. Everyone in the room was beside themselves with joy.

Diedra couldn't understand what all the commotion was about. "What's going on?" She tried to ask amidst the realization that she was unable to speak due to the presence of a tube inserted down her throat. She began to panic as she tried to ascertain what was happening. She reached for the tube but James held her hand and spoke soothingly to her. "It's okay, Babe. I've got you. They had to intubate you, but the nurse will be in to remove the tube. Just relax. Look at me." he said as he spoke softly to her.

Dr. Howard, Dr. Rodney Howard, and one of the obstetrics nurses entered the room along with a lady Diedra recognized to be a neonatologist at the hospital and another gentleman. She began to panic again and tried to speak with the tube in.

"Easy now, Diedra, I need you to relax so we can examine you, and then Dr. Brown will extubate." Everyone, except for James, was directed to leave the room. Dr. Brown, who explained he was an anesthesiologist, performed an assessment followed by the extubation procedure. After he completed the procedure and ascertained that Diedra was breathing without issue, he explained that a nurse would be in for therapy later. Then he left the room as the others reentered, followed by Pastor Vaughn and Pastor Mckinney.

Diedra looked apprehensively at the two Pastors. "Later? What is he talking about?" Diedra asked. "I want to go home," she said hoarsely, as she attempted to sit up.

"You gave us quite a scare, there Ms. Lady," said Dr. Howard gently.

"What is he talking about James? I had the best sleep I've had in weeks. I sat up for a while last night reading my Bible, highlighting scriptures and reading them out loud. I read the 27th Psalm and then I went to sleep."

James looked uneasily at Dr. Howard, and then turned to Mrs. Daniels. She started to speak but then she got choked up and couldn't. Robert Daniels crossed the room to his daughter and said.

"Baby Girl, do you know where you are?"

"Well, obviously, I'm still in the hospital on the obstetrics ward," she replied. "But why are you all here? And why are you all looking so…" She stopped in mid-sentence and began to panic again. It couldn't be her baby. She knew she was okay, she saw that in her dream. She reached up and grabbed her abdomen and felt the familiar bump.

"The baby is okay, Babe. Our little miracle is a fighter just like her mother." James said.

"So what's wrong?" she asked.

Dr. Howard began to explain. "Diedra, you suffered from placenta abruption. Shortly after you arrived last night you went into severe distress. You were actually in preterm labor. Fortunately, you came in early enough to prevent any damage to the fetus, but you did lose some blood, and your blood pressure dropped so low that you slipped into a coma. You even stopped breathing, so we had to intubate you. We have been monitoring the baby, as well as yourself, all night and from all indications, she's fine. We really couldn't make sense of it. We could not understand why you went under or why we couldn't wake you. We thought we were losing you. But even more baffling, was the fact that your baby was not impacted at all. The contractions stopped on their own and she seems to be fine."

"I don't understand." She reached for her Bible and James handed it to her. "I sat right here in this bed and went through this Bible last night; reading and highlighting scriptures. 2nd Chronicles 20:15." She turned to the page and found the scripture but it was not highlighted. "I'm sure that was one of them. I also read and highlighted 2nd Corinthians 10:4; For the weapons of our warfare are not carnal but mighty through God to the pulling down of strongholds."

James shot a glance across the room at Brea, as Diedra turned through the Bible and found the verse. It was not highlighted either.

"I just don't understand," she said.

"What else did you read?" James asked

"Isaiah 54:17"

"No weapon formed against you shall prosper and any tongue that rises up against you in judgment, you shall condemn," said Cassandra.

"That's right."

"Diedra, you said you read the 27th Psalm."

"Yes," she said. And then she quoted the entire scripture.

James turned and looked at her and asked in surprise, "When did you learn that?"

"Last night!" she insisted.

"Did you also read Psalm 34:19?"asked Brea.

"I did. Many are the afflictions of the righteous but the Lord delivers them from them all."

"Diedra honey, those were some of the verses the members of the prayer chain were speaking over you," said Cassandra softly.

"Glory!" shouted Lee Beverly.

As the realization of what had happened settled over her, tears started streaming down Diedra's cheeks. Pastor Vaughn and Pastor Mckinney started praising God and the others joined in.

Diedra felt that same peace fall over her that she had felt through the night. She remembered the dream she had within the dream. She understood why they could find no issues with her baby girl; because those who were for her were greater than those against her. She now understood that she had had a supernatural experience.

"Mike. I want to speak to Mike," she said.

James, Brea and Cassandra looked uncomfortable. "Don't you remember Dee? Mike's in a coma." Brea replied weakly. She didn't want to tell her that the last thing she had heard was that things were not looking good for him. His doctors were beginning to lose hope.

"Please call him. Call Saint Francis Hospital," Diedra insisted.

Brea shot pleading glances at James and Cassandra, and James nervously said, "Just call the hospital please."

Brea picked up the phone, shakily, and began to dial the number. Cassandra, noting her friend's apprehension, took the phone from her and waited for someone to pick up. Once the operator answered the line on the other end, she informed her that she was calling to check on the status of a patient. She gave her his name and room number and they put her right through. She thought that was odd, but she waited. Perhaps his wife or another family member would answer. She was startled by the deep male voice that answered the phone.

"Oh you must be Ike. I'm calling to check on Mike."

"Who is this?"

"This is Cassandra Smith. I am a friend of Brea and Diedra's."

"Breanna Thomas and Diedra Davis?" he asked excitedly.

"Yes."

"Are they with you now?"

"As a matter of fact they are? May I ask who I'm speaking with?"

"Well, who were you trying to call?" he asked lightly.

At this point she was getting annoyed. "I was trying to inquire about my friends' friend Mike, who was supposed to be in this room," she said.

"Well, I think I'm just fine, but those pesky doctors insist on running more tests."

"Excuse me? Aren't you supposed to be in a coma? I mean…" She just stopped in mid- sentence and handed the phone to Brea who was beside herself with joy. Both of her friends were wide awake and alert.

"Mike, I am so glad to hear your voice," she said, between sobs.

"You know you can't keep a good man down. No weapon formed against me shall prosper. For the weapons of our warfare are not carnal but mighty through God to the pulling down of strongholds."

"Amen," she replied through more tears.

"Let me speak to him." Diedra said through tears of her own. Brea handed Diedra the phone and sat beside her on the bed, across from James.

"Mike," Diedra said tentatively.

"Ms. Dee!" he said.

"You sure don't sound like someone who's been in a coma for a couple of weeks," she sniffed.

"And you don't sound like someone who was in my dream last night," he responded.

"What do you mean?"

"I had a dream last night, but it wasn't really a dream. You were there and then I woke up." He hesitated and then he asked. "Ms. Dee, are you expecting?"

James' head was next to Diedra's and he could hear everything said on the other end of the line. He and Diedra exchanged a confused glance. How did he know about her pregnancy?

"Yes, she said hesitantly."

"Have you been having medical issues?" he asked.

"Yes," she replied.

"But you know it's already been taken care of don't you?"

She hesitated for a moment and then released a deep breath as she replied, "Yes, I do."

"No more stressing, no more worrying. You know your sword, the Word of God, is sharper than any two-edged sword the enemy might bring against you. You just have to trust in Him and keep speaking life over you and your child. The troubles you have seen up to this point you will see no more."

"Mike," she said.

"Yes."

"What did you dream?"

"I dreamt that I was behind a row of Palm Trees and the wind was blowing against them in angry gusts but they stood strong. I felt like you were there but I didn't see you. I knew the Palm trees were the prayers of all our friends praying for me and praying for you. I started praying and agreeing with their prayers. Early this morning I just woke up. My wife called for the nurse and she came in and extubated me and then notified the doctor. After they examined me, they left us here and we prayed in the spirit for the next few hours.

Afterwards, I told my wife that I believed you were in a spiritual battle and your health and your unborn baby were under attack. I told her I believed you had had a turn-around last night and I wanted to call to encourage you. We have been calling both you and Brea's telephone numbers all day."

"Actually, we are at the hospital ourselves," said James into the phone. "We had a serious scare with Diedra last night but it is all good now. She does need her rest though. I know she's going to want to talk to you more about this. I don't know how long she'll be in the hospital so we'll give you the number here." He was well aware of the bond his wife shared with the man on the other end of the line. And he appreciated what he had done for her.

"He's right, Mike. I am so glad to know you are okay and I do want you to call me back. Here's Brea," she said as she handed her friend the phone back. James gave Diedra a long hug, his father walked over and hugged Diedra, and suggested that the grandparents take the boys to dinner while Diedra and James got some rest. They would get the triplets from Cassandra's house, where Nicholette was keeping them. Then after dinner Diedra's parents would return home with all the boys. Her visitors expressed their gratitude for Diedra's miraculous recovery. They each filed past her, hugging and kissing her before they left the two of them alone.

James leaned over his reclining wife and laid his head across her chest as they both fell asleep. Diedra woke up first. She began to pray out loud.

"Lord,

I thank you for your mercy and your grace. I thank you for holding on to me even when I let go of you. I thank you for the hedge of protection you have placed around my life and the people you have placed in my life to pray with me, for me, and over me. You have shown me time and time again that you are fighting my battles and now I see that you have already won. You have watched over me and kept me and especially at those times when I felt defeated, you already had things worked out. I thank you for this man you designed just for me. I thank you for my beautiful boys who have all been a blessing to me. I thank you for this little miracle that I am carrying and I thank you for protecting her. She will live and she will not die.

Lord, I thank you for purpose. I thank you for the gifts you have placed in me and I thank you for revelation. My trust is in you and I know that you are in control of all things pertaining to me. Even when it looks as if things are bad in the natural, you are using that for my good. With that, I thank you for the struggles. I thank you for the lessons that sometimes hurt. I sincerely forgive anyone who has hurt me in the past and I pray for their deliverance.

Amen

James woke up just as the hospitality attendant was bringing in dinner. He got up from his chair and pulled the tray over to the bed so she could set Diedra's meal in front of her. To his surprise, she had a tray for him as well.

"Dr. Howard said you wouldn't leave your wife's side, and you need to eat as well," she explained.

"Thank you. Dr. Howard was right."

James watched Diedra closely as they ate in silence. Perceiving that she had had some sort of spiritual encounter through the night, he observed that her whole countenance had changed. After they finished their meal, James set their trays outside the door. Both Dr. Howards entered the room to assess mother and child. They explained that they had agreed to keep her for one more night. If she did not have any episodes through the night and her baby continued to thrive, they would release her in the morning.

"Do you feel like talking?" James asked, once they were alone.

"What do you want to talk about?"

"I want you to tell me what happened to you last night. I sense a profound change in your demeanor." Diedra nodded her head and smiled at her husband as she attempted to gather her thoughts.

"I get it James." she said softly.

"You get what?"

"Jesus loves me. He really loves me… Diedra Davis. Just like Dr. Howard says. Before I was ever formed in my mother's womb, he knew me and he pre-destined me. He knew the path my life would take, but he had a plan all along, and he still does." She reached out and softly stroked James cheek as she continued. "He knew you would come along to love me through all the hurt and disappointments of my past."

"I wish I could remove all the hurt and pain from your life."

"But that's part of who I am. There has been a purpose in my struggles, and now I know God is in control. The enemy has been trying to convince me that I am defeated. That this baby would not survive, that I would not survive. He has even tried to convince me that our marriage would not survive. Those are all lies from the pit of hell."

God loves me and he wants what is best for me, and everything that has happened in my life is working together for my good. I speak life over my pregnancy, our marriage, our children, our careers, our extended families, and our friends."

"Amen," he agreed.

"James, I have been delivered from the spirit of fear that has engulfed me."

"Praise Jesus!" he said excitedly. "So how did you come by all this revelation?"

"I believe God has been trying to speak to me through my dreams. Sometimes when I wake up, I don't even remember what I dreamt but I just have a sense of something. I just thought of it as intuition. But lately, I've been dreaming about my grandfathers and they have been trying to tell me something. For the past few days there has been a sense of urgency surrounding them, but I didn't understand until today. When I realized that my dream last night had been within a dream, and it coincided with the prayer line and Mike's experience, I understood that God has been trying to tell me all along that though the enemy is attacking me, he will not win."

"Can you tell me about the dreams?"

"It's all connected. The dreams, the prophesies, even Kayla's dream of having a women's ministry. Do you remember when I told you about the day Mike and Ike prayed over me and Brea? Mike said it was time. Brea thought that meant it was time for us to move back home. Ike said he kept hearing Tamar. That didn't make sense to any of us. Now ten years later it has all come together. Everything we have learned about Tamar, the meaning of the name, and how it played out in my dreams. You heard Mike say he dreamt that he was behind a row of palm trees and I was there somewhere, right?"

"Yes, I heard that."

"Well I have been dreaming about palm trees as well." She shared with him all the dreams she had been having with her grandfathers, leading up to the night before. She told him about the clouds, the palm trees, the shadowy figures, and the prayers.

It was all pretty fantastic but James could not deny that his wife had experienced a spiritual breakthrough. There was no denying that the peace that exuded through her was the result of a supernatural experience and he thanked God for it. They continued to talk about their life together and their plans for their family. Diedra agreed that she would go on maternity leave and she also agreed they would start planning to move into a larger home.

They took phone calls from friends and family members as they began to settle in for the night. Diedra thanked them all for their prayers. When James returned from the nurse's station after inquiring about extra pillows, he found Diedra on the phone with Mike. She had him on the speaker phone as they discussed their experiences the night before and everything that had led up to it. Before they hung up, Diedra said a prayer for him and his family.

The next morning John entered the room as they were having breakfast. "Well I'll say! Some people will do just about anything to get out of work," he teased as he entered the room.

"I know, right? What's a little coma if it will keep me out of work?" she shot back.

"Come on in!" invited James. "She gave us quite a scare last night, but thanks be to God, she is okay now."

"What happened?"

"I have a lot to tell you John, and I will. But right now I just want to thank you for being a friend that cared enough to share the word of God with me and to pray for me and my family."

"Of course. That's what we as Christians are supposed to do. Share the good news. It's not some secret we should keep to ourselves."

"Amen." Diedra and James both agreed. They visited for a few minutes, then they prayed and he left.

Shortly after the hospitality attendant had removed their breakfast trays, Dr. Howard came around to see her.

"We are going to try to get you out of here as soon as possible today. It looks like the weather is going to take a turn for the worse and I don't want you to be caught out in it," he said after he completed his examination of her.

"Yes, I think I heard one of the nurses say they are expecting ice," replied James.

'Now I want you to stay off of your feet as much as possible. If you can't do that I'll have to admit you." he threatened.

"Yes sir," she agreed.

"I'll make sure of it," James promised.

Soon after that, Diedra was discharged from the hospital and she and James headed home. They arrived to find the boys at home with their grandparents. All of the area schools had been closed early due to the threat of severe weather. As soon as Diedra was settled in, their parents headed for their own homes. Fortunately, Mr. Davis and Mr. Daniels had gone to Wal-mart and picked up enough groceries to last the family a month if need be.

## CHAPTER 17

DIEDRA SAT IN THE OVERSIZED armchair with her feet resting on the ottoman and the triplets snuggled in around her. The family gathered in the den to discuss the recent events, and how they would proceed forward.

"You boys are going to have to help me take care of your mother for the next few months," James informed them. "She is going to have to take it easy and she won't be able to do the things you're used to her doing for you."

"Yes sir. We can help take care of the triplets," replied Austin.

"I'm counting on it," said James.

"Maybe we should quit the track team," offered Adrian.

"That won't be necessary," Diedra reassured him. "We just want you to make sure you do your chores without us having to get after you and help out with your brothers when you are here. You don't have to sacrifice your own activities."

"Your mother's right. Just be the responsible young men we know you are, and we will get through this as a family."

"We also want you to agree with us as we pray that this little miracle is healthy and strong." Diedra said.

Austin walked across the room and placed a hand on his mother's abdomen declaring, "This little miracle will be blessed and highly favored." And then he kissed Diedra on her cheek and returned to his seat.

Adrian followed behind him and declared, "Strength and honor are her clothing." And he kissed her on her cheek as well.

James and Diedra looked on in amazement, as they were pleasantly surprised by their sons. They were flabbergasted, when the three younger boys expressed their desire to bless the baby. One by one they placed a hand on their mother's abdomen and declared, "Miracle! Happy! Loved!"

The grandparents had already spoken to the boys about praying over the baby and they had helped them to choose declarations to speak over the little miracle. From that point forward, each one of them made a point to speak a declaration over the baby at least once a day.

The winter storm rolled in just as predicted. Within days the entire county was shut down. This was a storm like none other in their lifetimes, not in Alabama. And they were not prepared for it. The temperatures had dropped down to well below zero and the ground was quickly covered in snow which soon turned to ice. The snow continued to fall through Friday and was a foot deep in places. Some areas reported thunder and lightning. The television screen was plastered with scenes of major roadways at a complete standstill, with cars scattered haphazardly across the roads, either abandoned or occupied with stranded travellers. Residents across the state had been advised not to attempt to get on the roads unless it was an emergency. Emergency crews were operating 24/7 to rescue stranded travelers and restore power where needed.

Thanks to the forward thinking of their fathers, the Davis family had no pressing need to leave the house. James moved the chaise lounge to the den so Diedra could rest among the family throughout the day.

Saturday morning James and Diedra were relaxing comfortably on the chaise lounge, watching movies, while the triplets played on the floor in front of them. They had just watched Dirty Dancing and now they were watching The Five Heartbeats. Adrian and Austin, who had already developed cabin fever, had been in the garage all morning.

"What are they doing out there?" James asked. "Do you think maybe they got so bored they decided to clean the garage?" he quipped.

"Anything is possible, but that's highly unlikely. Sorry,"

Austin and Adrian burst into the room in an excited frenzy.

"We found it!" they both exclaimed.

"You found what?" asked James.

"Our old sled. For a minute there we thought it was gone, but we finally found it in the back corner of the garage under some old tarp," said Adrian.

"Yeah, now we can have some real fun. Who wants to go sledding?" Austin asked the triplets.

"Sledding? What's that?" they asked.

"Yeah, what is sledding?" James asked. "We don't know nothing about no sledding in Alabama," he said only half-joking.

"It is the perfect time to learn." Diedra said. "You should go with them to take the triplets out. I'm sure they will love it. Just be careful."

"We will. We'll find a small hill for them. Austin and I have been dreaming about getting a sled on Horseshoe Hill out at Eastwood School ever since we moved here. I wish you could come out with us, Mom. It would be like old times."

"Yeah, just like the good ole days." Austin agreed.

"Yes, that was fun, but I believe my sledding days are over." she replied. "You all go and have fun."

James and the boys bundled up and went out for the afternoon, leaving Diedra home alone. She turned off the television and pulled out her journal and started reading through it.

"*Someday you will write a book about it.*"

She recalled James words to her. As she read the pages of her journal, she realized that this was it. Her book was already on the pages of her journal. She believed her story would help other women who were navigating this road we call life. But it wasn't finished yet. There was more to tell; more to be revealed to her.

"Lord, I pray that you will give me the words to share the story you want me to write. Amen." She prayed as she began to write.

Tuesday morning the roads were still closed. By this time, most people had grasped the severity of the situation this "Thunder Snow" had brought to their area. The only ones who ventured out onto the roads were emergency personnel, and those few individuals with vehicles equipped for the road conditions as they were. The governor had declared a state of emergency.

Over the weekend, Adrian and Austin had put the sled to good use. They used it to pull groceries from Wal-mart for some of their less prepared neighbors. After they finished their tasks, they spent Saturday afternoon in the town square participating in a snowball fight.

Church was cancelled Sunday. Diedra had to reschedule her doctor's appointment that was supposed to have been Monday, and by Tuesday, she had become restless. She had not set foot out of the house since she returned home from the hospital the previous Thursday. But she had been able to read through her journals and formulate an outline for her book. She was excited. For years she had believed she had a novel inside of her waiting to go on paper, but every time she would get an idea, it would never go anywhere. Now she realized that her story was literally just that; her story. It just seemed to flow from her effortlessly. She would sit at her desk for a period of time and then retire to the chaise lounge to rest, and then back to the desk.

James kept the triplets occupied whenever Diedra was at her desk. When she wasn't reading or writing in her journal, she was studying her Bible. He welcomed the opportunity to spend this quality time with his sons. He also appreciated the opportunity to observe his wife. She seemed to be doing surprisingly well, considering the scare they'd had just one week earlier. It seemed the headaches had stopped all together. She was resting well, and he sensed a level of tranquility in her that he had not observed in... well, ever.

By Wednesday, the snow and ice had melted and it was practically as if the storm had never occurred. The schools had reopened and James would return to work the next day. Both Dr. Howards stopped by the house to check on Diedra. They concluded that mother and child were both doing remarkably well.

## CHAPTER 18

THE NEXT COUPLE OF MONTHS were pretty uneventful. Diedra continued to follow the direction of both her doctors and the baby seemed to be thriving. The best estimate Dr. Howard was able to give her for a due date was early to mid-June, around June 10th he guessed. They would continue to monitor her closely and try to pinpoint a due date when she reached her third tri-mester.

James was excelling on his job at the Depot. He learned that he was under consideration for a position he had forgotten he'd applied for. It would be a huge leap forward in his career. He and Diedra prayed about it and gave it over to God. They agreed that what was for him was for him, and God was going to take care of them regardless of any natural circumstances.

Their friends and family had really stepped up to insure that Diedra was able to stay off her feet, per doctor's orders. Her mother and her mother in-law cooked and cleaned for them. James would drop the triplets off at daycare each morning and Cassandra would bring them home in the evenings. Adrian and Austin did an excellent job of keeping the little ones occupied when they were home. Brea took over the track team and coached them to a winning season. James reluctantly took Diedra to a couple of the meets on the condition that they would have to leave if she became overly excited.

In April, Diedra's friends planned a Baby Shower for her, along with Mrs. Davis and Mrs. Daniels. They wanted to surprise her, but by that time, Diedra was truly homebound. The only time she left her home was for her doctor's visits. So they agreed to have a small gathering at Diedra's house.

## May 1

AT SIX O'CLOCK IN THE morning Diedra rolled over and eased herself up to a sitting position. She sat on her side of the bed peering down at her swollen abdomen.

"I don't even recall having this issue at the beginning of this pregnancy, but you are certainly making up for it now, aren't you Baby Girl?" She thought to herself as she gingerly stood to her feet and made her way to the bathroom for what seemed like the 10th time already. For the past week it seemed that this baby was resting squarely on her bladder. Her ankles were swollen. Her nose was stopped up and she couldn't take any medication, and of all things, her breasts were leaking. It seemed like all of a sudden, her body had just gone haywire. She tried to maintain a positive demeanor but her emotions were erratic as well. She couldn't help it. Dr. Howard said it was just hormones and it would level out after she had the baby. "Please explain that to my poor husband and sons." She had pleaded.

This morning while she sat in her bathroom she suddenly felt an overwhelming urge to cry. She didn't know why. She just felt like crying, so she did. She sat right there on the toilet and cried until she felt she had no more tears. She blew her nose, and then she got up and washed her face and brushed her teeth before she walked back into her bedroom.

When she returned to her bed she found James, wide awake, with all five of her sons. Each of the boys gave her a big hug before she climbed into the bed. James had his Bible open in his lap to Proverbs 31. Once she reentered their bed, he began reading to them. He read the entire chapter, verses one through thirty-one. After he finished reading he said a prayer and they each spoke a blessing over Diedra and the baby.

She couldn't help it. She started crying all over again. But this time they were tears of joy and gratitude. She thanked them all for being such a loving family, and knowing just what she needed when she needed it.

James leaned over and kissed her on the forehead as he placed his arms around her. "Your day is just beginning. Today, we want to honor you and show you just how much you are appreciated and loved; starting out with breakfast in bed." He gestured to the boys and Adrian held the door as Austin led Travis, Trevor, and Tremaine to retrieve the TV trays from the hallway. They returned with wheat toast, fruit bowls, cereal and orange juice.

After breakfast, James sent the boys to go 'clean their rooms' while he remained with Diedra. He explained that she was not to venture away from the bedroom until lunch time that afternoon, at which time they would have a formal brunch in the dining room. Since they had not been out to dinner in months, he and the boys had decided they would dine out at home today. And yes, they were all dressing up, but in the meantime, he would stay with her and keep her company.

James and Diedra remained in the room until about mid-day, at which time they started to prepare for their brunch. She was concerned about the triplets but he insisted that the twins would be able to handle getting them ready.

"I don't even know what I'm going to wear," she stated. "I haven't dressed up in months. James, it was really sweet of you to plan this brunch but I may not even have anything to wear," she insisted as she walked over to her closet. When she opened the closet she found a peach chiffon dress with a sheer coat, and matching shoes and purse. The dress itself was a spaghetti strapped dress with multiple layers of flowing fabric and it was gorgeous. "Where did this come from?" She asked incredulously. "Honey I love you to the moon and back, but I know you didn't pick out this dress!" she said.

"I don't guess you know as much as you think. I did pick that dress…with a little help from Marsha at Dillards to make sure the size was right."

"You bought this from Dillards?" she asked frowning ever so slightly.

"It was on sale," he responded.

"That's my man!" she replied. "You know what to say."

She was grinning from ear to ear the entire time she was getting ready. It felt good to get dressed up for a change. She had been stuck in this house for so long, some days she didn't even bother to change out of her pajamas. James always seemed to know just what she needed. She was one lucky lady.

She put her hair up in a ponytail with curls cascading over the top of her head and she put on a little light make-up, some lipstick, and eye liner. Once she was ready, she stood in front of the mirror turning from side to side. For the first time in months she felt pretty. Poor James, he had to be tired of seeing those pajamas and sweats.

James walked up to Diedra and hugged her from behind, placing his hands lightly over her large abdomen. "You are always beautiful to me," he said. "But when you dress up like this you get an extra sparkle in your eyes that is so, so captivating."

"You definitely know what to say," she replied as she turned her head up to kiss him. He turned her around to face him and kissed her tenderly. Just then someone knocked on the door.

"Who is it?" asked James.

"It's me, Travis."

"And me, Trevor."

"And me, Tremaine."

"We are ready for brunch!" they all squealed.

James walked over and opened the door and the three little boys came bouncing into the room. Trevor stopped and looked at Diedra. "You look pretty." he said in awe.

"Aww, you are so sweet, baby. Well, you three are quite handsome." she gushed as she leaned over to pat him on his cheek. Meanwhile, Tremaine could not stop touching the fabric of her dress.

"I like it, Mommy," he said. Tremaine continued to rub his hands across the chiffon as they prepared to leave the room.

"Where are Adrian and Austin?" she asked.

"In the dining room with…"

"They're probably waiting for us in the dining room." James interrupted Travis. "I told you we planned a special brunch with all your favorites today." He placed his hands on Diedra's shoulders as he guided her toward the door. He leaned over and whispered in her ear. "Now the boys and I put a lot of effort into pulling this off for you today, so I want you to close your eyes and do not peek until I tell you to."

They headed down the hall to the dining room. James continued to guide Diedra as he covered her eyes. Once they reached the folding doors to the dining room, they found Adrian standing outside. James gave him a nod and he opened the doors as James removed his hands from Diedra's eyes and she was startled by the loud scream of "Surprise" that burst from the room.

Diedra looked around to see her parents along with James' parents and their friends and other family members. "You guys!" She blushed. "What is all this?" she asked, taking in the pink décor around the room. When she spotted the beautiful cake in the form of a stack of white gift wrapped boxes with pink ribbons, and the pile of actual gifts in the corner of the room she started crying all over again.

"What's wrong?" asked Cassandra. "Too much?"

"No not at all. It's perfect. It's all perfect. I am totally overwhelmed that you would do all this for me. Thank you so much," she said as she went around the room hugging each and every one of them. "James, you didn't do all this did you?" she asked.

"Ha! Not hardly. This was all courtesy of these ladies right here." he said, gesturing toward his and her mothers and Diedra's friends. And... in the interest of full disclosure, I didn't pick out the dress either. That was Cassandra and Kayla. You know I don't know nothin'bout pickin' out no dresses!" he said to everyone's amusement.

"Okay, this is what we are going to do." Mrs. Daniels announced, clapping her hands together. "Brunch will be served, now. Then the men can retreat to the den and the ladies to the living room for the baby shower. Fill free to come back in for refills or seconds. We will let you know when we're ready to cut the cake and open the gifts. Children first, boys come on and get your plates and then the man of the house will bless the food."

"I think I am going to defer to my wife this time." James stated as he looked into Diedra's eyes and squeezed her hand." To their surprise, Diedra complied. She held onto James' hand as she closed her eyes and began to pray.

"Lord,

I thank you for everything you are doing in my life today and everything you have done in my life to get me to the place I am right now.

You have been in control from day one. From the moment I was formed in my mother's womb, you knew me and you had a plan.

You knew the choices I would make, good and bad. You opened the doors I needed to go through and you closed the doors that were not for me. Each of my experiences had a purpose in your plan for my life. Remind me daily that what the enemy means for my harm, you will use for my good. And even when he thinks he's winning in the natural, you have already won.

Lord, help us all to focus on you...To yield our desires to your will. Teach us to forgive and to love others as you love us.

Thank you for this little miracle we are here to honor today. Thank you for the hedge of protection you have already placed around her.

Lord I thank you for placing me in the midst of people who are spirit filled, praying believers. I thank you for a loving family of spirit filled believers. I thank you for allowing us to see glimpses of what you are doing in our lives.

I pray for my family and friends, that you allow them to see you at work in their lives.

Lord, I ask that you would bless this gathering today and bless the food as we partake, may it provide nourishment and strength to our bodies. And bless the hands that prepared it for us. Thank you Lord and in Jesus' name we pray.

"Amen"

"Amen!"

"Amen!" James said out loud. And to Diedra he said, "I am so proud of you Babe. You have really grown these past few months and I see it every day."

Mrs. Daniels and Mrs. Davis walked over to James and Diedra and Mrs. Daniels said, "You two have a seat in the place of honor in the living room and we will fix your plates. Don't worry about the little ones. Their big brothers will take care of them. You just relax and enjoy your day. And yes James, it is your day as well."

Just then, they heard the doorbell ring. Rodney III had arrived with Victoria, Nicholette and Jasmine.

Diedra and James sat in the living room in full view of the activity in the other room, relishing the entire affair.

"We are truly blessed aren't we?" Diedra said, absentmindedly rubbing her hands across her abdomen.

"Yes we are. We have a beautiful family and wonderful friends," replied James.

Cassandra and Brea brought in TV trays and Mrs. Davis and Mrs. Daniels set their food before them.

"Umm, sourdough biscuits! I haven't had these in so long. Thanks Ma," said James. He and Diedra had agreed not to tell his mother that Diedra had figured out her 'secret' recipe years ago. Mama Lee, are these your orange pancakes?" he asked Mrs. Daniels. "It's on now!" he exclaimed,

"Everything is perfect." Diedra said, eyeing the spread of cheese-scrambled eggs, sausage links, scattered hash browns, grits, fruit, and juice. "You two know better than anyone what we like. Thank you both," gushed Diedra.

As the guests settled in to enjoy the food, the children retreated to the den after stopping by Diedra to bless the baby. Adrian came along first and the rest of them followed suit, all the way down to Diedra's sister Beverly's two year old daughter, Ashley, who always did everything Trevor did."

"Her children arise up and call her blessed." Pastor McKinney said, as he observed the procession.

"And her husband also," added a smiling James.

"Amen" Said Mr. Daniels, beaming proudly at his daughter.

After the meal, the ladies began to prepare for the shower activities, and the men retreated into the den. A few moments later the men returned to the living room. "Ma, I don't think you thought this out too clearly," James told his mother.

"What's wrong, dear?" Mrs. Davis asked innocently.

"The children have the television tied up with video games, and they are sprawled all over the den. What are we supposed to do?"

"Oh that does present quite a conundrum." she said thoughtfully. "I guess you can join us in here for the shower."

"Ha! Robert I told you they had something up their sleeves." Josiah Davis whispered to Diedra's father. "I promise you, Ruth is a meticulous planner."

"Yes, Lee Beverly is as well." Robert chuckled.

"James, I want you to stay with me. This is your baby too." Diedra smiled at James.

"Seriously, Babe?" James asked incredulously, "I'm starting to feel like I've been duped." he said, looking at his mother as he went back to his seat.

"That's because you have, son," his father replied. "This whole set-up... and I do mean set-up, has your mother's name all over it." He chuckled as he returned to his own seat next to his wife.

"Well, I think it is just perfect." Diedra exclaimed.

"The only thing perfect about this is you." James whispered into Diedra's ear as he leaned over and stole a quick kiss.

The doorbell rang at the side door and Austin rushed to answer it. The adults in the other room heard all the squealing and excitement from the kids and since Beverly was the closest she went to see what the excitement was about. She returned to the room with a strange expression on her face leading Shar, who had just arrived in from Atlanta looking like she stepped off of a Fashion Fair runway.

# CHAPTER 20

DIEDRA STOOD UP AND WALKED across the room to hug her friend. "Now it really is per...fect" she said, pausing in the middle of the word as she saw Derek follow in behind Shar.

"Derek, what are you doing here?" she asked.

"I was in Atlanta and Shar told me she was coming to see you, so I offered to drive down with her to see my boys. Is that ok? I'll probably stay in town a few days so we can go car shopping. You know I promised them on their birthday that I would buy them cars this summer."

"Yeah, whatever, just remember we agreed that you would be practical," replied James. "Since the boys are kind of occupied right now, you're welcome to join us for my wife's baby shower. Grab a seat man." He gestured toward an empty seat on the other side of the room.

"Thanks, I will."

"He could at least have the decency to look uncomfortable," Cassandra whispered to Shawn.

"Diedra, I hope you don't mind. But my car is in the shop and you know I really hate driving this far if I don't have to. I mean, you know I would have, but when Derek offered to drive me down. I said, 'What the hey? He gets to see his sons and I get to see my friends.' Win, win!" she said with a toss of her long silky hair.

"Shar do you mean you couldn't rent a car?" Cassandra asked, incredulously. "I mean seriously, if you're struggling like that, I could have lent you some money."

Shar turned her attention to Cassandra and coolly responded. "I am sure you're aware that I am well able to afford a rental car. I actually did try to rent a limo, but the services I usually use were all booked up for this weekend. So, like I said, why drive, if I don't have to."

"Girls, girls! You two haven't changed a bit. You are too much alike." Mrs. Daniels interrupted. "I am glad to see you all together again. It's been too long." She said as she walked over and gave Shar a hug. "Shar, you look lovely, and Derek you're looking good too."

Diedra walked back to her seat saying, "Mama is right. It has been way too long since we've all gotten together. We have got to do better."

"I agree," said Shar. "Diedra, you are absolutely glowing. I'm glad to see you're happy and well."

"Thank you. I am that," Diedra replied, squeezing James' hands.

"So has everything been going well physically? No issues?" she asked.

"Not since that night in February. She's thriving and so am I, thank God," she replied as she patted her stomach tenderly. "No more headaches and no more episodes. The doctors are monitoring me and they say we're both doing remarkably well."

"Well praise God!" exclaimed Shar.

"All day every day!" replied James.

The Baby shower itself, was pretty uneventful. They played typical shower games. Some, the men participated in, and some, they sat back and observed. They shared childbirth stories that had Brea and Shar, both contemplating the benefits of remaining childless; while all the men expressed their appreciation at having the 'easy part'.

Robert Daniels even shared the story of Lee Beverly's first delivery, and how they had been in such a panic to get to the hospital after her water broke, but her uncle who was transporting them, had taken his sweet time getting them there, making several stops along the way, insisting that she would have plenty of time since it was her first child. As it was, she barely made it back to the examining room before Reggie decided to make his appearance.

Diedra and James received some beautiful gifts for their baby along with precious words of wisdom.

In the afternoon, guests started leaving. After the elder couples left, Rodney III drove all of the young people to the movies. Beverly and her family had to drive back to Savannah and James' sister, Esther, and her husband had to get back to Huntsville. In the end, the remaining couples at the house were Diedra and James, Cassandra and Shawn, Brea and Michael, Sherry and John, Kayla and Rodney, and Shar ...and Derek?

The group sat around talking about all that had taken place in the earlier part of the year. They told Shar and Derek about their church and their Life Group. Diedra told them about Valentine's eve at the Sun Dial and her scare a few days later. Shar was fascinated by the revelation of their Women's Ministry, Daughters of Tamar. Shar and Derek had some stories to tell as well. And it seemed that quite a few of them were shared experiences.

"It's been quite a year so far, hasn't it?" Shar exclaimed. She and James were in the kitchen getting a refill on their frappe.

"It has, but we're all the better for it." James replied. "I've watched Diedra grow in leaps and bounds right before my eyes. She is a far cry from that wounded young lady I met 10 years ago. I thank God for her, daily."

"Yes, it's a beautiful thing when you find that person God designed just for you. No matter what they've been through or what they may have done in their past; it's all part of who God designed them to be."

"Are you speaking from experience?" he asked.

Before she could answer, John entered the room. "Man, your wife is waiting for her drink. She said to tell you it doesn't have to be measured out perfectly. Just throw a scoop of ice cream in the cup and pour some ginger ale over it."

"I hear you," he laughed as he picked up the glasses and headed back into the living room.

Shar stood over the sink, deep in thought, until she was startled by a masculine pair of arms that encircled her waist. She jumped slightly, before she pulled away and said. "Not here, someone might see."

"Too late," said Cassandra as she, Shawn, and Brea entered the room. "I knew there was something going on between you two. Out of all the men between Atlanta and Los Angeles, you just had to have Diedra's sorry baby daddy. "

Shar was taken aback. "It, it's not like that, Cassie. And Derek takes very good care of those boys. He and Diedra just weren't meant to be. They were both young, and sometimes relationships just don't work out," she stammered.

"Are you seriously saying that to me right now? This man has steamrolled his way through Diedra and Brea's lives and now you're letting him into yours."

"Brea? What does Brea have to do with anything?"

"Oh, you don't know?" Cassandra asked, looking directly at Derek.

Derek turned on Cassandra. "Cassandra, why don't you mind your own business? You're always running your mouth about things that don't concern you. Your fat a…"

Out of nowhere a fist flew across Derek's face and landed squarely on his mouth, sending him sprawling across the room. Shar screamed out loud, and Brea stood off to the side looking as if she were the one who had been struck in the face. Shawn stood squarely in front of Cassandra with his arms crossed in front of him and his chin resting on one fist, as Derek scrambled to regain his footing. The rest of the men rushed in from the other room and James and Rodney grabbed Derek as he lunged toward Shawn.

"Let him go," Shawn said calmly as he glared coldly at Derek. "That's my queen!" he said, emphatically pointing a finger at Cassandra, but staring directly at Derek. "Don't let the swirl fool you. What? Did you think that just because I'm white you could disrespect my wife… right in front of me? NOBODY is ever going to disrespect her. Not while I'm around. Let him go!" he demanded.

"No sir! You better take that mess over to Brittany Downs," James said to Shawn. "This ain't the hood. You won't be getting any street credit here. Not in my house." James stood between the two men. "Now would somebody tell me what is going on in here? And I'm telling you right now. If anything is broken. You're paying for it."

"I'm sorry, James. I will be happy to pay for any damages I may have caused," Shawn replied, just as Diedra made it into the room.

Meanwhile Shar grabbed a paper towel off the counter, wet it at the sink, and started tending to Derek's busted lip. "You so deserved that," she whispered. "I should punch you myself, talking to my friend like that. And what's this about Brea?" she asked as she dabbed a drop of blood off of his lip. "Never mind, we'll discuss that later, but right now, you owe my friends an apology."

"I'm sorry baby," he whispered.

"What are you apologizing to me for? I'm not the one you disrespected," she whispered back.

"Damages? What's going on in here?" Diedra asked as she slowly entered the room.

"I don't know Babe. It appears that Mr. Golden Gloves had a flashback."

Diedra looked around the room at Shawn standing protectively in front of Cassandra, Shar nursing Derek, and Brea standing off to the side ringing her hands and looking like a deer caught in the headlights. She observed that Shar and Derek seemed to have a genuine connection.

Michael walked across the room to Brea. "Are you okay?" he asked as he pulled her into a protective hug. She allowed him to hug her as she stood stiffly, her tear filled eyes on Diedra. She realized the only way Cassie could have possibly known about her affair with Derek years ago, was if Diedra had told her, since Cassie and Shar were in DC when the three of them were in Connecticut. All these years and she'd never said a word.

Diedra nodded reassuringly at Brea as she spoke. "If you all would excuse us, I would like to speak with Derek alone," she said.

James looked searchingly at his wife.

"Obviously, you don't have to leave if you don't want to, but I would like for you to give us a moment," she said softly.

"If you insist," he said, then he headed out of the room. He hesitated at the door and glanced back at her. She nodded and smiled reassuringly at him before he disappeared through the doorway.

As the others filed out of the room, Brea and Shar, both hesitated. "It's okay," she reassured them.

Once they were left alone in the kitchen, Diedra pulled a chair out at the table in order to sit down. Derek rushed to her side to assist her as she sat down.

She looked up at him with a puzzled expression, her head tilted to the side, squinting and shaking her head in disbelief.

"What? Does that surprise you?" He asked. "I'm not that boy you knew years ago, Dee. I have grown up. Granted, I still have a lot of growing to do," he said, reaching up to touch his lip. "But I'm getting there."

He walked around to the other side of the table and took a seat across from her. His lip was doubled in size. "Are you okay?" she asked.

"I'm fine, why?" Derek asked. She looked at him pointedly. "Oh this?" he said touching his lip. "This is nothing. He barely touched me."

"If you say so," she replied.

"So, what's up, Dee?" he asked lightly.

"I don't know Derek. You tell me. What was all that commotion in here earlier?"

Derek reached across the table placing a hand over Diedra's, "Dee, I'm sorry. I didn't mean to disrespect or hurt you by coming here today. The last thing I wanted to do was to cause you any heartache or pain. I apologize if I was insensitive. I just thought maybe enough time had passed…"

"Slow your roll, Derek," she said as she removed her hand from his. First of all, you need to stop calling me Dee. My name is Diedra or Mrs. Davis, to you. You don't get to call me any cutesy little nicknames anymore. And second… What are you talking about? You have been here plenty of times before."

"What about Shar?" he asked.

"What about Shar? She knows she's always welcome here."

"Did it bother you to see me show up with her?"

"Why would it? I know you two are friends, and that you see each other often."

"What if we were more than friends?"

"Are you more than friends?"

"Would that bother you?"

"Why would it?"

"Because, I know I hurt you."

"Why did you hurt me, Derek?"

"Because I was young and didn't know how to do any better."

"Do better now, Derek. Be better."

"I am sincerely trying. I know I've made a lot of mistakes, mistakes that I can't go back and change. But, I've learned to stand up and take responsibility for my actions and accept the consequences. I know I handled things terribly when you had Adrian and Austin, but I've worked hard to ensure that they will never know lack again."

"You do realize that your presence is worth more than anything you can buy them?" she asked.

"I hear that. But, your husband stepped up, and I realize he has been an excellent example for them. I never wanted to confuse them."

"Why would they be confused by having two positive role models actively involved in their lives?" she asked. "James is raising them, and he's doing a superb job of it. And they love him dearly. But, good, bad or indifferent, you will always be their father. What type of father, is up to you."

She continued, "Now I love my husband, completely, and HE is the love of my life. What you need to understand is… though you harmed me greatly, I realize that it is not my place to pass judgment on you. If it is God's plan to bless you… in any area of your life, then, his will be done. That has nothing to do with me or his plans for me.

Do you understand what I'm telling you, Derek?" She looked at him intently and said, "Even though we will always be connected through our sons, that emotional bondage I was shackled in was broken years ago. And although I never told you, I forgave you years ago."

He sighed deeply, and then he spoke, "I never realized how much I needed to hear that until you said it. Thank you, Dee- er Diedra."

"You're welcome, Derek. So…what about you and Shar? Is it serious?"

"Huh?"

"You heard me, are you in love with her?"

"Do what?"

"Are.. you.. in.. love.. with .. her?" she repeated very slowly.

"I think I am."

"Why aren't you sure?"

Derek searched Diedra's face, attempting to decipher where her head was at. "I've never felt like this before." he said slowly. "I mean, this is different. She's different…uh, I'm sorry." He dropped his head in embarrassment. He paused a moment and then he looked her in the eyes asserting, "It is awkward saying this to you, but yes, I do love her and I am going to marry her…if she'll have me."

"No need to be sorry. What happened between us was ages ago, Derek. We were just children playing grown folks games. We are all older now. Knowing you, and knowing her as well as I do, I think she just might be the one for you. Just respect her enough to be totally honest with her, I mean totally honest, no secrets."

The rest of the group sat around the living room, engulfed in deafening silence for what seemed like an eternity. Finally, "What do you suppose they're talking about?" asked Sherry. She sat on the couch with John, Brea, and Michael.

"Yes, what do you suppose, Shar?" Cassandra, who was sitting directly across from them on the loveseat, asked. "Two guesses, Brea. What do you think Diedra would want to talk about to Derek, alone?"

"How would I know? I'm no psychic." Brea snapped.

"Cassie baby, you know I love you, and I will always stand up for you, but you are wrong and you are being very messy right now. Ease up, okay." Shawn told his wife.

Rodney stood up from his seat and gestured toward Kayla. "Honey, I think it might be time for us to call it a night."

"Oh no, you two stay right there. I have a feeling that before this evening is over we are all going to need prayer." James told him.

"Are you sure?"

"Definitely."

"Don't be ridiculous." Shar said as she jumped out of her seat and headed back to the kitchen. "I'm going in there."

Brea and Cassandra followed behind her. Michael and Shawn followed behind them, leaving James with Rodney, Kayla, John, and Sherry. "You might as well go after them, James. We'll be out here. I promise we won't leave." Rodney told James.

"You might want to go ahead and get that prayer going," James murmured as he followed the others into the room.

Shar burst into the kitchen spitting out words like a rapid-fire machine gun. "Diedra, I'm sorry, I should have told you sooner, but Derek and I are together and I think I'm in love with him, I know I am, and I love you and I don't want to hurt you or lose our friendship but, I want him in my life, I'm sorry he hurt you, but you can't always choose who you fall in love with." She sucked in a deep breath after she finished her speech. She stood there in the kitchen, tears streaming down her cheeks, waiting awkwardly for her friend to respond.

Brea stood behind Shar trying to process the information that had been revealed throughout the evening. Evidently, Shar and Derek were a couple. Diedra and Cassandra knew about her own involvement with Derek years ago. All these years, and no one had ever said a word. She watched as Derek stood up and embraced Shar, gently guided her over to the table, pulled his chair out for her and helped her take a seat. She stared intently at them and then she asked, "Are you pregnant?"

Once again, Shar was caught off guard. She shook her head as Derek laughed and wiped her tears. "It's not that type of relationship," he said. "Shar and I have been friends for years. We have truly grown up together. She's actually my best friend. I think we are in this for the long haul. We believe we are at a point in our lives where we understand what it really takes to make a relationship work."

He looked lovingly at her before he continued, "We agreed years ago that we would not leave the friend zone, as she calls it, unless we were serious. You all know Shar's stance on sex outside of marriage. It still hasn't changed and I respect that. For years we dated others and we remained friends. But at some point, we realized that we wanted to be exclusive. I mean I felt like she was cheating on me whenever I saw her with another man. So I had to really explore my feelings for her. I didn't want to hurt her."

He looked at Diedra and then Brea. "I know I can't change what I've done, but I don't have to repeat the mistakes of the past," he said. He turned to Brea as he said, "Brea, I realize I was selfish and I put you in a difficult position and I am sorry for that."

"I'm the one that put you in the difficult position Brea, and I'm sorry," blurted Diedra.

"What do you mean?" Brea asked Diedra.

"When you first introduced me to Derek, I decided he was going to be my boyfriend. I knew you two were close, but never once, did I ask you if you had feelings for him. I saw the way you looked at him, but I just ignored it and pre-tended that since you never said anything, there wasn't anything there."

Now Diedra's eyes began to glass over. "Do you remember that last summer when the three of us came from Storrs together? I slept in the backseat most of the way down and most of the way back. But I was awake enough to hear the way the two of you interacted. You were closer to him than I had ever been. I heard you admit that you had feelings for him and I heard him say that you were the one he should have been with. After that, my plan was to dump him before he dumped me, but then we returned to UCONN and I found out I was preg-nant, with twins no less, and I just couldn't do it. I wanted my babies to have two parents."

Brea was dumbfounded. "You never said a word!" she finally said.

"What was I supposed to say? I was in an emotional tailspin. I was angry, hurt, embarrassed, scared, and guilty, all at the same time. I was angry at myself for allowing myself to get caught in the situation I was in. I was embar-rassed that Derek was able to walk away so easily, and I was hurt that he had chosen you over me. I tried to push you away, but thankfully, you wouldn't let me."

"Diedra, you're like a sister to me and I never wanted to hurt you. I am so sorry."

"Everything turned out as it should," said Diedra. "I never knew real love until I met James." She beamed as she looked across the room at her husband and said, "I really am blessed."

Cassandra stood near the door with Shawn. She could see that Diedra was at peace. She was a far cry from the girl that had driven down to DC that day years ago and ranted and cried about the betrayal of her boyfriend and her friend.

Cassandra didn't think she had ever seen her friend that upset, not ever! More than upset, she was angry. Diedra and Cassandra had been through a lot togeth-er, good times and bad. As young girls they had experienced the loss of Diedra's grandfather, who was as close to Cassandra as her own grandfather. After Big

Daddy's death, Cassandra had offered to share her grandfather with Diedra. Years later they shared their grief over the death of Cassandra's grandfather.

The two young women, along with Brea and Shar, had shared most of the joys and sorrows of growing up as young black women in the sixties and seventies, military brats at that, moving from one base to the next. Fortunately for them, they seemed to land in the same places, which was a fairly rare phenomenon. Diedra was one of the strongest women Cassandra knew and for something to have this strong an effect on her it had to be serious. Diedra could usually find humor in just about any situation, but not this one, not this day.

She had been devastated by the revelation that Derek was going to leave her for Brea, along with the fact that she was pregnant with Derek's child. Diedra had realized that even though Brea had carried feelings around for Derek since she was twelve, he was the initiator of their little interlude. Although she felt no less betrayed by Brea, she would eventually have to forgive her. She understood that the devastating loss of Brea's mother that summer had left her vulnerable.

Shar just happened to be away that weekend, and Diedra had sworn Cassandra to secrecy, and they never spoke of the affair again.

"Shar, I am sorry for the way I've acted toward you and Derek today. I just want you to be happy, and if Derek makes you happy…then who am I to judge?"

Derek had his arm around Shar as he spoke, "Thank you, Cassandra. I understand completely where you were coming from, and I apologize for what I said to you earlier. Like I told Diedra, I have grown up a lot, and this lady right here has been a very positive influence in my life, but I still have a lot of growing to do." He turned to Shar and said, "Yes, it's true. Brea and I were involved. You know we were friends before any of you arrived to Nurnberg. I always thought she was cute but she seemed too young and innocent for me. You remember how she was when you met her."

"I was a tomboy with pigtails." Brea said absently.

"Exactly! You were like a little sister to me and we were always close. Then by the time we were at UCONN, you had blossomed and Diedra and I were drifting apart." He turned back to Shar, "Brea and I had always been close and our friendship turned to attraction."

"Sort of like you and I?" Shar asked guardedly.

"Sort of, but on a more superficial level. What you and I have is built on years of learning each other and growing together. At the age of 21, I was living in the moment. I had no concept of what a lifetime commitment involved. I wanted fun and relaxation, not hard work and difficulties.

At this point in my life, I understand that a relationship worth having is a relationship worth fighting for, and I am ready to fight with you and for you. I love you Shar."

Every woman in the room was crying. They all gathered around Shar, hugging and congratulating her.

Suddenly, Shar turned to Brea. "What about you Brea? Are you happy?"

Brea glanced over at Michael and exhaled deeply, "Yes, I am," she said thoughtfully. "I really am." Then she gave Shar a big hug and said, "I am happy for you as well."

"Have you told your parents?" Cassandra asked.

"Not yet, you know the Colonel doesn't think anyone is good enough... But Derek! With his past... Oh, He is definitely going to blow a gasket. But he is in no position to pass judgment on anyone. I just don't want to deal with that drama yet. Right now I'm just happy to be able to share with my friends." She squealed with delight as she said, "Oh Diedra I'm so happy to be able to share this part of my life with you. I have missed you all so much! And now that Derek is moving to Atlanta, we will be able to come down much more often, and you can come to Atlanta as well."

"Are you moving in together? What about the twins? Do they know about your relationship?" Brea asked.

"No we're not moving in together. We haven't told them, but they're pretty sharp. Based on some of the conversations we've had, I believe they suspected that we were more than friends." Derek shared. "I'm sure they'll be happy for us. They've been trying to play match maker for years."

"Diedra smiled as she recalled that when she and James first got married, Adrian had asked her if 'Aunt Shar' could marry his daddy. She had forgotten all about that.

"So are you two going to get married?" asked Shawn.

"We haven't discussed it," replied Derek.

"Well, don't you think you need to?" asked James.

"Certainly,"

"But that will be a private conversation, not a group deliberation." Shar interjected.

By this time, the rest of the party had entered the room. They filled them in on what had taken place. Someone asked if Rodney had been aware of the relationship and he admitted that he had noted the chemistry between them years before, but realized it would be an awkward situation. As the evening wound down, they gathered around the table, the ladies seated, with their men standing behind them and James suggested that Rodney lead them in prayer.

"Are you seriously going to pray right now?" asked Derek. "What? You don't get enough in church?" he quipped.

Rodney replied, "From the outside looking in, one would think it odd that we pray so often. They don't understand that this is not something we do out of tradition or habit. They don't know that God is real in our lives and we pray to Him because we recognize his presence and we acknowledge His power."

"Amen," agreed John.

"How can we not thank Him for his love that flows through us and to us? How can we not thank Him for His mercy and His grace? How can we not thank Him for ordering our steps and protecting us from dangers, seen and unseen? We know that even when in the natural, it looks as if Satan is winning and we are faced with trial after trial, and sometimes even calamity, God has already won. What the enemy has meant for our harm, God uses for our good. You all know my father's favorite scripture, 'Before I formed you in the womb I knew you, and before you came forth out of the womb I sanctified you and ordained you a prophet unto the nations.'

God's plan for us is to give us all a future and a hope. How can we not praise Him even in the very midst of our troubles?" He stopped and looked around the room and smiled as he said, "It's true. This joy that I have, the world didn't give it to me and the world can't take it away," quoting a hymn from their youth.

"I'm sorry, I just felt led to say that," he continued. "If you are not walking in the full confidence of your salvation, if you don't have the certainty of God's manifested presence in your life, then you might not understand why we talk about Him like we do or why we pray to Him like we do. But don't take my word for it. Read his Word. It is available to each of us in the Bible." He exhaled deeply. "Taste and see that the Lord is good." Then he bowed his head down and said, "Let us pray." There was a pause as they waited for him to begin.

"Father,

I thank you for your mercy and your grace. Thank you for your presence in our lives. Thank you for forgiving our sins and saving our souls. Thank you for dying on the cross so we could live.

Lord we want to do better. We want to be better. We long for an intimate relationship with you. We want you to guide our lives because we know we cannot do this without you. Lord tame our fleshly thoughts, our conversation, and our actions. Help us to focus on you so we will not be so quick to react with anger, resentment, or even rebellion. Help us to walk in your love. Help us to be vessels for you to love others through. Lord, we want to serve you in spirit and in truth. We want to walk with you daily. Help us to lay all of our burdens at the cross and let go of any feelings of anger, resentment, hurt, or unforgiveness that may linger in our hearts.

In Jesus' Holy name we pray,"

"Amen, Amen, and Amen," they all said in unison.

Shar felt something wet drop on her shoulder and she looked up at Derek who was wiping away at a continuous stream of tears. "What's wrong?" she asked him.

"I don't know," he replied. "I just can't stop it."

"Aww, baby," she said as she stood up to hug him. "That's the Holy Spirit. You just bask in that for a while."

Everyone gathered around the couple again, either hugging them or shaking their hands, congratulating them on all that was happening in their lives.

"Are we cool man?" Derek asked Shawn.

"I'm cool if you are," he replied. "I've got no beef with you, but I will always defend my wife."

"I respect that man. I was out of line and I apologize." The two men shook hands and the entire group moved back into the living room to enjoy the rest of the evening.

## CHAPTER 21

TIME SEEMED TO STAND STILL as Diedra waited for her due date to arrive. By the end of May she was the one with Cabin Fever. She had been stuck in the house on partial bed rest for three months, but it seemed like three years. She was so ready for this baby to arrive. At least, once she had her daughter to care for, there would be a break in her routine.

She had made some good progress on her book though. Shar had been shopping it around to some friends in Atlanta who were in the publishing business. A couple of them seemed genuinely interested. They would not commit to anything until they saw the finished product. Understandable.

Shar had been coming into town more often since she and Derek broke the news of their relationship. Diedra could not recall the last time the four ladies had spent so much time together. It was like old times. Good times! Brea, Cassandra, and Shar would come over to keep her company and they would hang out like a group of school girls.

"I like her," James had told Diedra about Shar. "I never really got to know her too well before. She seems to fill in a missing piece in your group. There is an impenetrable bond between you ladies that is pervasive whenever the four of you get together. You feed off of each other in a good way."

"Yes, I didn't realize how much I missed her until she was back. But you're right, no matter how long we stay apart; we always fall back into step when we get together."

On this Saturday afternoon, Diedra was at home alone. James had taken the triplets to the Talladega Superspeedway with his old friend David, who was in town to visit. The twins were at a pool party.

This was the first weekend since her shower that Cassandra, Brea, and Shar had not come over. She had spent the morning getting things ready for the arrival of her daughter, who was due to arrive by C-section, in less than a week. She was going through her suitcase for the hundredth time, trying to determine if she'd selected the right outfit for her baby to wear home from the hospital, when her mind drifted back over her life.

She thought about all that she and her friends had been through together and the paths their lives had taken. The loss of Brea's mother and Shar's parent's separation after they returned from Germany had been two pivotal events in their lives. Shar had always been fiercely competitive but professionally, she was driven; determined that she would never be dependent on another human being for her livelihood.

Growing up as a bi-racial child to a single parent had been difficult enough for Brea, but her mother's death had left her alone and vulnerable. And try as she might, to put up a tough exterior, her friends, her true family, knew that she had a gentle and loving heart.

"Hmph! And here we are, after all these years, still together. Who would have even guessed?" She tenderly folded the pink onesie she was holding and placed it back in the suitcase before she went to her desk and began to work on her manuscript.

# CHAPTER 22

DIEDRA WAS STILL SITTING AT the desk when she thought she heard the front door. She assumed it was Adrian and Austin coming in from the pool party. She heard the muffled sounds of multiple voices coming from the other room but neither of her sons came in to greet her as they usually did.

After a while, she got up from her chair and went into the living room. Adrian, Austin, Rodney, Nicholette, and Bianca were all huddled around Victoria who was visibly upset.

"Is everything alright?" she asked.

"Yes ma'am," replied Rodney. "She'll be okay."

"Are you sure you're okay, Victoria?" she asked, looking closely at the young girl. "Adrian, is there something I need to know?"

"Yes ma'am," he replied. "I can't lie to my mom," he said to the rest of the group. "Besides, we can't just leave him there."

"Leave who where?" she asked. "Did something happen at the pool party?"

Adrian stood up and paced across the floor wringing his hands and shaking his head.

"Why did he do it? I just don't understand?" he said as he wiped a hand across his eyes.

"Why did who do what?" Diedra felt a tightening in her stomach that caused her to gasp as she walked over to her son. She grabbed his hands, led him to a chair, and placed her arms around him.

"It's okay, baby. I'm here and I've got you. Now somebody please tell me what happened." They all looked dumbstruck as Adrian attempted to explain what happened.

"The police officer, he didn't have to do what he did."

"Police officer! Son, what are you talking about?"

"He was like, out of his mind, Ma!"

"Did he hurt you, Adrian?"

"No ma'am, not me." He shook his head agitatedly. "We should have never gone to that party. They don't even want us out there." He said though glassy eyes.

Diedra winced as she straightened up and looked intently into her son's eyes. She didn't know what had happened at that party, but something had certainly had a devastating impact on all six of the young people in her living room that day. Seeing the looks on their faces had such a distressing effect on her that she wasn't certain if the pain that stabbed through her heart at that moment was emotional or physical. She had never seen any of them like this before. Especially Vitoria; she was traumatized.

"Victoria," Diedra asked as calmly as she was able. "What happened to you at the pool party today?"

"Forget about me! If he could do what he did to me, in front of all those people, who knows what is happening to Junior!"

"Junior? What does Junior have to do with anything?" Junior Johnson was one of Rodney's friends from school. He was a nice enough kid.

"He got in a fight with a white kid at the party and someone called the police and they came and arrested him. He didn't start it and they wouldn't even listen to our side," Victoria explained.

"I should have never left them there," Rodney said. "My Dad is going to kill me," he cried.

"Surely, Victoria has been at the city pool without you before."

Each of the teens dropped their head at the mention of the words 'city pool'.

"What's that all about?" she asked. "You were at the city pool weren't you?"

They all looked around at each other and dropped their heads again. "Speak up! Adrian, Austin, somebody better tell me something," she said sharply.

"Mom..." Austin said hesitantly, "The summer kickoff party was at Dixie Falls."

This time the pain was unmistakably real. Diedra felt a sharp pain shoot through her side from around her back, and she gasped in pain. It wasn't something that they talked about, but people in Jacksonville knew that the water slide at Dixie Falls in Draper was not for everyone. It was one of the lingering vestiges of segregation. Black people did not frequent Dixie Falls. They couldn't, unless they were a guest of one of the "members". Adrian and Austin had been invited to a few birthday parties out there when they were younger, but she only allowed them to attend if she was able to take them herself.

"Are you okay, Mrs. Davis," asked Bianca. Diedra took a deep breath and held fast to her composure.

"Nobody move," she ordered as she pulled herself up and went into her bedroom to make a telephone call.

When Diedra returned to the living room, she had her purse and keys in hand. "Let's go. You can tell me the details in the car."

"Mom, you're not supposed to drive," said Austin.

"It's not recommended, but it's not prohibited. Neither of you is in any condition to drive. Let's Go!" They knew better than to protest any further. They each got up and followed Diedra out to the garage. She stopped and scribbled a quick note for James on the message board in the kitchen on her way out the door. When she reached the driver's side door of the minivan, Adrian and Austin both ran over to assist her into the vehicle.

On the way to the Draper police station, Austin explained to Diedra that they had gone to the city pool first and there were only a bunch of little kids there. Junior had reminded them about the summer kickoff party out at Dixie Falls that several of their classmates had invited them to. Their friends insisted it would be okay.

They were all getting along fine until Buddy Ray, one of their former neighbors, had arrived with some of his cousins. Right away, they had started harassing them.

"Why didn't you just leave?"

"Because Rodney had taken me to the store," explained Bianca.

"What did you have to go to the store for that couldn't wait till later?" she asked.

"It was kind of an emergency," she ducked her head slightly. "We weren't even gone 20 minutes."

"Mrs. Davis, when we got back, there were police all over the place. Before we could even get into the parking lot I got stopped, and they even made Bianca and I get out while they searched the Navigator. Like they thought we had drugs or something. One of them even asked me how I was able to afford a ride like that." Rodney added.

"Why were the police there?" she asked.

"That Stevie Ray! He just wouldn't back off. We kept telling him to leave us alone," said Austin. "We even told Buddy to tell him, but he just kept coming at us, making racial remarks."

"What kind of racial remarks?" she asked.

"He called us all the n-word. He told us we should all go back to the projects where we came from. Except for Nicholette, he said she could stay and be his date."

"Okay, so that wasn't cool. But you couldn't just ignore him?"

"We tried to. Junior tried to laugh it off. He told him it was true, he did live in the projects, but he could go where he pleased. But then Stevie just got bolder. He even touched Nicholette."

"What do you mean, he touched her?"

Austin was visibly embarrassed. "I mean he touched her, inappropriately, on her backside. I told him he better leave her alone."

"But he did it again anyway," chimed in Adrian. "But the second time, before anyone could say anything, Junior punched him in the face. They were going at it pretty hard until someone broke it up. They told us we had to leave, but we couldn't because our ride wasn't there."

Diedra shifted in her seat, trying to get comfortable as she maneuvered the minivan down the highway.

"Then the police showed up because someone had called them about the fight. We saw them pointing at us and then at Buddy and his friends. The one guy took one look at Stevie and walked over to us cursing and yelling at us. He grabbed Junior and told him he was under arrest for assault. We kept trying to tell him that he didn't do anything and he told us to get our a-words out of there," he continued.

"We told him our ride wasn't there and he said he didn't care, if we didn't leave we were going to go to jail too," added Nicholette. "Then we just started walking toward the highway and Victor…"

"I called him Barney Phyfe," Victoria blurted out.

"You what!?"

"The whole thing was so stupid. He told us to leave there, like we were supposed to walk down the highway in our swimming suits. I just said, "We better go because 'BARNEY PHYFE' said so." I know I shouldn't have said anything but that was sooo stupid Mrs. Davis. Ooh! It made me mad."

"Then somebody laughed. I think that's what really made him mad," added Nicholette.

"Mom, the next thing we knew, he came and grabbed Victoria and dragged her back saying 'I told you to get you're a-word out of here.' Then he grabbed her hair and slung her down to the ground and handcuffed her like he was hog-tying a calf at a rodeo or something!" exclaimed Austin.

"Surely you are exaggerating! Why would he manhandle a little girl like that?"

"Mom, I'm telling you, he was even kneeling over her with his knee in her back."

"I'm sorry Austin; perhaps in the heat of the moment, things just seemed more intense. I find it hard to believe, in this day and age, that a law officer would treat a child in the manner you've described. Not even in Draper."

"It's true!" they all chimed in."

Diedra pulled into the parking lot of the Draper police station. She eased into a parking space in front of the small, austere, building, and put the minivan in park. She looked around the vehicle at the faces of the young people with her. She was certain she had done the right thing in calling Shar, but how long would it take her to get there? And what was she supposed to do about Junior? Hopefully Shar would be able to reach the other kid's parents and they would be there shortly.

She turned off the ignition and placed her keys back in her purse. She said a quick prayer as the teens jumped out of the minivan, and Austin ran around to assist her as she exited the vehicle. By the time they reached the door to the building, Adrian was holding it open for her. Diedra led the group to the front desk and she asked to speak to someone in charge.

Diedra stood at the counter for several minutes waiting for someone, anyone to acknowledge her. There were two officers at a desk several feet behind the counter where she stood.

"Are those all her kids?" the younger one asked the other.

"Probably so."

"Look it therr! She got her own rainbow coalition."

"Yeah, she's probably here to post bail for one of her baby daddy."

Both men laughed softly.

"You know I can hear you right?" she asked. The two men looked at her and then at each other and shrugged.

"We'll be wit cha in a bit," the older officer replied.

Diedra directed the teenagers to take a seat while she stood in front of the counter shifting her weight from one foot to the other...waiting. She breathed through another wave of pain while she waited for the officer to assist her. Finally, the younger officer walked over to the counter and addressed her.

"Kin I help you?" he asked briskly.

"I am here to inquire about Junior Johnson," she responded.

"You family?"

"No"

"You a law-yer?"

"No"

"Then I cain't help ya."

"Is there a supervisor here?"

"Yeah, but he's busy."

"I'll wait," she said and then turned and walked over to join the teenagers at a row of straight back chairs lined up in front of the wall across from the counter.

Just as she sat down, the door opened and a young lady with sweat soaked blonde hair, about Diedra's age and obviously pregnant, but not nearly as far along as Diedra, entered the building with a young man about Adrian and Austin's age. They were both dripping in sweat. The twins identified them as

Buddy and his mother. As soon as the woman approached the counter, the officer came over and offered her assistance. When she asked to speak with a supervisor, he walked to the front of the counter and led her around to the other side to the older officer's desk and pulled a chair out for her.

"Did you see that?" Adrian asked.

"Hush boy." Diedra scolded him and they continued to wait. She had hardly recognized Eliza Ray. She had not seen her or her son since her husband had lost his job at the Cotton Mill. Their family lost their home and had to move out to Draper on his family's property.

Buddy eased over to them, hesitantly, looking down at his shoes as he spoke. "Hey Austin, what'r you doing here?" he asked.

"What do you think, Buddy? We're here to see about Junior," Austin retorted.

"Yeah, me too. I told my mama what happened at the party. Sorry 'bout my cousins."

"Why didn't you say something then?"

"You know Stevie; he ain't gonna listen to nothin' I say. After y'all left I had to fake sick just ta get Wendell to take me home. Then, me and Mama had to walk clear over here." He continued to make eye contact with only Austin as he spoke. "I'm real sorry, man. I didn't think what happened ta Junior was right... or Victoria or... Nicholette either." He turned and hurriedly walked away, joining his mother and the police officer.

Eliza sat at the desk speaking with the police officer while Diedra and the group of teenagers waited. Occasionally Diedra would pull herself up out of the uncomfortable chair and walk around a bit before she would sit back down.

A tall athletically slim fellow with sun bleached hair coupled with a deep tan, entered and walked directly around the counter. "Hey there, Robby! What brings you out here on a Saturday afternoon?" the Sergeant addressed him.

"I need to speak with you, Earl." He said as he pulled out a handkerchief and wiped it across his sweat soaked face. This air in here sure does feel good," he added.

"That it does, that it certainly does. It's hotter than all get out outside but it's cool as can be in here. Well, what can I do you fer?" he asked.

"I understand there was some sort of fracas out at Dixie Falls," he replied.

"No big deal; just a couple of thugs out there tryin' to stir up trouble. My officers took care of it."

"Were there any arrests made."

"Just one. A boy assaulted another party goer. We have him in custody."

"But I told you, he didn't start it!" exclaimed Eliza.

"According to my officer's report, he threw the first punch, therefore, he was arrested."

"Where is the young man, now?"

"In a cell where he belongs."

"Where is the young man he was fighting?"

"Safe at home, I assume. He was the victim."

Diedra tried to listen to what they were saying but was unable to hear much over the hum of the air conditioner.

Rodney and Kayla Howard burst through the door followed by the Smiths. Brea was a few steps behind them with Junior's mother.

"Daddy! Victoria screamed as she ran into her father's arms. Rodney III walked sheepishly over to his mother.

"We came as soon as we got the word." Kayla told him. "Your father was at the church and he insisted that I wait for him to return."

"Yes, and we were in Anniston ourselves, and didn't get the message until we arrived home." Shawn said as he held Nicholette.

Brea observed the surprised and disapproving look the two officers shared when they noticed Shawn and Cassandra hugging their daughter. Robby caught that too. He walked back around to the front of the desk and greeted the group.

"You must be Ms. Johnson," he said to Junior's mother as he reached out a hand toward her.

"Yes, I am Shyanne Johnson," she replied.

"I had to work today, and Officer Thomas came and found me at Federation Motors."

"Well it is nice to meet you, although I'm sorry it's under these circumstances." He told her while shaking her hand vigorously. "I am…"

"I know who you are. I seen your picture in the paper," she told him. "What happened?" she asked nervously. "Officer Thomas told me she thought Junior had been arrested. Junior is a good boy," she continued. "He has a temper but he don't get into no trouble and he never causes any."

"Well ma'am, Sharnell Jackson called me. She really wasn't sure of the details herself and I just got here, but I'm going to try to help straighten this mess out."

"That really wasn't necessary," Brea whispered as she pulled Robby aside. "I'm sure Shar can handle this."

"I'm sure she's capable, but she's not here. So would you rather that young man spend one minute more in a cell than he has to, while we wait for her arrival from Atlanta, or are you willing to put your personal grudges aside and allow me to do my job?"

"Officer Thomas, if he can get my boy out of there, please let him."

"Ma'am, it's really up to you. Do you want me to function as your family's legal counsel?"

"Yes, yes."

"Whatever!" Brea exclaimed, throwing a hand up in the air as she walked over to Diedra. Then Robby returned to the police officer.

"Are you alright?" Brea asked Diedra. "You look pale."

"It's been a stressful afternoon, but I'm okay," she replied. "I'm just glad you all arrived when you did. "I was really beginning to lose my patience." She massaged the back of her waist and stretched a little. "Brea, you should have seen the way they have ignored me since I've been here. They acted like I was invisible or something."

"I'm not surprised! Look at where you are. I know you told Shar not to, but I called the track and spoke with James."

"How did you manage that?"

"I identified myself as Officer Breanna Thomas of the Jacksonville police force and I informed them that his very pregnant wife had an emergency." She observed the expressions of shock, disapproval, and gratitude as they played across Diedra's face. "All true," she said. "I am Officer Thomas, you are very pregnant, and this is an emergency." She smiled reassuringly at Diedra. "Not to worry though, once he came to the phone, I explained to him what I knew about the actual situation; which wasn't much, by the way. What exactly happened?"

"We'll talk, I promise."

The other two couples had gotten the story from their own children and they were thoroughly upset, but at this time, Junior was the primary focus.

"Look here! I don't care what your name is, that doesn't mean you'll get special privileges here! The judge will set bail Monday morning and that's that!"

They all turned to see Robby and the sergeant, facing off, faces red, and sweat dripping, apparently oblivious of anyone else in the room.

"Earl, you are denying my client's due process and I won't stand for it!"

"Tell it to the judge!" the officer smirked, "Monday Morning!"

Robby started to yell something else, but then he stopped, took a deep breath and said, "Earl, as God is my witness, that young man will not spend tonight in jail. You don't think my name means something in this town? Try me!"

Earl stood in front of Robby with his arms crossed in front of him, rocking back and forth on his heels, looking intently at Robby. "Now son, you know your granddaddy doesn't have the same sensibilities as you."

"Are you sure about that, Earl?" Robby asked as he reached across Earl's desk to pick up his phone. He dialed a number and someone answered fairly quickly. "Is he in?" he asked. "May I speak with him please?"

He spoke with the person for several minutes, and from his demeanor and tone, it seemed that Earl may have been correct in his assumption. Earl sat back in his chair, placing his feet up on his desk with his hand behind his head, watching smugly as Robby tried to convince the person on the phone to intervene on his behalf.

"If you care half as much about your family as you claim to care about this town, then now is the time to show it. You need to do something… quickly," he said, just before he slammed the phone back down on the receiver. He turned around without looking at Earl and walked back across the room to Ms. Johnson. Robby reached behind his head and rubbed the back of his neck as he rotated his head and shrugged "Ms. Johnson, for some reason, they are dead set against us seeing Junior, and this has me concerned. But I promise you, he will not spend one night in jail."

Just then, the phone on the desk rang and Earl answered it. He had a short muffled conversation, which mostly consisted of "yes sir," and "no sir," on his part. It ended with, "right away sir." He hung up the phone and called Robby back to his desk.

The officer picked a pencil up off the desk, and twirled it around angrily between his fingers. "You think your Hot Stuff don't you boy?" he asked him angrily. "How are we supposed to keep our women and children safe from these thugs, if you bleeding heart liberals continue to interfere with the performance of our duties? They got to know they can't just go around assaulting our children."

Robby calmly replied, "It's not your duty to play judge and jury, Earl, Due process is for everyone."

He threw the pencil down on his desk. "David, take Mr. Draper and his client back ta see the suspect."

Robby and Ms. Johnson followed the young officer back to Junior's cell. When he stopped in front of the cell, Ms. Johnson gasped loudly as she faced her son sitting on the cot, leaned up against the wall for support. She hardly recognized him. His right eye was swollen shut and his jaw was grotesquely swollen. There was a pool of blood on the floor where he had spit periodically.

"I guess Stevie did get a few good licks in," the officer quipped.

"Has he been seen by a doctor," Robby asked angrily.

"Well no. He didn't ask for one," he said as he opened the cell door.

Junior's mother ran across the jail cell to her son who was barely responsive. She attempted to ask him questions until Robby stopped her. "It looks as if his jaw might be broken," he said as he pulled a cell phone out of his pocket. Ms. Johnson and the police officer both looked at him in surprise. "What? Have you ever tried to slam a cell phone?" he asked.

He dialed 911 and ordered an ambulance to be immediately dispatched to the station. They waited with Junior for the ambulance that arrived in minutes. Immediately after the EMTs went back to Junior's cell, James came running into the station with the triplets in tow. "What happened? Where's my wife?" he asked in a panic.

"I'm right here," she said weakly. He swooped her up in his arms just as she was about to collapse.

"What is it, Babe? I'm here," he whispered softly in her ear."

"I'm just so tired," she said weakly through short breaths. "I'm, I'm in labor, James."

"How far apart are your contractions?" he asked as he walked her back to her chair.

Rodney noticed them and asked, "Hey how are you doing over there?"

"She's in labor," James replied.

"Probably brought on by the stress of the afternoon. Why didn't you say something?"

"I...I, just had to be sure all of our children were okay," she said.

"How far apart are your contractions?" Rodney asked.

"They're getting pretty close," she said, wincing as she felt a sharp pain start in the small of her back and circle around her stomach. And then her water broke.

"Whoa!" said Trevor as he pointed at her. "Mommy's having an accident."

"You come with me." Austin picked him up in his arms, while Adrian and Bianca picked up Travis and Tremaine and took them off to the side, away from Diedra and all the commotion.

"Considering the stress you've been under today, you need to get to the hospital as soon as possible."

"Do we have time to go home and get my suit case?" Diedra asked.

"You probably can, but given your history, it's probably best that you get to the hospital and get monitored as soon as possible." Noting the alarm on their faces, he continued, "I'm not saying it's an emergency, I just think you should take every precaution." Then he looked up and said, "Thank you Lord for your divine intervention."

A young police officer came through the door. "Good Golly! What's with all the fancy cars outside?"

Earl nodded toward the group huddled in prayer in the middle of the room, "Just the SCLC and 'Atticus_Finch' over there."

He turned to the group and grinned broadly when he saw Shawn. "Hello, Major Smith!" He shook his hand heartily and turned to Cassandra, "Mrs. Smith, it's good to see you both again."

"Yes! Boyd Hannah, right?" replied Cassandra. We haven't seen you since you graduated. I thought you were commissioned into the Army.

"Yes ma'am. I'm in the Reserves."

"Good for you!"

"What brings you out here?"

"I'm sure your co-workers will fill you in," Shawn said, as Junior was rolled out on a stretcher.

Shyanne Johnson left in the ambulance with her son, Junior, and Robby gave Eliza Ray and Buddy a ride home in his Jaguar. Then he headed to the hospital.

Kayla drove Adrian and Austin home in James' Maxima so she could pick up her son's Navigator, and they could pick up their mother's suitcase. The rest of them headed directly to the hospital.

Shar and Derek arrived at the hospital at the same time as Diedra and James' parents. Diedra and James had just gone into the delivery room and the growing crowd was gathered in the lounge, anxiously awaiting the new arrival. They realized that once she gave birth to her daughter, the doctors would finally be able to do more extensive testing to determine the extent of her brain cancer and plan for surgery. They all gathered together and Mr. Davis led them in prayer again as they asked the Lord to guide the doctors in the performance of their tasks, both on Diedra and Junior, who was also in surgery.

# CHAPTER 23

Dr. Howard Sr. examined Diedra and determined that she was indeed, fully dilated, but her baby was breeched. He considered attempting to turn the fetus, but the stress of the day had caused Diedra's blood pressure to rise, and he didn't feel that a normal delivery would be feasible. He advised Diedra and James that a C-section would be the best for both mother and child.

Diedra opted to have an epidural. When they placed her on the operating table, Dr. Brown, the anesthesiologist attempted to explain the procedure to her. In the middle of his spiel, Diedra suddenly arched her back and yelled, "Oh, I feel like I have to push."

"Hold on!" Dr. Howard said as he walked around to check her. "Looks like this little girl has decided she's coming, feet first, no less," he exclaimed.

He delivered the baby with much less problem than he would have anticipated with a breech birth. Because of the manner of her delivery, James had to wait for the nurses to care for his daughter before he was able to hold her. She received an Apgar score of 9, which was phenomenal. Her lungs were good and strong. And when he did get to hold her, she grasped his thumb with a surprisingly strong grip.

By the time they presented her to Diedra, exhaustion had taken over and she had fallen asleep. She woke up just long enough to give her a light kiss and tell her and James that she loved them. James followed the nurse to the nursery and there, he showed his beautiful daughter to his friends and family.

"Here comes the proud father!" exclaimed Shawn as James entered the room.

"Congratulations man!" said Michael as he walked up to him and shook his hand. He had been at work all afternoon, and had headed for the hospital as soon as he got off.

James was beaming! He loved his sons, but a daughter! This was a feeling like none other he had ever known. He didn't even realize he was crying until his father handed him his handkerchief saying, "I know, son, I know. This is some kind of special." And then he hugged him in a tight embrace and said, "Son I am so proud of the man you are and the father you are. I just want you to know that."

"I want to see Mommy!" cried Tremaine.

"She fell asleep. Let's go see if she's awake now." He picked Tremaine up and grabbed Trevor's hand while Austin and Adrian held Travis' hands as they followed behind them.

Derek watched on in awe.

"You are going to be a father like that someday," Shar whispered to him.

"How do you always know what I'm thinking?" he asked her.

"Because, I know you; I truly know who you are and I see in you the man God designed you to be, not the mistakes of your past." She locked his arm in hers and squeezed, smiling happily.

"Wake up Sleeping Beauty," James whispered as he kissed Diedra lightly on her forehead, followed by each of the boys.

"Where's the baby?" she asked as she struggled to open her eyes. She smiled softly at her family, basking in the realization that she was the most fortunate woman in the world; second only to this little miracle she had just given birth to. She was certainly going to be spoiled from every direction.

"She'll be in shortly. I think the nurse said it was almost her feeding time. But first, we have some business of the utmost importance to tend to," James said in a solemn tone.

Diedra frowned slightly and asked, "What sort of business?"

"Everyone is waiting to come in and visit, but…" he hesitated.

"What is it James? You're making me nervous."

The slightest hint of a smile curled up from the right side of his mouth and his right eyebrow arched as he said, "How is she going to receive visitors when she doesn't even have a name?" He smiled fully. "I know with all that was going on; you didn't want to give her a name before she was actually here, but she's here now, and she needs a name." He reached out and held her hand and asked, "What are we going to name our baby, Diedra?"

"She has a name!" cried Trevor.

"What are you talking about?" asked Adrian.

"Her name is Miracle!" he explained. "You said it, you said it," he said pointing around the room. "Even Grandma said it. Everyone called her Miracle."

"We said she is a miracle, we didn't say her name was Miracle, silly." Adrian told him. Diedra and James looked at each other and smiled.

"I think it fits," he said.

"I think it's perfect" she agreed.

Just then, the nurse wheeled the baby in to the room followed by Dr. Howard. "Here's our little miracle," he said as he entered the room.

"Yes she is!" laughed James and Diedra.

# CHAPTER 24

DIEDRA SAT ALONE ON THE beach watching the tranquil waters ripple gently under the clear blue sky. Her granddaddy and big daddy waved at her as they rowed away in their small boat. The frothy white clouds settled over her, soothed her soul. Their very presence seemed to reiterate her granddaddy's last statement to her. She smiled to herself as she remembered his words.

James woke up to the sound of a faint cry coming from Miracle's crib. He turned over and saw Diedra smiling in her sleep. He gave her a light peck on the forehead and jumped out of the bed and went to his daughter. "Good morning Beautiful Girl! It's just you and me this morning," he whispered to her as he reached into her crib.

It was Labor Day and it was a big day at the Davis house. God had shown up and shown out in so many ways in their lives. This was the first time they would be entertaining at their new home in Brittany Downs. James' cousin, Huey Davis, had built his fiancée, Darby Jones, a brand new house up in Heritage Highlands, right across the street from the Howards, as a wedding present. She sold James and Diedra her home which she had been awarded from her previous marriage, for the balance on the loan which was less than the market value of their house in Mecca Woods.

They decided not to sell their old house just yet though. They were going to keep it as rental property. They rented it out to Shyanne Johnson and her family, so she could move her family out of the projects. She was currently in the midst of a civil case against the Draper police department for the abuse of her son, Junior. The arresting officers had claimed that he had sustained his injuries in the fight against Stevie. They had attempted to paint a picture of Junior as a thug who had trespassed onto the premises and started the fight with Stevie.

They almost got away with it too. But several people from Draper and Jacksonville came forward and reported that the group had been invited guests to Dixie Falls that day and Stevie had initiated the entire altercation. Then somehow, video footage turned up at the TV station clearly showing the events that took place at Dixie Falls, including the officer's unwarranted attack of Victoria. Diedra was brought to tears when she saw the video. She repeatedly apologized to all of the children for not fully taking them at their word on that day.

The video clearly showed that Junior had no injuries when the police arrived, and since they had all already gone on record, stating that he was injured before their arrival, the arresting officers were facing criminal charges as well. Rodney and Kayla, who had lawyered up the same day of the incident, were pushing for jail time for all the officers involved.

To distance themselves from the officer's actions, the police department had placed all of the involved officers on administrative leave the day the video came out. Boyd Hannah replaced the desk sergeant.

James' new position at the Depot came with a generous sign on bonus and that, along with the Advance that Shar was able to negotiate for Diedra's book, *Tamar's Dream,* enabled them to pay cash for the new house. When Huey and Darby first approached them with the proposition of selling them the house, James had pulled out an old piece of paper that he had kept from before they were married. It was Diedra's wish list for her Dream Home. He had promised her when they purchased their first home that someday she would have everything on that list.

He took the list with them when they went to look at the house. They were pleased to find it had everything on the list and more. This house was one of the larger homes in the subdivision with five bedrooms and four bathrooms, a full basement with a storm shelter, two gas fireplaces, a four car garage, and a chef's kitchen, all on a full acre, beautifully landscaped, corner lot with a pool and outdoor kitchen. There was plenty of room for the children to play and there was also a Rose Garden reminiscent of Elizabeth Park in Hartford. Diedra fell in love with it instantly.

But the icing on the cake was the master suite. It was a luxurious hideaway. It included a large main room, his and her bathroom, with separate vanity sinks, a jetted garden tub, a rainforest steam shower, and two large walk-in closets, and finally a bonus room that would serve as the perfect nursery. There was a balcony off the back of the bedroom that overlooked the pool area, with a clear view of the rose garden and the play area. The house was more than they'd ever dreamed.

Diedra did not go back to work after Miracle was born. They agreed she would stay at home with the children and continue her writing efforts. Her publisher was already inquiring about her next book. The first one had already generated a great deal of interest and it had not even been released yet. She would be giving out pre-view copies to their guests today.

All of their family and friends would be there to join them in celebrating all that God had done in their lives. Even Ike and Mike were in town. They were staying at the Victoria Inn with their wives. They had visited the church in Coldwater the day before and they loved it, as both Diedra and Brea knew they would. Diedra's brother and his family had flown in from California. He had already been in town a week and his family and friends had enjoyed spending time with him. He and Rodney had appreciated the opportunity to catch up.

Because it was such a large affair, and they were celebrating so many different events, Labor Day, the triplets fifth birthday, the release of her book, James' promotion, their new home, and Shar and Derek's engagement, Diedra agreed to let Shar and Brea hire an event planner. Shar insisted this would give her an opportunity to preview her wedding planner.

Diedra was awakened by the mixed sounds of a baby's cry and the hum of electrical equipment outside. She walked into the nursery to find James sitting in the rocker trying to soothe Miracle. Diedra stood in the doorway and watched as her husband sang a sweet lullaby to his daughter, while he gently rocked her, and rubbed and patted her back until she burped. Then she cooed softly and went back to sleep. He looked up and saw Diedra and smiled fondly at her. "She's had a restless night. I've been in here since three this morning," He whispered.

"What? Why didn't you wake me?"

"Because you needed your rest; I believe that was your first full night's sleep since she was born," he said as he laid his daughter in her crib. He walked Diedra back into their bedroom and over to the sliding glass doors that led to their screened in balcony. They watched as the workmen erected a Pavilion in their back yard. They could already smell the smoke wafting up from the barbeque pit.

"You have a big day ahead of you," he said, observing all the activity going on. "All of our family and our closest friends will be here to receive their copies of your book. How does that feel?" he asked. "I know I didn't write it, but I'm just as proud as if I did. And the triplets turn five today. They're in kindergarten! Can you believe that? And last, but certainly not least, Miracle's Christening. I think it's a blessing that both Pastor Mckinney and Pastor Vaughn agreed to conduct the ceremony together at our house." He stared out the window with his arms around Diedra, "You know, I think Mike and Cassandra were the perfect choices for God Parents too."

"I agree. Did you see how she took to him when he picked her up?"

"Yes I did. It was like she already knew who he was."

"Exactly," she replied reflectively.

People started arriving at around 11:00 that morning. The caterers would be changing up the menu as the day moved on. They would be serving from 11 to 11. So at any given time, guests would be able to find fresh food on the serving table. Shar had thought this would be a great opportunity to test out cake flavors, so there would be a variety of cake samples on the dessert tables. Guests could rank the flavors if they chose.

Shar and Brea were the first to arrive. They helped Diedra to ensure that all details were perfect; coordinating directions with the event planner. As soon as Brea walked in the door, Diedra noticed the rock on her finger. It was a perfect single carat solitaire. She hugged her friend and congratulated her. They would have two engagements to announce. Derek and Michael would arrive later; the two men had hit it off pretty well. The rest of the guests would trickle in throughout the day.

As Diedra was bringing Miracle downstairs to be near the festivities, she paused at the top of the landing, looking across the two story foyer to the picture window that was above the front door. The light shined down on the marble floors, causing them to sparkle like they were embedded with diamonds.

She saw her sons pull into the driveway in their new cars, Adrian in a black Camaro and Austin in a silver Mustang. They were bringing Victoria and Nicholette over early so they could get in the pool. Rodney III and Bianca pulled in behind them. Diedra smiled when she saw Junior climb out of the back seat and run around to open the door for his girlfriend. He was talking a mile a minute, bantering back and forth with Rodney III. There had been no lingering effects from his injuries, he was all set to begin his senior year, and though they were all elated to learn that he had already been accepted to Emory University along with Rodney, he had announced that he was waiting to hear from Howard University.

That afternoon, after their guests had toured the house, they had Christened Miracle Grace Davis, and her aunt Brea had given her the same gift she had given each of Diedra and Cassandra's children when they were born, a $10,000 check. Then, after they had celebrated the triplet's birthday and they had received more gifts than they would know what to do with, Diedra handed out autographed copies of her book. Derek and Michael stood up in the center of the patio next to the DJ and serenaded Brea and Shar with an off key but enthusiastic rendition of O'Bryan's 'You and I' followed by a much better dance to 'Wifey' by Next.

Brea and Shar were both blushing as each man placed a chair in the center of the floor and they walked them over to be seated.

Michael stood in front of Brea and started speaking from 1st Corinthians 13, "Though I speak with the tongues of men and of angels but have not love, I have become sounding brass or a clanging cymbal. And though I have the gift of prophecy, and understand all mysteries and all knowledge, and although I have faith, so that I could remove mountains, but have not love, I am nothing. And though I bestow all my goods to feed the poor, and though I give my body to be burned, but have not love. " he paused, and then breathlessly, "it profits me nothing."

Every woman there was in tears. Then Derek started speaking, and to their surprise, he picked up where Michael left off, "Love suffers long and is kind, love does not envy, love does not parade itself, is not puffed up; does not behave rudely, does not seek its own, is not provoked, thinks no evil; does not rejoice in iniquity, but rejoices in the truth; bears all things, believes all things, hopes all things, endures all things." The men stomped and cheered as the women clapped. Michael waited for the clamor to die down and then he continued,

"Love never fails. But whether there are prophecies, they will fail; whether there are tongues, they will cease; whether there is knowledge, it will vanish away. For we know in part and we prophesy in part. But when that which is perfect has come, then that which is in part will be done away."

Brea and Shar were both crying profusely at this point. Derek kneeled down before Shar and looked into her eyes, and continued as if they were completely alone, "When I was a child, I spoke as a child, I understood as a child, I thought as a child, but when I became a man, I put away childish things. For now we see in a mirror, dimly, but then face to face. Now I know in part, but then I shall know just as I am also known."

He stood up next to Michael and they simultaneously said, "And now abide faith, hope, love, these three, but the greatest of these is love."

Brea rushed into Michael's arms, and Shar into Derek's. They continued to stand together in front of everyone and then Derek gave a beautiful speech sharing that he was proud to announce that the beautiful Sharnell Jackson had made him unbelievably happy by agreeing to become his wife. He shared how she brought out the best in him because she saw the best in him and he knew there was a God because he felt his love through her every day.

Michael was next, he shared how his life began the day Brea walked into the Jaeger Haus and sat at his table. He said that he truly believed that she was the woman that God had designed just for him and he was grateful to have her in his life. And he looked forward to spending the rest of his life with her and raising a family with her. He told Brea that he knew how she felt about not having a family and he wanted her to know that he would always be her family.

Just then, Robby Draper stepped up and congratulated them both and he gave Brea a big hug that lasted so long, that it became sort of uncomfortable to watch. "I'm sorry," he said after he turned her loose. "I have wanted to do that from the first day I saw you."

"What?" said someone in the crowd.

"Huh?" said someone else.

"Robby, perhaps this isn't the time," said James.

"No, it is past time," he said. "I love you Brea."

James started coughing uncontrollably at that revelation. Diedra was confused. She wondered why Shar was grinning like a Cheshire cat. She and Robby had been close for years. "Did she know about this crush?" she wondered.

"You can't punish the rest of us for the actions of one ornery old man and a weak younger man," he continued. "If you continue to turn your back on the rest of us, you're no different from them. You have a niece right over there, that deserves to know her aunt," He said pointing toward his wife and young daughter.

"Ohh!" someone said as they began to understand.

"I told you she looked like those Drapers," someone else murmured.

"This is better than a soap opera!" someone else exclaimed.

Michael took Brea in his arms and held her for a few moments, gently wiping her tears before he stepped back and looked into her eyes. "You know he's right don't you? Baby I know how important family is to you, and I know how much it hurts you to not have family of your own, which is why you cling so tightly to your friends. And that's okay. They're great, and I know beyond a shadow of a doubt that they love you like a sister, but Robby is your blood and he's reaching out to you, in the open, in front of everyone... even your grandfather," he said as he turned her to face an older silver-haired white man in the back of the crowd.

Mr. Draper sat in his chair stone faced. He didn't say a word or even show any facial expression indicating that he was aware of what was going on around him.

"Why is he here?" Brea muttered.

"He is here, to give you the opportunity, to forgive him, if you so choose," said Robby softly.

"Remember baby, forgiveness is for us, not the other person." Michael whispered in her ear.

Those words struck a chord with Brea. Her mother used to tell her that before she died of breast cancer. "You have to forgive them, Brea, to free your heart from the blackness of bitterness."

Brea grabbed Robby and hugged him like she would never let him go. She thanked God for leading Michael to give her the best engagement present she could ever receive, her family.

Later that evening, a group had gathered back under the pavilion enjoying the cool evening air and listening to the smooth sounds of cool jazz playing through the air. Colonel Jackson proposed a toast to the newly engaged couples. He announced that he was proud to welcome Derek into his family. "Son, I know better than anyone, it's not how you start but how you finish that matters," He said as he smiled across the room at his wife.

"Here, here," agreed Diedra and James simultaneously, then they looked at each other and burst into jovial laughter.

They began to recount all the things that God had done in their lives, in the past year, in just the past three months even! After she gave birth to Miracle, she had gone back to the Kirklin clinic for a brain scan so her doctors could plan her surgery and they were surprised that there was no sign of a tumor anywhere. She and James believed she had been cured ever since that night in February.

She looked around the room with tears in her eyes. Her brother Reggie, whom she hadn't seen in years; Mike and Ike, the men who had been a Godsend to her years ago; Shar and Brea, two of her best friends, who were now engaged to two men who truly loved them, Cassie, who had been her first true friend and was still today one of her best friends. James, who had stepped into her life and loved her back into living. And Brea was united with the family she had never been a part of, even her grandfather who had refused to acknowledge her when her father was alive. Brea was probably more like him than any of his other children, grandchildren or great-grandchildren. Everyone in this room had been brought together for a purpose in God's plan for their lives.

"So what have you learned through all of this?" Mike asked Diedra.

Her granddaddy's words rang in her ears, "*No matter how big your dreams are, God's plan is greater.*"

Diedra gently bounced her daughter on her knee and said, "You know, I had another dream last night and I saw my grandfathers again. My granddaddy reminded me that dreams don't always come true and fairy tales aren't real. But my God is a God of Miracles! And he will always make a way."

And somebody said, "Won't he do it?" And they all said, "Amen."

TO BE CONTINUED...

THE BEST IS YET TO COME...

I AM TAMAR

I am not a weeping willow nor a shrinking violet.

Many have tried to break my spirit,

No matter what life has brought against me,

My spirit remains intact, and my will remains strong.

I am like butter that has been beaten and whipped into cream.

And cream always rises to the top.

I am a palm tree.

Storms may rage against me, and fierce winds may blow,

I sway back and forth, and I may even bend.

But I never, ever, break.

I am Tamar

By, Diedra Davis

Author of **Tamar's Dream**

Biblical Scriptures as they are referenced in this book

1. a three-fold cord is not easily broken." Ecclesiastes 4:9-12
2. And we know that all things work together for good to them that love the Lord and are called according to his purpose." Romans 8:28
3. Before I formed you in your mother's womb, I knew you. Before you were born, I sanctified you." Jeremiah1:5
4. that whatever we bind on earth will be bound in heaven and whatever is loosed in heaven will be loosed on earth.  Matthew 18:18
5. The bible says he who finds a wife finds a good thing.   Proverbs 18:22
6. That if thou shall confess with thy mouth the Lord Jesus, and shall believe in thine heart that God has raised him from the dead, thou shalt be saved.' Romans 10
7. He reminded them that the last thing Jesus said to his disciples was to go into all the world and spread the gospel. Mark 16:15
8. For we wrestle not against flesh and blood, but against principalities, against powers, against the rulers of darkness in this world, against spiritual wickedness in high places.  This battle is not yours, but God's, Ephesians 6:12
9. God, who forgives all your sins, heals ALL of your diseases.  He delivers you from all of your afflictions.  His plans for you are to give you a future and a hope. Psalms 103:3 & Jeremiah 29:11
10. "He will fill your mouth with laughter and your lips with shouting." Job 8:21
11. For whom he foreknew, he also predestined Romans 8:29
12. Jesus says with faith the size of a mustard seed we can move mountains. Our Father cares for the flowers in the field. How much more does he care for us and our needs. Jesus told Thomas 'Because you

have seen me, now you believe, but blessed are they that have not seen, and yet have believed.' Matthew 17:20, Matthew 6:26 & John 20:29

13. Look to the hills from whence comes your help. Not to the left nor to the right. Not even within your own might. Psalm 121

14. God has a plan for you and it is to give you a future and a hope. Jeremiah 29:11

15. because we are not of those who turn back to perdition, but we continue on to the saving of our souls. Hebrews 10:39

16. that God is not a man that he can lie and his promises will come to pass. Numbers 23:19

17. Regardless of the attacks of the enemy, we have this treasure in earthen vessels that the excellency of the power may be of God and not of us. 2 Corinthians 4:7

18. We are troubled on every side, yet not distressed; we are perplexed but not in despair; persecuted but not forsaken, cast down but not destroyed; always bearing about in the body the dying of the Lord Jesus, that the life also of Jesus might be manifest in our bodies. 1 Corinthians 4:8-10

19. For he shall be like a tree planted by the waters, and spreads out her roots by the river, and shall not see when heat comes, but her leaf shall be green, and it will not be anxious in a year of drought nor cease to yield fruit. Jeremiah 17:8" pg. 215

20. Oh you don't get it yet. But you will... That tree by the water is referring to a palm tree. Do you know what palm tree means in Hebrew?" "I never really thought about it," replied Diedra. "Wait for it... It means Tamar. In Christianity the palm tree has been used as the symbol for victory of the faithful over enemies of the soul." pg. 215

21. The Word says to study to show yourself approved unto God, a workman that needeth not to be ashamed, rightly dividing the word of truth." 2 timothy 2:15

22. . For the Word of God is quick, and powerful, sharper than any two-edged sword... Do you understand what I mean?" Hebrews 4:12

23. My people perish from a lack of knowledge, Hosea 4:6… and you have not because you ask not, James 4:3.
24. And remember that wisdom is the principal thing. Therefore, get wisdom and in all your getting, get understanding. Proverbs 4:7
25. "The power of life and death is in the tongue Proverbs 18:21
26. "Baby Girl there is life in the word. You've got to speak it." John 1:4
27. . You shall live and you shall not die." Psalms 118:17
28. The Word of God is living and powerful, and sharper than any two-edged sword, piercing even to the division of soul and spirit, and of joint and marrow, and is a discerner of the thoughts and intents of the heart. Hebrews 4:12,"
29. The battle is not mine but God's 2 Chronicles 20:15
30. For the weapons of my warfare are not carnal, but mighty through God to the pulling down of strongholds." 2 Corinthians 10:4
31. "No weapon formed against me shall prosper, and every tongue which rises against me in judgment I shall condemn." Isaiah 54:17
32. "Though I walk in the midst of trouble you will revive me. You will stretch out your hand against the wrath of my enemies and your right hand will save me. Psalm 138:7
33. "Many are the afflictions of the righteous but the Lord delivers me from them all." Psalms 34:19
34. "The Lord my God has given me rest on every side. There is neither adversary nor misfortune." 1 Kings 5:4
35. The troubles you have seen up to this point you will see no more." Exodus 14:13
36. "This little miracle will be blessed and highly favored." Luke 1:28
37. Strength and honor are her clothing. Proverbs 31:25
38. Her children arise up and call her blessed And her husband also Proverbs 31:28
39. What the enemy has meant for our harm, God uses for our good Genesis 50:20
40. Taste and see that the Lord is good Psalm 34:8

41. Michael stood in front of Breanna and started speaking from 1ˢᵗ Corinthians 13, "Though I speak with the tongues of men and of angels but have not love, I have become sounding brass or a clanging cymbal. And though I have the gift of prophecy, and understand all mysteries and all knowledge, and although I have faith, so that I could remove mountains, but have not love, I am nothing. And though I bestow all my goods to feed the poor, and though I give my body to be burned, but have not love. " he paused, and then breathlessly, "it profits me nothing."

"Love never fails. But whether there are prophecies, they will fail; whether there are tongues, they will cease; whether there is knowledge, it will vanish away. For we know in part and we prophesy in part. But when that which is perfect has come, then that which is part will be done away."

"When I was a child, I spoke as a child, I understood as a child, I thought as a child, but when I became a man, I put away childish things. For now we see in a mirror, dimly, but then face to face. Now I know in part, but then I shall know just as I am also known."

"And now abide faith, hope, love, these three, but the greatest of these is love."

# About The Author

DARLENE PRYOR WAS BORN IN Ancon, Panama in the Canal Zone. Growing up in a military family, she was fortunate to experience life both in Alabama and overseas in Germany.

Darlene's educational background consists of a Bachelor's degree in Corrections with a minor in Sociology and a Master's degree in Public Administration. She believes that everyone has a story to tell, and as the proud mother of five sons, who is also a breast cancer survivor, she draws from her personal experiences to write of love, redemption and restoration, with the intent of uplifting and encouraging her readers.

Darlene has completed her first novel entitled Dreams of Tamar; a compelling tale of a group of young Christian friends who learn the meaning of grace. Darlene is presently simultaneously penning her next endeavor, Dreams of Her Father.

Darlene Pryor currently resides in Lancaster, Ca.

Follow me on twitter @dpryorauthor

Follow me on Instagram @darlenepryorauthor

Visit my Facebook page Darlene Pryor The Author

Excerpt from Dreams of Her Father (working title)

## CHAPTER 1

ROBERT PULLED THE NEATLY FOLDED paper from the envelope that had his name printed across the front in bold letters, 'Robert Brian Draper Jr'. So cold and informal like a church announcement or a message from his school, Jax State. But it wasn't from church and it wasn't from the university either. It was from her. It was her final communication to him before she left. She had written the words neither of them had the strength to say, but both knew had to be said.

How could something as innocuous as a piece of paper have the power to tear into one's heart so deeply? Every time he read the words they stabbed at his heart again and again, threatening to slice it in two. He was already torn; torn between the love of his life who he could never have, and his wife, whom he also loved. It was true. He loved two women, two women as different as night and day.

Cindy, his wife, was soft spoken, shy and reserved. She wanted nothing more from life than to be the wife of Robert Draper Jr and the mother of his children. Cindy planned to have a house full of children and raise them right here in Jacksonville. She was even majoring in Home Economics. She doted on Robert and she hung on his every word, believing he was the smartest man she'd ever met. His dreams were Cindy's dreams and he knew she would support him in whatever he chose to pursue in life. They would have a good life together and he would be completely happy…if it wasn't for her.

Her! Her with the regal stature and the fiery eyes that seared right through his soul, daring him to do better, to be better. Challenging him to fight against everything he had ever been taught and everything that was expected of him as the son of the most powerful man in Calhoun County. She knew him better than anyone else. She wasn't blinded by some false sense of privilege, leading her to believe he could do no wrong. She knew his weaknesses and recognized his faults and she loved him anyway. She loved all of him. But she never asked him for anything. She never would. She just waited for him to step up on his own and claim her, pronouncing his love for her to the world. She didn't want anything from him but she expected everything.

If only he'd been stronger. If he'd trusted in their love: he could have stood up to his father. He could have walked away from his family and their money, and he and Josephine could have made a life together. But when his father threatened to disinherit him he realized he had to consider the future generations of his family, his children and their children. He had no right to deprive them of their legacy.

Now his child; Josephine's child, would be financially set for life, as long as his father never found out. Perhaps that's why she left. Maybe she realized that if she had stayed in Jacksonville he would not have been able to stay away and they would never have been able to keep their secret.

Robert unfolded the paper and read over the note once again…

Dear Rob,

As I sit here trying to write this letter, I struggle to put into words the feelings I want to express to you. (Funny right? Me at a loss for words.) Writing this letter is one of the most difficult tasks I have ever undertaken. From the time we were toddlers playing on your back porch while my Mama hung the laundry; you have been my best friend.

How do I say goodbye to the one who knows my thoughts before I speak them? How do I say goodbye to the one whose heart beat is synced with my own? You are everything I am not. We are two sides of the same coin. What's going to happen when we part? Will I be left with half a heart?

I don't want to leave, but I must. I can't stay here with our child and watch you build a life with Cindy. That wouldn't be fair to any of us, especially our child. So I'm leaving Jacksonville and I won't be back. There is nothing here for me anymore.

I don't blame you for anything. I am not angry with you. I know you are doing what you feel is best. And please don't be angry with me. I am doing what I feel is best for me and our child. I wish you a lifetime of joy, and I will forever love you.
Love always,
Josephine Thomas

Robert swiped a tear from his eyes as he tenderly folded the letter back into its original state. He still cried every time he read those words. It had been nearly a year since Josephine left, and even though he knew it was for the best, it still hurt just the same. The phone rang in the other room. He tucked the note away, safely in his wallet. That would be Cindy calling for him to pick her up from her doctor's appointment. She was four months pregnant with their first child. Although this child could never fill the void left by the one he would never know, his first born; he eagerly anticipated the day he would hold his son or daughter in his arms. Maybe, just maybe, then the sacrifice would be worth it...

www.ingramcontent.com/pod-product-compliance
Lightning Source LLC
Chambersburg PA
CBHW050036180626
46810CB00002B/751